The

TREASURE

Box

The
TREASURE
BOX

A Novel

Penelope J. Stokes

WESTBOW
PRESS
A Division of Thomas Nelson Publishers
Since 1798

visit us at www.westbowpress.com

The Treasure Box
Copyright © 2001 Penelope J. Stokes

Published by WestBow Press, a division of Thomas Nelson, Inc.,
P.O. Box 141000, Nashville, Tennessee, 37214.

Library of Congress Cataloging-in-Publication Data

Stokes, Penelope J.
    The treasure box : a novel / Penelope J. Stokes.
        p. cm.
    ISBN 0-8499-1705-0 (hardcover)
    ISBN 0-8499-4464-3 (trade paper)
    I. Title
    PS3569.T6219 T74 2002
    813'54—dc21   2001046668
                                                                CIP

Printed in the United States of America

04 05 06 07 08 PHX 6 5 4 3 2

For Helen,
whose greatest gifts to me are
the Treasure Box
and
our lifelong friendship

ACKNOWLEDGMENTS

Special thanks are due to certain people God has placed in my
life, people who remind me that mystery, miracle,
and wonder still exist in the world:

My Covenant Group—Cindy, Kay, and Kirstin—
who dare me to grow with their spiritual questions,
their intellectual honesty, and their love;

Carlene and Sandi,
who wouldn't let go until I found my joy
and reconnected with my soul again;

Ami and Lil,
who challenge me to the best in myself and in my work;
and B. J., who cheers me on.

Thanks, too, to Henrik Ljungstrom,
Webmaster of http://www.greatoceanliners.net/.
His excellent Web site provided me with invaluable
information (as well as many hours of fascination),
and his personal assistance in research made my
work on this novel much easier.

Wonder is the basis of worship.
—THOMAS CARLYLE

1

VITA'S TREASURE

Vita? Vita, it's Mary Kate. Are you there?"

Vita Kirk grimaced and kept on typing. On the tinny answering machine speaker, her sister's voice sounded even more whiny and insistent than it did in real life.

"I know you're there, Vita. You're always there. For heaven's sake, pick up the phone!"

Vita whirled in her chair and scowled at the machine. She had bought the thing for the sole purpose of screening calls from her garrulous editor Nick, who kept phoning at all hours trying, in his words, to "establish rapport" with his most prolific writer. Rapport. Vita didn't want rapport. She wanted to be left alone.

And now the contraption's bright red eye blinked off and on, signaling that a recording was in progress. A recording of the voice she hadn't heard in ages but still recognized—that familiar, high-pitched mewling. Mary Kate's voice.

"Vita, please." Her sister's tone shifted—less petulant, more desperate. "I need to talk to you. It's about Gordon."

Gordon. Vita's stomach twisted, and her mind lurched into reverse—back sixteen years, to 1985.

Sixteen years and a hundred lives ago. How old had she been—twenty-two, twenty-three? Old enough to have finished her B.A. and begun working on her master's in English literature. Old enough to know better when Gordon Locke had swept into her life like a brash young Byron and demanded her undivided attention.

"Go out with me," he had said, gazing into her eyes across a small battered table in a secluded corner of the student union. "I won't take no for an answer."

Did anyone ever say no to Gordon Locke, Duke University's golden boy and most eligible bachelor? A Ph.D. candidate in anthropology. Five years Vita's senior. Handsome, brilliant, with those amazing, mesmerizing blue eyes. He was perfect. And certain of everything.

"Marry me," he said six months later, looking into her eyes the very same way across the very same table. "I won't take no for an answer."

Vita hadn't even thought of refusing. With Gordon, everything was yes. Yes to his proposal. Yes to a deadly dull administrative job in the chancellor's office so that she could support them while he finished his degree. Yes to putting her own studies on hold. It would all work out, Gordon assured her.

Vita believed him. After all, she had looked into his eyes and

2

seen the certainty there. Except that when she brought him home to Asheville, he had looked into someone else's eyes. Mary Kate's.

In 1985, Mary Katherine Kirk had been a not-quite-twenty-year-old beauty. The year before she had taken third runner-up in the Miss North Carolina Pageant and declared her primary interests to include modeling, fashion design, and world peace. Could she have been more unsuited, Vita wondered, for a learned anthropologist? Didn't Gordon need someone who was his intellectual equal, a scholarly woman, educated in literature and the arts? Someone who could hold her own in the academic world—or at least carry on an intelligent conversation?

But there was no wisdom in love. Gordon married Mary Kate six months later, in a simple ceremony with the bride's sister as reluctant but dutiful maid of honor. The last twist of the knife.

Vita had seen Mary Kate only twice since the reception—once at their father's funeral in 1989, and a year later at their mother's. Her sister still lived in Asheville, barely thirty miles from Vita's home in the small town of Hendersonville. Thirty miles . . .

"Vita, I'm going to keep talking until you pick up the phone. This is important. Gordon is in the hospital."

Vita snatched up the receiver, and the answering machine beeped loudly before shutting off. "All right, I'm here. What is it? But make it quick; I'm working."

"Gordon's had a heart attack. He's in the cardiac unit at Mission Hospital."

"I'm sorry to hear that." Vita kept her voice low, calm.

"It wasn't a bad one, fortunately. He was playing tennis, and—"

Vita's mind conjured up an image of Gordon in his tennis whites, tanned and shining, a young Robert Redford, his blond hair damp with sweat and ruffled by the wind . . .

"Vita, are you there?"

"I'm here."

"I need someone to take the twins for a few days. They're on break from school, and—"

The twins. Little Gordy, the flaxen-haired image of his dad. Mary Vita—so named, Vita was certain, as a vain attempt at reconciliation. They had been toddlers at Mother's funeral; they would be eleven or twelve by now.

"Surely you have someone else who could look after them," Vita suggested.

"We have friends at the university, of course, but—"

Friends. The same ones—at least some of them—who had once orbited around Vita and Gordon. They had transferred their loyalties to Mary Kate as easily as Gordon had transferred his affections.

But Vita hadn't been surprised. At Duke, they were Gordon's friends all along, faithful followers of the golden boy. Some of them had even wrangled teaching positions and moved to UNCA after Gordon had received his appointment there. For years now they had all lived together in a closed little academic enclave, an intellectual and social ghetto.

4

Vita returned her attention to Mary Kate. "So call one of them."

"But they're not family." Her sister sounded uncertain. "And besides, they're busy people. They've got their own—" She bit back the rest of the sentence, and Vita heard the sharp intake of air.

"Go ahead and say it. They've got their own lives. Unlike me."

"I didn't mean it like that. Vita, please. I need you to do this."

"I'm sure you can find someone else. Someone more appropriate." She hung up the phone and turned the volume on the answering machine down to zero.

⌒

An hour after her conversation with Mary Kate, Vita was still steaming, still trying to settle down to work. But her concentration had been broken, her momentum interrupted. At last she gave up. She might just as well get some errands done and try to start fresh in the afternoon.

With a collapsible shopping bag draped over her shoulder, Vita left the house and headed toward town. It was a perfect April day, with dogwoods blooming and ornamental pear trees shedding their petals on the breeze like pink confetti. Between the trees, in the distance, the mountains rose up in lush blue-green layers. To Vita's eyes, they always looked like women napping, their rolling dark hips and rounded shoulders gently rising and falling against the blue dome of sky.

Hendersonville, North Carolina, lay nestled in a hollow of

the Blue Ridge—the kind of place where people still sat on benches along the treelined streets or chatted around open-air café tables. Main Street hosted the Apple Festival in fall, the Bluegrass Festival in spring, and the Antiques Festival somewhere in between. Visitors flocked in for the celebrations, and some of them decided they had found heaven—or Mayberry—and simply stayed. Low crime, wonderful weather, stunning mountain vistas—what could be better?

But Mayberry had its drawbacks. For one thing the place, in the parlance of the locals, "had got overrun with foreigners." Translation: wealthy retirees, attracted by the temperate climate and natural beauty of western North Carolina, had flocked in with their New York and Florida money and driven real-estate prices through the roof. Traffic had doubled. On weekend afternoons, you'd have to stand in line for half an hour just to get a table at the Park Deli. Finding a parking place on Main Street was a major life accomplishment.

Fortunately, Vita didn't often have to worry about parking. Her house was only four blocks from Main, in a sedate, shaded neighborhood just off Church Street. She had purchased the home ten years ago, before real-estate prices had skyrocketed—a small two-story Victorian with a wide front porch, an Italian marble fireplace, and all its woodwork intact and unpainted. And close enough to town that she could walk most anywhere she wanted to go.

Vita was just about to cross Church Street when a pickup

truck roared through the light, blaring its horn. She jumped back, her heart hammering, and realized that she had her mind not on traffic but on Mary Kate. And Gordon.

For a minute or two she stood on the corner with her eyes closed, forcing herself to take deep, cleansing breaths. She had to calm down. Obsessing about her sister didn't do her blood pressure any good, and it might kill her cold if she stepped in front of a speeding car.

She waited for the light to turn green, then looked both ways—twice—before jogging across Church Street and up the hill toward Main. She dragged her thoughts away from Mary Kate and forced herself to make a mental "to do" list—get a few groceries, stop by the drugstore, perhaps drop in at Hap Reardon's antique shop to look around. She could get her errands done and be home before the town clock chimed noon, then have a bit of lunch and get back to work.

As she passed the courthouse, a young couple came out the doors and onto the sidewalk, holding hands and smiling at one another. The man held up a marriage license and beamed in Vita's direction. "We're getting married!"

Vita thought about Gordon and raised one eyebrow. "My condolences."

She walked on without another word, and when she turned her head, she could see out of the corner of her eye the two of them standing there, staring in her direction and whispering.

People always whispered behind their hands when Vita Kirk

7

was around—words like "bitter" and "withdrawn" and sometimes even "crazy." Vita knew what they said. But she had trained herself not to care. Caring just made a person vulnerable.

It all came down to practicalities, in the end. You could put your hand to the flame and get burned, or you could keep your distance and stay safe. Vita had been burned more than once, and she had learned her lesson: Wrap yourself in enough layers, and you won't freeze to death. But even if you're shivering, stay away from the fire.

True, she felt the chill sometimes, but for the most part she had trained herself to ignore it. She had her books to keep her company and a job that allowed her to explore the world without ever setting foot off her own front porch. Her systematic, orderly existence suited her quite well, thank you very much. It wasn't everything, but it was enough.

For years now Vita had written travel guides for a small publishing company in New York City. Vita wasn't oblivious to the irony—a travel writer who never went anywhere. Still, it was interesting work and it paid the bills, and she learned a lot in the process—information that convinced her, had she needed any persuasion, to stay right where she was. She knew, for example, how many tourists got mugged annually in airports and alleyways and city parks, how many wallets were lifted during tours of cathedrals and shrines and palaces. She had at her fingertips data that would make the most seasoned traveler quake with fear: the percentage of airline pilots and railroad engineers who came to work drunk or hung over; the number of burglaries per day in hotel rooms across America; the statistics on extramarital affairs aboard luxury cruise ships.

If everybody knew what Vita Kirk knew, they'd stay at home, too.

But she had plenty of other reasons to keep to herself—and not just the Gordon–Mary Kate fiasco, either. Other losses, other pains—places in her psyche she'd rather not revisit. Gone, but not forgotten, like a childhood scar that twinges when the seasons turn, like bursitis in the elbow that shoots a spark of pain to signal an approaching storm.

It was better to let the past remain buried, where it belonged. Hanging around the cemetery only invited the ghosts to come home and take up residence.

The bell over the door jingled as Vita crossed the threshold of Pastimes, the tiny, cramped secondhand store at the south edge of Main Street. Pastimes billed itself as an "Antique Shoppe and Purveyor of Attic Treasures," but in reality it was more of a junk store, crowded to capacity with mismatched china and crystal, tarnished silver and chipped flower vases, gaudy lamps and discarded furniture.

A year ago, Vita had purchased five place settings of an English china pattern called "Her Majesty's Garden," and every now and then she dropped in to see if any additional pieces of the pattern had come into the shop. Not that she needed more than that; she never had company to dinner, and she always washed and dried her single plate or bowl before she retired for the night. In truth, one place setting would have been enough for Vita. But she valued symmetry, and five dinner plates in a glass-front china cabinet made for a lopsided display.

"Well, if it isn't Miss Vita Kirk! What might I do for you today?"

Vita turned from the haphazard arrangement of china on a rickety shelf and repressed a frustrated sigh. The last thing she wanted this morning was an extended conversation with Hap Reardon about her "adorable little Victorian cottage" and how some piece of leftover memorabilia that had just come into his shop would be an "absolutely perfect accessory" to her decor.

As Reardon approached, all Vita's natural defenses slammed around her and bolted into place. The man had no boundaries, no concept of personal space. He was forever backing her into a corner, encroaching upon her territory until she would either buy what he suggested out of sheer desperation, or make a panicked exit without having the leisure to look around.

Vita didn't know why she put up with it. The china, she supposed. No place else in town carried antique china settings, and although she might be able to track down the pattern on the Internet, she had better things to do with her time than spend hours on-line in a bidding war with some anonymous competitor who used the handle "eBay Baybee."

Besides, she occasionally did find genuine treasures in Pastimes, and at bargain prices. When she had first bought her house and was attempting to furnish it, Hap had come up with a fine old claw-foot table just perfect for her dining room. It had been stored in a chicken house and was covered with bird droppings, but a good washing revealed it to be solid oak. She had gotten it for a steal—sixty-five dollars, including Hap's time in loading it into his pickup and delivering it to her front door.

Clearly, he had hoped to be invited in. He had stood there on one foot and then the other, grinning and thrusting his hands in and out of his pockets. At last he had cleared his throat and said, "Well, I guess that'll about do it. Unless you want me to set it up in your dining room. I could do that for you. If you want." When Vita said nothing, he blathered on, anxious as a seventh grader on his first date. "We could have coffee—or something—if you want, that is. You know, try out the new table, like a—well, like a test drive. See how it works." Still Vita waited. "Or whatever," he went on. "You know, if you wanted to—"

When he finally ran out of both words and nerve, Vita gave him a five-dollar tip, sent him on his way, and wrestled the heavy oak table into the house on her own. Three weeks later, when she had found six pressed-back chairs to go with the table, she had brought them home herself, two by two, in the backseat of her ten-year-old Toyota. She wasn't taking any chances that Hap might latch onto the wrong idea.

But no matter how much Vita discouraged Hap Reardon's earnest attentions, he never seemed to get the message. Apparently he did not share the rest of the town's opinion that Miss Vita Kirk was a cynical, bitter woman who had best be left alone. Even outright rudeness didn't seem to dissuade him.

"Searching for china this morning, Vita?" he asked cheerfully, bearing down on her with that infuriating effervescent grin. "Her Majesty's Garden, isn't it? I'm afraid I don't have any more pieces of that particular pattern at the moment, but I've just had a new shipment of—"

Vita whirled on him. "Listen, Hap," she hissed. "I'm simply looking around, all right? Go on back to your cash register. I'll let you know if I find something."

The smile never faded. He touched a fingertip to an imaginary hat brim and took a step back. "As you wish, Vita. Call me if I can be of assistance." He retreated to the high counter to unpack a box of small figurines. But she could feel his gaze still on her, boring into her back as she turned away.

She let out a disgusted snort and moved into an alcove of the store, as far away from him as she could get. Just because they were both middle-aged and alone was no cause for him to take on like a love-struck teenager. Hap Reardon ought to know better, at his age. Or at the very least, he should have sense enough to realize that she was not now, nor ever would be interested. She had made that abundantly clear.

On the wall just above the shelves, a round beveled mirror caught her image and reflected it back to her. Vita inspected the frame for a moment, considering whether it might fit in that empty space above the stair landing, then suddenly realized she was scrutinizing herself. As she peered into the spotted, yellowed glass, the image that stared back at her could have been the portrait of a Victorian woman. A thin, narrow face with high cheekbones and a faint frown line between the brows. Dark hair parted in the center and pulled back rather severely from the face. And a smaller figure in the distance over her shoulder—a round-faced man in a vest and white shirt, with blondish hair and blue eyes. Hap. Looking up. Watching her from behind.

Vita immediately dropped her gaze and moved to a shelf stacked with small wood and metal boxes. She knew exactly what she wanted—something to store CD programs and computer disks. A place for her research files and software and the disks that held travel books in progress and completed manuscripts. A writer these days might need to be high-tech, but she didn't have to lose her taste in the process. Vita deplored the ugly, brightly-colored plastic things they sold at the discount stores, or the more expensive but equally vulgar cases made from fake wood. It had to be something that was durable and functional but wouldn't offend the eye, preferably an antique that would complement the decor of the house.

The shop's dust filled her nostrils and aggravated her allergies as she examined the small containers, and she silently maligned Hap for never cleaning the place. Then she forgot Hap, forgot the mold and dirt, forgot everything as her eyes lighted on the box.

Ten inches long and six inches wide, the ideal size—just high and deep enough to accommodate a CD in its plastic jewel case. Made of heavy tin and painted a light sea blue, it was crafted like a small treasure chest, with brass fittings on the corners, brass handles on each side, even a tiny brass keyhole and lock. But the best part about it was that, across the sides and back, an antique map of the world covered the little chest. A travel writer's dream. The artist had carefully painted in tiny mountain ranges and blue rivers and the islands of the Pacific. There was even a dragon in the waters, reminiscent of the old sailors' maps which warned *There Be Dragons Here* at the point where vast oceans dropped off the precipice of a flat, two-dimensional earth and fell in a roaring cataract into the netherworld.

The box was made to order for an office in a Victorian house. She retrieved it, holding it gingerly by the brass handles, then stood up to make her way toward the cash register.

When she turned, however, she found herself nose to nose with a tall man, exceedingly old, whose bright brown eyes pierced into hers. He wore a high-necked collarless shirt and waistcoat, a black swallowtail coat, and a silk top hat. If Vita hadn't known for certain that it was the twenty-first century—and Vita knew everything for certain—she would have instantly assumed him to be a nineteenth-century gentleman. In one arthritic hand he car-

see pg. 215

ried an ebony cane with a figure of a bird worked in brass on the handle. He lifted the cane and tapped lightly on the top of the box—once, twice, three times.

"Take care," he warned in a low, whispery voice. "You hold in your hands something more rare and valuable than you can possibly comprehend."

Vita stared at him. "Do you care to elaborate, or do you merely intend to stand there blocking my way?"

"Elaboration," the man said, "is unnecessary. Eventually, you will understand." He gave a slight bow and raised the cane to the brim of his hat, then moved into a side aisle to allow Vita to pass.

Vita resisted the impulse to turn and look back at him as she headed for the counter. The old man gave her the creeps, and she simply wanted to get out of there as quickly as possible.

Hap Reardon, however, seemed determined to waylay her. "Ah," he sighed wistfully as she set the box down in front of him, "the Enchanted Treasure Box."

"I beg your pardon?"

He took a stained rag and wiped off the top of the box. "See?"

Vita looked. Sure enough, across the top of the metal box was painted an embellished baroque scroll, with Gothic lettering that said, *Enchanted Treasure Box.*

"It's a Victorian memorabilia box," Hap explained. "A place to save important things like photographs and poems and"—he gave her a broad wink to go with that ubiquitous smile—"love letters."

15

"It's the right size for CDs and computer disks," she said. "How much?"

Hap thought for a minute. "For you, Vita? A dollar."

"A dollar?" she repeated.

"Too much?" Hap grinned at her.

Vita hesitated. Rare and valuable, the fellow in the black coat had whispered. Was it possible he was some kind of expert, an antique dealer giving her a tip? "The old man back there said—" She turned and looked over her shoulder.

"Old man?" Hap peered toward the back of the shop. "I didn't see anybody come in. I was in the back for a few minutes, but I would have heard the bell—"

"Never mind." Vita shook her head. "It doesn't matter."

"A box like this has held generations of memories, a hundred years of love," Hap went on. He raised his eyebrows, and his face took on a faraway expression. "Don't you find it a little mysterious and compelling? Who knows what stories this box holds? Who knows—"

"Who cares?" Vita thrust a crumpled one-dollar bill in his direction. "Are you going to sell it to me, or aren't you?"

"Oh, I'll sell it to you, all right," he said softly. "In fact, I'm delighted to sell it to you. I think you're just the right person to have it." He took her dollar, carefully wrapped the box in a length of wrinkled butcher paper, and handed it over. "Let me know how it works out for you, will you?"

Vita didn't answer. Hap's cheery farewell mingled with the

jangling of the overhead bell and the slam of the door as she made her exit.

~

Vita did not go to the grocery store, as she had originally intended. She had endured enough of humanity for one day, and she could do without the few things on her list until later in the week. She still had chicken and rice casserole left from last night, and some pasta and vegetables from the night before.

As soon as she arrived home, Vita went straight to the kitchen sink and unwrapped the Treasure Box. The first item on her agenda was to get the multiple layers of dirt and mold removed, then organize her disks and CDs and select the right place in her office to display her new find.

Cleaning the chest brought some pleasant surprises. The colors brightened up considerably under a gentle buffing with rubbing compound. The artwork survived intact, and Vita discovered that the appealing little dragon at the edge of the sea actually had a smile on its face. Under several spots caked with mold, she uncovered a blue whale spouting a flume in the Atlantic, an elephant raising his trunk at the tip of Africa, a tiny pod of sea lions lounging on the beach in the Bahamas.

And underneath the lid, a small inscription, in the same Gothic lettering as the banner on the outside. At first she could barely read it, so obscured was it by time and the accumulated dirt of ages. Then, gradually, it appeared more clearly:

17

~ ~ *Love Is the Key That Unlocks Every Portal.*

Vita's mouth went dry, and the old man's words came back to her: *"You hold in your hands something more rare and valuable than you can possibly comprehend."* A twist in her stomach, some involuntary synapse in her brain, triggered a flood of adrenaline. For an instant the metal box felt red-hot—or perhaps ice-cold, for in the first moments of trauma the mind cannot always distinguish between the two.

But cold or hot, the sensation shocked her. She dropped the chest with a clatter into the kitchen sink. For a moment she stood staring at the maxim, then reprimanded herself for her foolishness. It was just a pathetic, maudlin aphorism created by some teary-eyed Victorian. Nothing more.

Vita was no sentimental fool. She had chosen the box for utilitarian purposes. If it turned out she had gotten the bargain of the century and the little chest was worth a bundle, so much the better.

She set the box aside, went to the refrigerator, and peered in. As soon as she had finished lunch, Vita would take it to her office, file her computer disks and CDs in it, and do a little research on Victorian memorabilia boxes.

It was time to find out whether or not this Treasure Box was valuable, after all.

2

THE PORTAL

When she entered her office with the antique box, Vita cast a fleeting glance at the answering machine. Before she left for town, she had erased her sister's voice from the tape, and now the light glowed a steady red. No new messages. Good. That meant Mary Kate had given up.

She sat behind her desk and stared out the window for a moment—not that she could see much. Vita's office had once been a large sunroom on the southeast corner of the house, surrounded by windows on two sides. But the sunlight rarely got in anymore; she had let the privet hedge next to the foundation grow up until it wove into a living curtain of green through which no prying eyes could penetrate. Someone walking by on the sidewalk might see a pinpoint of light or two peering out, like separated stars in a near-empty galaxy, but they couldn't see Vita, and she couldn't see them.

With the Treasure Box at her elbow, she spent an hour and a half thumbing through her large collection of books about antiques. By the time she had turned the final page of the last one, she had a stack three feet high on the floor beside the desk. She had located two dozen or more Victorian memorabilia boxes, ranging in value from a few dollars to several thousand, but nothing resembling the box she had discovered at Pastimes.

Heaving a sigh of frustration, she loaded her arms full and began replacing the books on the shelves that lined the two walls not taken up by windows. Her eyes lingered on a framed bulletin board filled with postcards, visual representations of places she had written about in the past: the Eiffel Tower in Paris, the Trevi Fountain in Rome, an estate in the Cotswolds that had been turned into very affordable holiday cottages, a beer garden in Munich, a dairy farm in Wales. All places as familiar to her as this room . . . except that she had never seen a single one of them.

But that was one of the wonders of the modern world, wasn't it? Vita didn't actually have to *go* anywhere. She could just log on, click a few buttons, and through the magic of virtual reality, experience whatever her heart desired without the claustrophobia of crowded airports or the inconvenience of delayed flights or the worry about lost passports or stolen funds.

The Internet. Of course! Maybe her reference books didn't have the information she needed, but she knew where to go to find it. If there was anything to be learned about the value of the Treasure Box, she'd uncover it on the Web.

She hastily finished putting the books away, sat down in front of her computer, and logged on. From a long way away, she heard a faint rumbling noise—was the area due for a thunderstorm? She clicked a cloud icon on the screen: sure enough, the weather service predicted "the likelihood of precipitation in the afternoon and early evening, moderate to heavy in some locations, with significant electrical activity." Translation: a good chance for a thunderstorm.

Vita considered whether or not she should shut down her computer. Two years ago, her hard drive had been scrambled by a power outage, and three months' worth of research had been lost. Still, this probably wouldn't take very long, and she had a new surge protector in case of power spikes or brownouts.

She logged onto eBay and ran a general search for "Victorian memorabilia boxes," but the offerings were meager. A general Web search through various antique sites seemed more promising, but after thirty-five minutes of sorting through photographs which seemed to take forever to download, she came up empty-handed.

Raindrops began to spatter the windowpanes, and the thunder drew closer. Just one more attempt, and then she'd shut down. She exited the current site and tried a more specific search, using the words from the lid of the box: Enchanted Treasure Chest.

The screen shifted, and as her cursor turned into a rotating hourglass, a notice came up on the bottom of the screen: *Downloading . . . 2%, 6%, 10%. Remaining time: less than one minute.*

Vita drummed her fingers impatiently. She must have hit the right one this time.

Rain pelted against the glass in force now. A heavy cloud cover shrouded the room in gray, and she heard lightning crack in the distance. But the storm was still far enough away; she wasn't about to shut down now.

A Web site filled the screen, a star-studded sky with a banner across the top that read, *Welcome to the Enchanted Box: Antiques for the Electronic Age.*

Vita scrolled down through the site map. Furniture, jewelry, art, estate pieces. Nothing about nineteenth-century memorabilia. She was just about to click on the link to "Accessories" when she saw it. In the upper right-hand corner of the home page, a tiny moving icon. A box. A small blue box with some kind of writing on the top, opening and closing, revolving on its axis.

She rolled her cursor to the top of the page, hovered over the moving icon, and watched as it turned into a little white hand with one finger pointing upward. "Yes!" she whispered. "It's a link."

This had to be it.

She held her breath and clicked the icon. At the same moment, a writhing bolt of lightning struck the tree outside her window. Thunder rattled the house, the lights went out, and the computer screen faded to black.

⌒

When the lightning hit, Vita felt a tingle come up through the mouse and keyboard into her arms. She shut her eyes and put her hands to her temples, praying—if you could call "God, no!" a prayer—that she hadn't fried the motherboard. ⌐

A minute passed, then two, while she sat there holding her head. She was just reaching for the telephone to call the power company when the lights flickered back on. The surge protector on her computer desk gave a faint little beep, and its red light changed to green, a signal that electricity had been restored and everything was all right. Maybe.

Vita pushed the button to restart her computer, and while it booted up, she rose and went to the window to see if she could assess the damage from the lightning strike. But the thick hedge screened the yard from view so effectively that she could see only dark shapes. Behind her, she heard the characteristic beeps and clicks as the computer went through its start-up procedures. She let out a sigh of relief, went through the dining room, and stepped out onto the front porch.

Although threatening clouds still hung in the sky, the storm had rolled through quickly, and the rain had stopped. Everything had been washed clean; the air smelled charged and fresh, like the atmosphere of a younger, more vibrant world. The roof seemed intact—that was a good sign. One massive limb, almost large enough to be a tree in its own right, had fallen from the big oak tree in the side yard, but there was no other damage as far as Vita could see. She went back into the house, latching the screen behind her but leaving the door open to let in some of that fresh air.

Her computer had finished its boot-up and gone to a screen saver. Vita took her place at the keyboard. She had lost the Web site when the power went down, but now that she knew where to look,

23

she could get it back easily enough. Right now she needed to make sure her new project files were intact, or she would have to recreate more than a month of work on the Alaska project.

She could just imagine the conversation with her editor: "Nick, it's Vita Kirk. I'm—well, I'm going to be a little late on my deadline. You see, lightning struck my hard drive, and—"

Sheer genius, Vita thought. Almost as convincing as "the dog ate my homework."

Vita touched the Enter key, and her screen saver disappeared. But instead of the familiar desktop with her program icons around the perimeter, she found herself staring at a dark blue screen studded with tiny white stars. It looked a bit like the home page she had been on a few minutes before, except that there were no headers, no menus, no nothing—just a tiny keyhole in the center. But how had she gotten back on-line without logging on?

She rolled her pointer to the top left of the screen, hoping for a drop-down menu that would let her exit the program. Nothing. She went to the bottom. No response there. She pressed Escape, even unplugged the telephone line, but nothing helped. At last she simply shut down and started the computer again. There would be a delay while the automated disk-scanning program checked out her hard drive for damage, but it couldn't be avoided.

Vita waited and watched while the scan-disk program went through its survey of the hard drive, exhaling a sigh of relief as the titles of her familiar programs and working files flashed by. So far so good. The dog hadn't eaten her homework after all.

The safety protocol finished, and her desktop flickered on the screen for just an instant. But before she could open a single file, it was gone again. The same blue-black sky with its scattering of diamond-like stars filled the monitor.

Great, Vita thought. *Somehow, between the storm and the lightning strike and the icon on the Web site, I've managed to download a virus. I just hope I can get rid of it before it eats any of my hard drive.*

But no matter what she tried, she could not access her anti-virus program or any of the other programs installed on her hard drive. Over and over she rebooted, but every time with the same results. The virus didn't seem to be doing any damage; it was simply blocking her from entering her own computer.

"All right," she muttered to herself after the fifth attempt. "If I can't get *around* it, I suppose I'll just have to go *through*."

She sat there for a long time with her hand poised on the mouse, staring at the screen. The field of stars looked so deep— three-dimensional, as if you could reach out and touch them, as real as actual constellations in the night sky. Was that the Big Dipper over there on the left? And Orion? And the North Star? Did she really see a comet shoot by?

Vita shook herself back to reality. It was a Web site, for heaven's sake. A sophisticated one, but still, they could do almost anything with computers these days.

She peered at the central icon, which seemed to have grown with every attempt to shut the program down. When she had first seen it, it had been tiny, no larger than a single lowercase letter on her word processing program. Now it dominated the center of the screen, and she could see that it, too, had depth and substance, like the starry sky. It was three-dimensional, an ornate brass keyhole on a carved backplate—the kind of keyhole one might find in an elaborately appointed Victorian home. Vita's own house had none of those touches, but she had seen them before. And now she saw something else—light streaming through the keyhole. Not one of the myriad of stars in the background, but living light, as if there were something on the other side, something you would be able to see if you put your eye up very close.

She rolled her pointer to the center of the screen, directly over the light, and waited. But instead of turning into a hand, the cursor transformed into something else: a key. A large, ornate brass skeleton key. Before she could quite absorb the reality of this metamorphosis, a low, whispery voice emanated from her computer speakers:

"Love is the key that unlocks every portal."

With her heart pounding and her blood pumping in her ears, Vita touched the mouse and slipped the key into the lock.

For a moment, nothing happened. And then, as if an invisible door were swinging open in the night sky, a crack appeared. Golden light streamed out in a narrow beam. The portal grew larger. The crack widened and widened until the door stood fully open and filled the monitor in front of her. The light became brighter and more intense, so dazzling that Vita had to put her hand up to shield her eyes.

The door began to rush toward her at great speed. Vita grabbed at the edge of the desk to keep from falling. Though her rational mind knew that she was sitting perfectly still, safe in her chair in front of the computer, her body experienced all the sensations of motion, as if she were in an Imax Theater or a very fast express elevator. Her head spun, and her stomach floated for a second or two.

And then she saw inside.

"Inside" seemed to be a rudimentary kind of workshop, a small room with stone walls and exposed beams and a rough table in the center. At the table, surrounded by a scattering of tools and a bright kerosene lamp, a man in shirt sleeves sat motionless with his head bent over a box—a small metal chest painted blue. In his hand he held a paintbrush, and there were flecks of gold-colored paint in his thinning brown hair.

Vita ran her cursor in circles over the scene, pausing on the box, the lamp, the paintbrush, the table, even the man himself, to see if she could get a link that would allow her to exit the program. But nothing worked.

The voice came again, low and entreating: *"His name is Jacob Stillwater. Watch and learn."*

Then the flame of the lamp began to flicker, and the man began to move.

3

THE TINKER

Jacob Stillwater leaned over his bench and inspected his handiwork. "Ah, my little Sophie," he murmured to himself, "if you ever doubted that you are the glory of your father's heart, know it now." He stepped back, put his hands on his hips, and smiled. "A labor of love—for your birthday."

Vita drew closer to the monitor and peered at him. He was an ordinary-looking fellow, not especially handsome or well-built. A slight middle-aged paunch showed beneath his work apron, and a bald circle at the back of his skull made him look a little like a tonsured monk. Still, he had a pleasant expression, warm brown eyes, and a genuine smile. From the rafters over his head hung the products of a tinker's trade—hammered copper pots and pans, strainers and serving spoons, bridle bits and ornamental brasses. And on the worktable in front of him sat a sea blue box, painted all around with a map of the world and adorned with brass corners and brass handles and a tiny brass keyhole.

Vita inhaled a quick breath. It was the Treasure Box. *Her* box.

Beyond the single window on the far wall of the workshop, daylight faded into dusk, and Vita watched as the man reached to turn the kerosene lamp brighter. This was an odd sensation—not like viewing a movie, exactly; more like slipping uninvited into a stranger's private spaces. Like voyeurism.

She drew back sharply as a door creaked open, and a stout gray-haired woman entered the shop. "Good evening, Bridget," Jacob said. "Is dinner ready?"

The woman gave an awkward curtsy. "Aye, sir. Or nearly so. Miss Sophie is setting out the table and slicing the bread."

"I'll be right along." She turned to go, but he called her back. "A moment, please. Take a look, Bridget. Will she like it, do you think?" The woman drew near the worktable. "Take care not to touch it," he warned. "The paint's not dry yet."

Bridget made a circuit around the table, looking at the box from all sides. "Ach, Mr. Jacob!" she exclaimed at last. "'Tis a work of art, it is. That child's got an imagination that won't be stopped, as well as a taste for adventure. It'll be her dearest treasure, and that's the truth."

Jacob grinned and put a hand on Bridget's shoulder. "It's her tenth birthday, and I want it to be special."

"As special as the child herself," Bridget agreed. "I'll be making her favorite dinner—glazed pork roast and mashed potatoes."

"Pork roast?" Jacob shook his head. "We can't afford—"

"Tush, now," Bridget interrupted. "Don't you go poking your

nose into my business, if you please. As it happens, the butcher's got a fondness for me shepherd's pie."

"And for a certain Irishwoman, too, if I'm not mistaken." Jacob pinched at her cheek, and she slapped his hand away.

"Ach! He's an old fool, he is, but I'm not above a little honest bartering to get my girl a roast for her birthday. If he's enough of an eejit to think something else is like to come of it, it's his own fault, and none of mine."

Jacob laughed. "Bridget, you're a wonder."

"I am," she declared. "And don't you be forgetting it." She smiled at him and lowered her voice conspiratorially. "I'm making her an applesauce spice cake, too, from the last of those apples I canned last fall. Sophie's little friend Rachel Woodlea will be joining us, as well as Rachel's sister Cathleen. It'll be a regular party, with streamers and hats and favors—some of those silvery crackers with the toys inside. I saved a few over from Christmas."

"Sounds perfect. I don't know what we'd do without you, Bridget."

- "A widower with a child needs a housekeeper, sir," she said in a no-nonsense tone. "Anyone else in my position would have done the same."

"I don't think so," he objected. "You love Sophie as if she were your own. And you take such good care of us. You're not a housekeeper, Bridget. You're a member of the family."

She ducked her head. "Does my heart good to hear you say so, Mr. Jacob. I do love that child with all my heart, that's God's

30

certain truth. And don't you worry yourself about her birthday. It'll be a celebration to end all, I promise you."

"I'm sure it will. Just keep her out of my shop until tomorrow night, will you? I want my gift to be a surprise."

"Aye, sir. And a fine gift it is. Now, if you're ready, dinner is waiting."

Jacob turned down the lamp wick until the flame sputtered out, and Vita's computer screen went dark.

Vita stared at the black monitor, trying in vain to sort out her feelings. By rights, she ought to feel confused or frustrated or even angry at not being able to get into her own computer. But her prevalent emotion at the moment was simply disappointment at the brevity of the scene.

She blinked and looked around her. The storm had passed on through, but night was falling, and a chilly breeze blew through the screen door, raising goose bumps on her arms. She got up and shut the door, turned on a few lights, and headed for the kitchen to find something to eat. The leftover chicken casserole would do. She heated it in the microwave, poured herself a glass of milk, and returned to her office.

The computer screen was still black, as if the system had gone to sleep. Gingerly she touched the Enter key, not in the least certain whether she hoped for more of Jacob Stillwater or a return to her familiar desktop programs.

The monitor faded back in. This time the scene was different: a larger room than Jacob's workshop, but crafted of the same rough stone. On the far wall, a small fireplace held a smoky peat fire, with a mismatched collection of threadbare furniture arranged before the hearth. In the foreground, a trestle table was set with a humble meal of boiled potatoes, beans, and a crusty loaf of homemade bread. At one end of the table, a small girl with auburn curls and dancing brown eyes stood slicing the bread, shifting impatiently first on one foot and then on the other.

Vita took a bite of the lukewarm casserole and leaned back in her swivel chair to watch.

⌒

"Papa! Papa!" Sophie dropped the knife onto the table with a loud clatter and ran into her father's outstretched arms.

"How's my girl this evening?" Jacob embraced her and gave her a kiss on her sun-freckled nose.

"I'm just fine, Papa," she said, twining her arms around his waist. "I made the bread all by myself almost, and helped Bridget beat the rugs."

Jacob glanced over her head toward Bridget, who moved a small vase of wildflowers to the center of the table. "Is that right, Bridget?"

"Aye, sir. A regular little helper, that one."

Sophie wriggled out of her father's arms and picked up the long bread knife. "Like this, Papa—bam! Bam! Bam!" She brought the flat of the knife down on top of the loaf, sending bits of crust flying. "The dust went everywhere! It was fun."

Jacob threw back his head and laughed. "I'm sure it was, love. But you'd best leave the bread intact if we're to have supper tonight."

"Whatever you say, Papa." Sophie seated herself primly at the table and batted her eyes at him. "You know what tomorrow is, don't you?"

"Tomorrow?" Jacob winked in Bridget's direction. "I believe tomorrow is . . . Friday."

"And what else?"

"Laundry day," Bridget chimed in.

"And what else?"

"Hmm." Jacob scratched his head. "Market day in the village?"

Sophie rolled her eyes. "No, no. Think hard, Papa. It's something about *me*."

"About you? Give me a hint."

"It's a special day."

"Special day, special day—" Jacob pretended to wrack his brain. "Does it have something to do with a number? Maybe—two numbers?"

Sophie let out a giggle. "Yes."

"Could it be—no, it's inconceivable. Tomorrow couldn't possibly be Sophie's *birthday!*" He bent over her and tickled her until she howled. "And you're going to be—what? Nineteen? Twenty-six? Fifty-four? I forget."

33

"Silly Papa!" Sophie panted between squeals of laughter. "You know. It's 1910. The century is ten years old, and so am I. Or I will be tomorrow."

Jacob took his place at the table and regained his composure. "My little girl—ten years old! I can hardly believe it. I can still remember you in your mother's arms—" He stopped abruptly and swiped at his eyes.

"Let's have supper before it gets cold," Bridget said quickly. She sat down, and they all joined hands.

"God of the Universe," Jacob prayed, not bowing his head but letting his gaze drift from his daughter to Bridget to the food on the table, "you give us many gifts. The bounty of the fields for our nourishment, the warmth of family, the joys of work and play. Thank you for all these blessings, for laughter, and for love. May we ever live with a grateful heart. Amen."

"Amen," Sophie echoed and began heaping potatoes on her plate.

~

A grateful heart . . .

The words gnawed through Vita's stomach lining like a parasite. She could recall—faintly, like the echo of a childhood taunt—a time when she, too, had uttered such prayers. A time when gratitude to a benevolent Higher Power came naturally, freely.

Once upon a time, Vita Kirk had believed in God, had

embraced the fairy tale with all the credulity of the green and gullible. Sunday school, children's choir, confirmation class. Prayers at home around the dinner table and at bedtime. Vita had conversed with the Almighty, and the Almighty had heard and answered. Or so she assumed.

But she had been much younger then, much less experienced in the futility of hope.

And now she looked at Jacob Stillwater and wondered: *What does this man, this tinker, have to be grateful for?* His home was little more than a hovel. He made pots for a living, and if the scant dinner upon his table was any indication, a meager living at that. His wife was dead, her tasks taken up by a crude, beefy-faced Irish washerwoman. The only birthday gift he could afford to give his daughter was a tin box made in his pathetic little shop. A place to keep her treasures—in the unlikely event that she had any treasures to keep.

Vita picked up the box and held it in both hands, considering the labor that went into its creation. Despite herself, a stab of pity knifed through her. Poor Jacob. He could have been an artist, could have given himself to painting or goldsmithing or jewelry making—something that would have lifted him out of his poverty, anything besides hammering out cheap cooking pots for others as wretched and miserable as himself. The man was trapped in a life of squalor and deprivation. And yet he smiled broadly, laughed warmly, and prayed his little ritual of thanksgiving with sincerity. He didn't even know enough to realize what he was missing.

She lifted the lid and considered the epigram: *Love Is the Key That Unlocks Every Portal.* If Jacob Stillwater had written those words, surely the irony had escaped him. Love hadn't unlocked his prison door. If anything, it had confined him to a constricted, dead-end existence—caring for his daughter, longing for his wife, scrabbling for a foothold to make it through each day.

For a long time Vita sat there, staring absently at the box, her mind filled with images of Jacob and his paltry, mundane life. After a while the computer gave a whirr and a whine and began to transfer itself into standby, its "sleep" mode.

She shut down the system and glanced at the clock. Nearly midnight. A few blue-white tendrils from the streetlight on the corner crept into the room through the high hedge against the windows, but they did little to dispel the night. Except for a single desk lamp, the office was dark. Reflected in the glass Vita could see herself, cradling the Treasure Box in her arms—an obsolete tintype come to life in the modern world.

She pulled the chain on the desk lamp, plunging the room into blackness, and groped her way up the stairs to her bedroom.

4

THE CELEBRATION

Vita slept sporadically, her dreams invaded by images of a little brown-eyed girl in patched hand-me-downs running across a flowered hillside, carrying a small blue box under one arm. At the far side of the meadow near a gently flowing stream stood two people—a man in dark brown trousers and a forest green shirt, and a woman in a pale yellow-green dress.

Vita instinctively surmised that these were the girl's parents. They stood waving and laughing and motioning for her to come to them. But just as the child reached her mother, the woman in the flowing green dress turned into a weeping willow tree on the bank of the stream. Her branches brushed the girl's hair as she ran past, and the father, a bit beyond the water's edge, metamorphosed into a stout oak. The child splashed through the shallows, climbed into the lower branches of the tree, and sat there, swinging her legs and singing a sad little song.

When she awoke, Vita couldn't remember the words or the

tune; she could barely remember the dream, but a sense of urgency seized her. Despite all logic, she felt a sense of foreboding, a premonition of something that would happen to little Sophie—or to her father Jacob. What about the birthday party and Jacob's gift of the Treasure Box? Was the dream some kind of omen, some—

With a huff of disgust, Vita came to her senses. She got out of bed and stalked to the bathroom, carrying on an internal argument as she brushed her teeth. *These aren't actual people, Vita,* she told herself. *This is a story, a computer fabrication. A virus.* Maybe in the clear light of morning she could find a way to get around the electronic infection, to neutralize it and get back to work. Back to the real world, the world of deadlines and contracts and word counts. Back to a world that made sense.

She brushed out her hair with a vengeance, then without bothering to pull it back, threw the brush down on the dressing table and left the bathroom. Still in her pajamas and slippers, she padded downstairs, turned on the computer, and went to the kitchen to make coffee while the system booted up. When she came back to her office with a steaming mug, the monitor displayed no program icons, no desktop. Only that dark blue screen full of blinking constellations.

Vita sat down at the keyboard and stared at the stars, and all her self-directed anger drained away. In a sudden moment of clarity she realized that she wasn't the least bit disappointed. The Alaska project would just have to wait.

She hit the Enter key and waited as the starry sky faded to gray and the interior of Jacob Stillwater's house came into view. The setting was, as Vita had predicted, a party—Sophie's tenth birthday party. What Vita hadn't expected and couldn't explain was that this time when the scene unfolded before her, she perceived far more than she should have. Two of the people she had never laid eyes on before, yet she knew—without knowing *how* she knew—that they were Sophie's best friend Rachel and her sister Cathleen. She knew that Cathleen Woodlea dominated Rachel, and that Rachel, a mild-mannered child, usually gave in to her sister's bullying. She could understand it all, without being told.

When she had taken her first glimpse into Jacob Stillwater's workshop, Vita had felt a twinge of shame, and wondered briefly if watching him and his little family could be considered prying. Now, not only could she see the faces and hear the conversations, she could even see into the minds and hear the inner thoughts of Jacob and Sophie and some of the others—like a voice-over in a movie script. She felt Jacob's pride and loneliness, his grief over his wife's absence, his anticipation of presenting to Sophie his gift of the Treasure Box. She sensed Bridget's love for them both, and her longing for a family of her own. Her own heart beat in time with the rhythms of Sophie's giddy excitement and the underlying sadness of missing her mother.

Vita didn't have the faintest idea how to handle this new source of information. Accustomed to a world barely wide enough for one, the sheer claustrophobia of having that space invaded by

39

other minds and hearts and lives should have overwhelmed her. But her fascination was stronger than her fear. Besides, she couldn't abort the program, couldn't shut it down. She might just walk away, but she was certain that whenever she came back, it would still be here—asleep, on standby, waiting for her to wake it up and set it in motion again.

What else could she do but drink her coffee, sit back, watch, and wait?

Vita counted only five people gathered around the trestle table by the hearth. Only five, and yet the stone-walled room seemed crowded to capacity. At the head of the table sat ten-year-old Sophie, presiding over the slicing of a cream-frosted spice cake. Paper streamers hung from the rafters, and tiny bits of confetti and small toys from the broken silver crackers littered the table. To Sophie's right sat her father Jacob, and to her left, Rachel. Cathleen perched primly on the rough wooden bench next to her sister, and at the foot of the table stood Bridget, beaming broadly over the celebration.

"The biggest slice goes to Papa," Sophie said, cutting an enormous slab and setting it in front of her father. "Thank you, Papa, for the party." She cast an adoring look in his direction. "And thank *you,* Bridget," she said, smiling and passing a second piece of cake down to the housekeeper. "It's the most wonderful birthday ever."

She cut two more slices for Rachel and Cathleen, exactly the same size, and set them on the table in front of the two girls. Cathleen eyed Rachel's cake and, when she thought no one was looking, switched the two pieces. But Sophie noticed, and frowned.

"I brought you a present, Sophie," Rachel said, her voice shy and whispery. She reached into her pocket and pulled out a small battered box, tied with a piece of cotton string.

Sophie cradled the box in one hand and fingered the string. Although Cathleen liked to put on airs and pretend she was superior to everybody else, Sophie knew the Woodlea family was little better off than Sophie's own. They couldn't afford to buy a gift for a ten-year-old. For a split second she began to protest—until she caught a glimpse of the look in Rachel's eye. Whatever was in the box was important to Rachel—too important to be diminished by a well-meaning refusal.

"Thank you, Rachel." She leaned across the table and hugged her friend, then gently untied the string and lifted the lid. Nested in a bit of cotton was a small locket on a length of yellow knitting yarn. In places the silver plating had rubbed off, showing the base metal underneath, and Sophie recognized it immediately. It was Rachel's most cherished possession, a gift from her grandmother at Rachel's baptism. She always kept it hidden behind a loose stone in the cottage wall, where Cathleen couldn't find it.

Sophie held it up. "Oh, Rachel, I can't believe it. Your locket! Are you sure—?"

Rachel nodded mutely, her blue eyes shining. "Happy birthday," she managed in a choked voice.

Cathleen lurched to her feet and snatched the locket out of Sophie's hands. "Rachel, you idiot! You can't give her this! It's special. Mama will kill you!" She reached into the pocket of her pinafore, pulled out a rumpled wad of fabric, and tossed it in Sophie's direction. "Here, Sophie, you can have this."

It was a handkerchief doll, old and worn, created from a square of homespun dyed with tea. Sophie gazed placidly at Cathleen, then picked up the ragged doll and looked at it. One of its button eyes was missing, and its embroidered smile grinned crookedly on its cotton-stuffed head.

"I didn't expect a gift from you, Cathleen," Sophie said graciously. "But thank you very much." She sat down and smoothed at the doll's dress.

Rachel, however, was not to be denied. Sophie had never once seen her stand up to Cathleen, but clearly Sophie's birthday, in Rachel's mind, called for desperate measures. She forced Cathleen's fist open and retrieved the locket. "For your information," she grated through clenched teeth, "Mama *told* me I could give it to her. You'd have one, too, if you hadn't gone and lost yours." She turned back to Sophie and placed the locket in her hand. "Cathleen's right," she said. "This locket *is* special. That's why I want you to have it."

Sophie took it, and with great ceremony slipped the circle of yarn over her head. The small silver oval caught the lamplight and shone like pure gold. There was no question now of refusing the gift.

~

Jacob watched the scene with wonder, and with pride. How had his boisterous little girl grown into such a gracious, almost elegant young lady? It certainly wasn't because of anything he had taught her. Elena must have instilled those qualities in the child while she was still alive, in some magical moment between mother and daughter when Jacob wasn't looking.

Sophie hadn't argued with Cathleen over the locket, or insisted upon her own way. She hadn't refused it, which would have hurt little Rachel's feelings. She obviously cared much more for her friendship with Rachel than she did about any material gift. And she had a way about her of making people feel cherished and valued.

Jacob blinked hard, and his daughter's image cleared before his eyes. She had Elena's looks, with that thick auburn hair and dark, intense eyes. And more importantly, she had Elena's heart. She was, in all respects, her mother's daughter.

Sophie had been six years old when Elena had contracted tuberculosis and died. For months Jacob had wandered around in a dazed grief, barely managing to eat and sleep, let alone remember that he had a child who depended upon him for care. By the time he came out of his fog, Bridget had installed herself in the household and swept the child into a fierce embrace of nurture and comfort. But for all of Bridget's good intentions, a house-keeper could never take the place of a mother—or a father.

Like most men, Jacob had always left the bulk of Sophie's upbringing to his wife. But Elena was gone. Sophie needed a parent, and Jacob was the only candidate for the job. Fortunately for him, she proved to be an easy child, open and trusting and over-flowing with love. They began to take long walks along the river in the evenings after dinner. He taught her how to repair a leaky kettle and split firewood, and she instructed him in the finer points of hosting a tea party and making porridge without burn-ing it to the bottom of the pot. They talked. They giggled. They shared secrets. And Jacob discovered, much to his surprise, that fatherhood had rewards he'd never dreamed of.

He still missed Elena, of course, still thought of her every day and dreamed of her every night, still longed to see her smile at him over the breakfast table or feel her snuggle close for warmth on a cold winter's night. But in her absence, he began to understand his daughter in ways that many fathers never did.

Other men might measure wealth in terms of money or power or prestige. Jacob Stillwater's treasure had auburn curls and sparkling brown eyes and her mother's lilting laugh.

Ignoring Cathleen, who was still miffed about the locket, Sophie watched with interest as Papa went to the mantel and brought down a gift swathed in the same kind of thick white paper the butcher used to wrap the pork roast for their dinner. She eyed the bright green ribbon with delight, imagining how fine it would look twined in her hair when next she wore her good green dress for church on Sunday. Or perhaps she'd put Rachel's locket on it and tie it around her neck.

"This," Papa said, setting the gift in front of her with a flourish, "is for my darlin' girl." -

"Oh, Papa, thank you!" She loosened the bow and smoothed the ribbon against the edge of the table, then folded it carefully and laid it aside.

"Open it, Sophie!" Rachel insisted.

Sophie removed the paper, and for a moment or two she couldn't speak. It was the loveliest thing she had ever seen: a small chest, crafted in tin and painted blue, with a map of the world covering its surface and delicate brass workings at the corners. She knew instantly that Papa had made it with his own hands, and that made it twice as precious.

"Look at the dragon!" Rachel squealed. "And over here—an elephant. And the seals!"

"Sea lions," Papa corrected with a smile. "Where the elephant is, that's Africa." He extended a long calloused finger. "Here's England. We're right up here, amid these hills, near this little lake."

"Where's America?" Cathleen asked in a surly tone.

"All the way across the ocean, there." Papa pointed. "Are you interested in America, Cathleen?"

45

"I'm interested in anywhere but here," she retorted. "Anywhere a person's got a chance at a decent life. America's rich, don't you know? Gold for the taking, right out of the ground. Big cities with fancy homes and carriages and—"

Papa frowned at her. "Money isn't the most important thing in the world, lass."

"It is if you haven't got it."

She jerked the box roughly out of Sophie's hands and turned it around and around, scrutinizing it. "Where'd this come from?"

"Why, Papa made it, of course." Sophie grinned and kissed her father on the cheek. "Thank you so much, Papa. I couldn't have imagined a more special birthday present. I'll keep all my treasures in it." She retrieved the box from Cathleen's grasp, nestled the handkerchief doll inside, and laid the silver locket gently on top.

"It's just an old homemade box," Cathleen muttered under her breath. "What's so special about that?"

Sophie didn't answer. Cathleen could protest all she wanted, but nobody who was looking could miss the glitter of envy in her eyes.

5

CHILD'S PLAY

Sophie and Rachel sat cross-legged in the shade of a tall oak tree, giggling.

"Behold Titania, Queen of the Fairies," Sophie declared solemnly, settling the handkerchief doll into a forked space at the base of the tree. "And these—" She lined up a semicircle of acorns in the grass, with their little hats bowed down facing the doll. "These are her faithful fairy minions, who have come to do her bidding."

At first Vita thought she might be viewing the yard surrounding Jacob's cottage, for a stone's throw away she could see a sturdy hut with a thatched roof and wild pink flowers climbing over the doorway. But a woman, younger and thinner than Bridget, came to the doorway and stood there leaning on her broom, smiling at the girls. Rachel's mother, Rose Woodlea.

"Where's that sister of yours got off to?" she asked her daughter.

Rachel shrugged. "I don't rightly know, Mam."

"Well, if you see her, tell her to come inside straightaway. She left without finishing her work. There's wood and water yet to fetch, and I've got a colicky baby on my hands."

"Do you want me to do it?" Rachel got to her feet.

"No, child, it'll wait a while. You've done your own chores, like the good girl you are. There's no point to your doing Cathleen's as well. That girl takes on like the Queen Mother herself. She's got to learn responsibility, or she'll die a pauper." She shook the dust off the broom and went back into the house.

Rachel shot Sophie a black look. "Die a pauper? Not likely, that one."

Sophie reordered the fairy minions into two straight lines and then looked up at Rachel. "So where is she?"

"I expect she's down at the village green, making eyes at that almighty dolt, Rafe Dalton."

"Dalton? The landlord's son, do you mean?"

Rachel nodded and flopped down on the grass next to Sophie. "She's been after him for weeks." She tilted her head and took on a high-pitched, mocking tone: "Oh, Rafe, you're so handsome! Oh, Rafe, you're so smart!"

"Handsome? Smart?" Sophie grimaced. "He's dumb as a rock with a face like a draft horse. And Cathleen's only thirteen!"

"She doesn't care. He'll inherit his father's money and land; that's all she's interested in. And when she marries him, she'll be"—Rachel screwed up her mouth in disdain—"a *la-dy*."

48

"It'll take more than a rich husband to make a lady out of Cathleen," Sophie said.

⌒

As Vita watched the girls playing and laughing together, an unfamiliar emotion stirred within her, something akin to spring fever. She'd once had a friend like Rachel, so long ago it seemed like a wisp of smoke on the wind—not even a dream, just the echo of a memory of a dream. Hattie, the girl's name was—two doors down on East Chestnut Street in Asheville, in the neighborhood where she grew up. Hattie Parker . . . Parkinson. Or maybe it was Mattie. Vita couldn't remember.

But she could recall vague images of drawing hopscotch blocks on the sidewalk with brightly-colored wedges of chalk. Hiding under the porch in the cool semidarkness. Dressing up for Halloween in Mama's high heels and a musty-smelling fur cape from an old trunk in the attic. Putting doll clothes and a yellow bonnet on Harley, the Parkers' big gray tabby cat. Trading plastic rings from a Cracker Jack box and promising to be friends forever.

Forever. How long was that, Vita wondered, *in Cracker Jack years?*

⌒

Sophie and Rachel, with their heads together arranging Queen Titania and her acorn fairies, didn't see the attack coming. Suddenly

49

a foot slammed down onto the grass, crushing several fairies and grinding Titania herself into the dirt.

"You told, didn't you?"

Sophie looked up. Cathleen stood above them with both hands on her hips, her mouth twisted into a scowl and her cheeks the color of boiled beets. She glanced over at Rachel to see a look of sheer terror pass over the girl's ashen face.

"You told Mam where I was—with Rafe, down at the green!" Cathleen hauled Rachel to her feet and shook her. "You're going to pay for this, you are!"

Sophie jumped up and grappled with Cathleen, trying to make her let go of Rachel's arm. "Stop it, Cathleen! Rachel didn't tell your Mam a thing."

Rachel was beginning to cry. "Cath, you're hurting me."

Cathleen shook harder, digging her fingernails into Rachel's skin. "I'm going to hurt you a lot worse before this is over! Sweet little sister, who never does anything wrong! Perfect Rachel, Mam's pride and joy!" She began to pummel Rachel with her free hand, boxing her ears with a clenched fist.

Sophie latched onto Cathleen's flailing arm, and the fist connected with her nose. Blood spurted out, but Sophie held on. "Stop! Stop it *now!*" She heaved with all her might. Cathleen's grip gave way, and she reeled to one side and fell against the trunk of the oak tree.

For a minute she lay there, stunned and panting. Sophie turned away from her and went to comfort Rachel.

"Your nose is bleeding." Rachel dabbed with a hand at the sticky mess on Sophie's face.

"I'll be fine. Let me look at your arm."

The arm was bruised and bloody, marred by three deep gashes where Cathleen's fingernails had dug into the flesh. Fueled to a fury by white-hot indignation, Sophie whirled around to face Cathleen. "How could you? She didn't do anything."

"You stay out of this!"

"I will not! Rachel is my friend, and even if you are her sister, you've no right to—"

But Cathleen wasn't listening. She had risen to a sitting position, her eyes fixed on a point just beyond where the crumpled form of the handkerchief doll lay. Sophie followed her gaze.

The Treasure Box, her birthday gift from Papa, lay in the grass a few feet away.

"Leave it alone, Cathleen," she warned.

Cathleen lurched toward the box, grabbed it up, and was on her feet in a flash. "You want it back, you'll have to come and get it." She took off running with the box under one arm.

After a split second of hesitation, Sophie went after her, with Rachel close on her heels. She could see Cathleen up ahead, sprinting through the woods that surrounded the cottage, lifting her skirts to jump over a fallen log. But she managed to keep her in sight and could hear Rachel's labored breathing right behind her.

At last they slowed and came into a clearing on the bank of the river. A dead tree spanned out halfway over the water, and

Cathleen stood on the trunk, doubled over laughing at both of them. Then, as if in slow motion, Sophie saw her raise her hands and hold the box out in their direction. "Your precious little box that Papa made for your birthday," she mocked in a singsong tone. She put the box up to her ear and shook it. "I hear something rattling inside. A locket? Something special? Some *treasure* you just couldn't live without?"

"Give it back, Cathleen," Rachel demanded.

"Or what? You'll tell on me? You'll go crying to Mam?"

Rachel took a step forward. "It's not yours. It's Sophie's. And you know it's important to her."

"Rafe Dalton was important to me. But the two of you had to spoil that, didn't you?"

"We didn't tell. Now, give it back."

"You didn't tell? Oh, well, that explains everything. Mam just knew all on her own, right where to find me with Rafe, and when. Maybe she's got the second sight. Maybe she had a vision."

"Put the box down, Cathleen. Please. I beg you."

"You beg me? You *beg* me?" She laughed wildly, tossing the box from one hand to the other and moving in a bizarre dance up and down the tree trunk. "Beg some more."

"Please," Rachel repeated. "Please, put it down."

"All right, since you asked so nicely."

Cathleen held the box out toward Rachel, dangling it by one of its brass handles. Then, as Sophie watched in horror, she swung her arm out over the river and dropped it into the water.

"Nooo!" Rachel darted to the bank and plunged into the stream. For a moment or two she kept her footing, wading out into the shallows. Cathleen still stood on the fallen tree, laughing.

The bottom sloped down until the water rose as high as Rachel's knees, then up to her hips. As the weight of it caught her skirts, she slipped and fell, and her head went under. Spluttering and gasping, she came up with the blue tin box in one hand. "I found it!" she shouted.

Triumphant, she began struggling back toward the shore. Sophie buried her face in her hands, but when she looked up again, Rachel was staggering, pitching on the mossy rocks. She lost her balance, and as she went down, her head struck the side of a massive boulder, just a few feet from where the river widened and deepened and rushed downstream in a cataract of white water.

Before Cathleen could scramble down from the fallen tree, Sophie was in up to her waist, frantically trying to reach her friend. The day had been mild, but the water was like ice, and the current was a good deal stronger than she had expected. She could hear Cathleen behind her—no longer laughing, but screaming above the roar of the river: "Rachel! Rachel!"

At last Sophie got to her, and with some difficulty pulled her face up into the air. Rachel came to, coughing and choking and spitting out river water. When she finally found her feet and stood upright, she was still clutching the precious Treasure Box.

Cathleen waded out part way and stood knee-deep in the stream. "It's all my fault," she muttered. "I never should have . . . I'm sorry. I'm sorry."

Sophie gripped the boulder and watched as Cathleen put an arm around her sister and helped her toward the bank. Exhausted and shivering in the waist-deep water, she wanted nothing more than to go home to Papa, to be warm and dry and wrapped in a blanket by the fire.

"Come on!" Cathleen shouted from the bank, motioning for her to hurry.

But Sophie couldn't move. The hem of her dress, heavy with water and silt, seemed to be snagged on some outcropping under the surface. "I'm caught on something—a branch or a rock, I think," she called back.

"Well, pull it free." Cathleen's repentance apparently hadn't lasted very long; her annoyance was clear in her tone. "We need to go home. It'll be dark soon."

"I'm trying." Sophie tugged vainly at her skirt. "I don't want to rip my dress."

"Tear it, you little fool," Cathleen shot back. "Unless you intend to stay out here all night."

"I'll come help you," Rachel offered, her voice barely audible.

"You'll do nothing of the sort." Cathleen grabbed Rachel's arm to hold her back. "You're already soaked and freezing; we both are." She turned back to Sophie. "Pull harder."

A shudder ran through Sophie, whether from the cold or

from fear she couldn't tell. The sun was beginning to set, and a chill was closing in. The push of the river against her legs seemed to be growing stronger. Long dark shadows stretched over the surface, making it difficult to see. She took a deep breath, braced one hand against the boulder, and yanked with all her might.

She felt a rip, and the dress gave way. The momentum threw her backward into the current, and before she could regain her footing, the force of the water swept her downstream toward the rapids.

The monitor went black. Vita sat staring at it for a full minute after the image had vanished.

She shouldn't be surprised. Both logic and life experience had taught Vita that Murphy's Law was not merely some cynical philosophical construct, but an inescapable reality. If anything could go wrong, it would. Expect the worst, and you'll never be disappointed.

But she hadn't expected *this*. Somewhere, deep down in Vita's soul, in a place beyond the reach of experience and logic, a voice kept saying, *It wasn't supposed to happen this way.*

Rachel had saved the Treasure Box, and Sophie had saved Rachel. Weren't people supposed to be rewarded for their courage and their love, not punished by a capricious God or a heartless Fate? Where was justice? Where was simple fairness?

Vita pounded her fist against the keyboard, but nothing happened. The scene didn't resume. No fortuitous rescue. No happy ending.

Nothing.

Just the vacant computer screen, a black hole, a lifeless eye staring back at her from the depths of a senseless universe.

6

UNDER THE WILLOW TREE

The first rays of a salmon-hued dawn filtered in through the high hedges around Vita's office windows. After roaming around the house for hours, unable to concentrate, Vita had gone to bed in a black funk, determined to keep her distance from this computer and its virus and the compelling, disturbing images it pressed upon her mind. Yet after a sleepless and grueling night, here she sat, coffee cup in hand, as the sky lightened into morning and the clock chimed seven.

The computer was up and running, but so far nothing had happened. For thirty minutes she had waited, staring, while the monitor stared back, dark and unchanging. Maybe it was over. Maybe the virus had consumed her hard drive and there was nothing left.

Then she heard it—faintly. Muted sounds emanating from the dual speakers on the shelf above her head. Muffled footsteps. A rooster crowing. The bark of a dog.

The sounds drew closer, louder. She could hear voices now, although she couldn't make out the words. Shouting. Running. And above and behind the voices, a whooshing like static, like the white noise of a waterfall.

Or a river.

The screen brightened, and an image came into view. A riverbank, flanked by a stand of willow trees. In the middle of the stream, the water tumbled wildly over huge boulders and fallen tree trunks, but where the willows grew, their roots created a sheltered, placid pool. Long strands from the graceful branches cascaded into the shallow water, and light from the rising sun turned the pool to molten gold.

Vita looked closer. Something lay motionless in the water, half propped against the bank. A bedraggled doll, filthy and waterlogged, its dress torn to ribbons.

No. Not a doll. A child.

The footsteps accelerated, and she caught an echo: "Sophie! Sophie!" It was Jacob Stillwater.

"Here!" Vita shouted aloud. "She's over here!"

But of course, no one could hear her. This wasn't real. Still she couldn't seem to quiet the pounding of her heart or stem the surge of adrenaline that shot into her veins.

She could see Sophie's face more clearly now, pale and gray and crisscrossed with lacerations—from tree branches in the water, perhaps, or sharp edges of the rocks. Like a reflection in a broken mirror. Like the spider-web pattern of a shattered windshield.

Like Hattie.

The memory unfolded and settled down on Vita, a thick woolen blanket thrown over her head, cutting off both light and air. How could she have forgotten, buried that image so deep? The picture of Hattie Parker's face, scarred beyond recognition. Seventh grade. The year she lost her best friend without really knowing why.

Hattie had just turned thirteen, and puberty had not been kind to her. Awkward and homely and devastated by her parents' divorce, she had begun acting out—letting her grades slide, drinking on the sly, hanging around with older kids, a wild and rebellious bunch from high school.

Vita had caught up with Hattie at Little Pigs' Barbecue, a local teen hangout, the afternoon before their seventh grade history midterm. "Let's go home and study," she said. "You can have dinner at our house."

Hattie had refused. "Some of us are going out," she said, glancing over her shoulder at a gang of pimply-faced boys and longhaired girls who jostled one another on the hood of an old blue convertible. She didn't say so, but the message was clear: Vita was not invited.

"But it's a school night," Vita protested. "And the exam tomorrow—"

"You're not my mother, OK? So quit hovering." Hattie stormed away, and Vita went home to study alone.

The call came at 11:35 that night. A one-car accident, head-on into a telephone pole on a deserted road outside of town. The driver, a sixteen-year-old sophomore who had received his license five weeks before, had been killed instantly. Hattie had gone face-first through the windshield. Half a twelve-pack of beer lay on the floorboard, and six empty cans littered the backseat.

The doctor wouldn't let her into the room, but Vita went to the hospital anyway, every afternoon for a week. Not a single one of Hattie's new friends ever once set foot in the place. Finally the nurses let her go in—ten minutes, they said. No more.

The visit took less than five. Hattie sat propped up in the hospital bed, her face a patchwork of stitches and puckers and swollen bruises. It had taken the ER doctors nine and a half hours to remove the glass from her face and put her back together. Half an inch closer, and she would have lost her right eye.

"How'd you get in here?" she slurred, her mouth twisting in a direction it wasn't meant to go.

"I've been here waiting to see you every day since the accident. The nurses finally let me in." Vita set a small potted plant and a card on the bedside table. There were no other flowers in the room, no cards, no balloons. Just bare white walls and a hanging drip that went into a needle in Hattie's left elbow. Her eyes flitted back and forth from Hattie's ruined face to the window, to the muted television, to the foot of the bed. She didn't know where to look.

"Go ahead and say it." Hattie turned her head to one side and closed her eyes.

"Say what?"

"*I told you so.*"

"I didn't say that."

"But you thought it." She opened her eyes. "So high and mighty, Vita. Always right. Always in control."

Vita frowned. "I didn't come here to fight with you. I came because—"

"Because you wanted to see the freak? Well, go ahead. Take a look. Take a good hard look."

"You're not a freak, Hattie. The doctors can fix it. It'll take some time, but it'll be all right. At least you're alive."

"Yeah," she said. "Guess I should count my blessings."

"I'm so sorry, Hattie. I just want you to know that—"

"That you'll always be my friend?" Hattie interrupted. "Don't say it, Vita. Just don't. I can't stomach your pity. So just leave, all right?"

Vita left. For a while she held out hope that the accident might serve some good purpose, that she and Hattie could be friends again. But it never happened. Hattie recovered, got out of the hospital, and went on with her life—a life that no longer included Vita Kirk. Once, in high school, Vita saw her in the parking lot, getting onto a motorcycle with some guy twice her age. She wore a black leather jacket with a skull and crossbones embroidered on the back. The banner above the skull read *Scarface*.

Hattie lived, but the friendship died. Vita never really understood why. What she did understand was that when you cared about people and trusted them, they betrayed you. Always. One way or another, they always left you, always let you down.

~

By some miracle, the searchers found Sophie Stillwater in time.

"She's alive!" Jacob shouted as he gathered the limp, dripping body into his arms. "Thank God—she's breathing!"

He fought his way out of the tangle of willow branches and up onto the bank, and somebody tucked a heavy coat around the shivering girl's shoulders.

"Papa," she murmured. "I knew you'd come. I prayed, Papa, and Mama kept me safe until you found me."

Jacob pushed a sodden lock of hair away from her face. "She's burning up with fever. Let's get her home."

~

For ten days little Sophie floated between this world and the next, and although for Vita the timespan was compressed, she knew that the longer Sophie's fever continued, the less chance the child had of surviving. Rachel came every day and sat at her friend's bedside with the blue Treasure Box on her lap. Bridget hovered, feeding Sophie sips of broth from a spoon and cooling her brow with a damp rag. Jacob hung in the doorway with a bleak, haggard look on his face.

Then, on the eleventh day, Sophie's fever broke. The angry

red blotches on her cheeks faded. She slept—not feverishly, shaking with chills and sweats, but a sweet, deep sleep, twelve hours of it. She woke up hungry, ate soup, talked a little. Jacob and Bridget smiled again. Everyone breathed easier.

Everyone except Sophie.---

"It's pneumonia," the physician said, snapping his black bag shut. "She's inherited her mother's weak lungs, it seems. Keep her upright and quiet."

"But she'll be all right, won't she?" Jacob persisted. "She'll get well."

"It's possible her condition may resolve itself," the doctor said. "Only time will tell."

Sophie was lying propped against the head of the bed when Rachel came to visit. "I kept this for you," Rachel said, holding out the Treasure Box. "I dried it out and cleaned up the locket, but I'm afraid your pretty green ribbon got ruined."

"That's all right." It hurt to breathe, and Sophie was so tired she could barely talk, but she took the box and opened it. Inside lay the handkerchief doll, a bit the worse for wear, with the locket twined about its neck on a ribbon the color of mud. "I see you rescued Titania."

Rachel nodded. "And you rescued me," she choked out, fighting tears. "And now—oh, Sophie, I'm so sorry."

Sophie waved a hand to brush the words away. "There's nothing for you to be sorry about. It wasn't your fault. I'm fine. Honestly."

She fingered the locket, then removed it from the doll and placed it around her own neck. "I'll get a new ribbon. A pale green one, like—" She stopped suddenly. "Rachel, can you keep a secret?"

"You know I can. We're friends, aren't we? Best friends."

Sophie smiled. Even smiling hurt, but it was a good kind of hurt. "I saw Mama."

Rachel's eyes widened. "When? Where?" she demanded. "Oh, Sophie, do you suppose that means you've got the sight?"

"No. It wasn't like that. Not a vision, I mean. It seemed—well, like a dream, but very *real*." She sighed and leaned her head back against the pillows.

"Can you tell me?"

Sophie tried to take a deep breath, but her chest felt as if a heavy iron ball had settled on it. The air only went down as far as her breastbone, and all she could manage was a shallow little gasp. Still, she went on.

"I was in the river—it was freezing cold, don't you know, and I was terrified. I saw the rapids come up to get me, and then I was pulled down. Something was tearing at my face." She reached up and touched gingerly at one of the cuts across her cheek. "A tree branch under the water, I think. My head hit on something hard. And then she was there—"

"Your mother? She died when you were six."

"Yes, but I saw her." Sophie's eyes held Rachel's. "You do believe me, don't you?"

"Of course I do. Go on."

"She was standing on the bank, wearing a long, flowy kind of dress—the prettiest dress I had ever seen, a pale yellow green, so pale you could almost see through it. And her hair was loose—not tied up, like she usually wore it—so that it flowed too, around her shoulders and nearly down to her waist. She almost looked like—like a mermaid."

Rachel leaned forward. "And then what happened?"

"She opened her arms and began to sing to me, motioning for me to come to her. And then I was with her, and she was holding my head in her lap and singing, stroking my hair. I wasn't cold anymore. Not until Papa pulled me out of the water."

Talking so much wore Sophie out. It was getting harder and harder to breathe. Now the air only went down a little below her shoulders. But she had to finish.

She pushed the Treasure Box in Rachel's direction. "You're my best friend, Rachel. I want you to have this."

"I'll take care of it for you if you like," Rachel said, misunderstanding. "Until—"

"No," Sophie gasped. "It's yours to keep. Forever. So you won't forget me."

"Forget you?" Rachel's voice grew agitated. "I could never forget you!"

"Remember me," Sophie whispered. "Remember." She closed her eyes. "Can you hear it? The singing? It's so beautiful. So warm and flowy and green."

She wanted to tell Rachel more about the song, but the air had all gone out and wouldn't come back in again. Then she saw her mother coming toward her, smiling, her dress swirling around her like rivulets of water, like music on the breeze.

Like the branches of a willow tree in spring.

~

The light grew brighter and brighter until Vita had to shield her eyes from the monitor. When she looked again, the computer screen had gone black.

7

THE MORNING AFTER

Vita came to, groggy and disoriented, feeling as if she had been on a three-day bender. Yellow sunlight filtered through the sheer lace curtains and splashed across her comforter, bathing the room in a rose-gold brightness. She slitted her eyes and peered at the little china clock on her bedside table. Ten-fifteen.

Ten-fifteen? Impossible. She had gone to bed a little after nine the night before. How could she have slept the clock around, and then some? Rising early was something of a religion with Vita Kirk, or at the very least an obsession. She hadn't set an alarm in years, but she was always awake and moving by seven, even if she had worked until midnight. Only lazy people lolled around in bed after sunup.

She sat up and swung her legs over the side of the bed. Every muscle in her body protested. Her head throbbed, and her sinuses felt as though they were packed with concrete. She let out a groan.

No, definitely not a three-day bender. More like a six-car pileup, with Vita right in the middle.

Maybe a shower would help. She staggered to the bathroom and brushed her teeth while the water heated up. Once under the spray, she stood there for a full five minutes, barely moving except to turn and turn again so that the steaming pulse pummeled first her back and shoulders, then her chest. Her sinuses began to clear, and the pounding in her head eased a little.

But not the tightness in her chest.

Despite the losses Vita had endured in her lifetime, she had little experience of true grief. When Gordon chose Mary Kate over her, a cold blue anger rose up inside her, a wall of ice that shielded her and kept her invulnerable to the heat of any passion. By the time her father died, she couldn't feel much of anything. She could only watch with detached curiosity as her mother shriveled in upon herself like a night-blooming flower against the blazing noonday sun.

Sophie's death, however, had somehow pierced beyond the wall. Vita didn't know how it had happened, but she did know—instinctively, if not experientially—that this was what grief was like. A bottomless, empty pit. A raw place on the soul, an open wound that welcomed the purging burn from every tear.

Scalding water ran down Vita's face, and she tasted an unexpected mixture of shampoo and salt. For a long time she stood there, crying, until the shower turned tepid and she began to shiver.

I have to get hold of myself, she thought. *This is ridiculous. How can I weep so bitterly for a child I've only known through a few brief scenes on a computer screen?* And yet she could still see the little rag-doll figure lying among the willows, feel the weight in her own chest as Sophie's lungs fought for air, hear the song of the willow-woman as she sang her little girl into the great beyond.

Maybe it was because Sophie was so young. Or maybe it was because the friendship with Rachel called up painful memories of losing Hattie. Whatever it was, it was over. Sophie was gone. - - -

Vita turned off the water, toweled herself dry, and stood naked and chilled on the cold tile floor while she ran the hair dryer. The mirror was fogged with steam; she turned the dryer toward the glass and watched as her face appeared in an ever-widening circle surrounded by mist. Red-rimmed eyes set deep over high cheekbones. Wet, dark hair lying in disarray across her bare shoulders. For the first time in years, she saw herself as a portrait of weakness, of vulnerability.

Vita abandoned the dryer, went into the bedroom, and began opening drawers. Within five minutes she was dressed—black slacks, a matching turtleneck, a gray cable-knit cardigan. She brushed back her still-damp hair and fastened it with a rubber band at the nape of her neck, then glanced in the mirror over the dresser. Her face seemed to float above the high turtleneck, a white oval disconnected from the rest of her body. She gave a grunt of disapproval, made the bed with a few expert strokes, and went downstairs.

Vita was at the kitchen table when she heard the Seth Thomas on the living room mantel strike one deep bong. She glanced at the clock on the stove. It was twelve-thirty, and she was still sitting here, pushing around the remains of her scrambled eggs and fiddling with a cup of lukewarm coffee.

She was already nearly a week behind schedule on the Alaska project, but it seemed like a Herculean effort just to get up and walk into her office, much less do any real work. She took one last gulp of the coffee and grimaced as it went down cold.

Stalling wasn't going to help, and it wasn't her style, anyway. Writers had a reputation for sheer genius when it came to procrastination, but Vita had never counted herself among them. She was the one who always finished *before* the deadline. The practice made editors deliriously happy—they were so easily pleased—and kept work coming her way at a steady pace.

Exhaling determination on a sigh, Vita heaved herself to her feet and went to the sink. She scraped the remains into the garbage can, put her plate in the soapy dishwater, and poured herself a fresh cup of coffee. Then she gathered together all her resolve and made her way through the living room onto the sun porch.

The computer sat there, dark and silent, mocking her. The moment of truth. Time to find out whether the Treasure Box program had irreparably damaged her hard drive, or whether it had been a benign virus that, once gone, would let her access her working files.

She opened the top drawer of her desk and riffled through a stack of business cards until she found the one she wanted: Bits 'n Bytes, on Hendersonville Road. Home of Sandy the computer genius. "Don't go anywhere," she said to the card as she wedged it under the corner of the telephone. "If this doesn't work, I may be needing you."

She pressed the power button, then went back to her desk and picked up the folder marked *Alaska*. Behind her, she heard the computer booting up, but she kept her back turned while she flipped through the material. "I've got enough to begin writing," she muttered to herself. "Anything else I need, I can track down on the Internet."

When she heard the music that marked the opening of Windows, Vita swiveled back around toward the computer. There was her desktop, displaying the familiar wallpaper scene of the Blue Ridge Mountains, surrounded by program icons.

Vita stifled a rush of disappointment and tried to force herself to feel relieved. She had been right. The Treasure Box program—or virus, or whatever it was—had vanished. It was time to forget about Sophie and get back to work.

Biting her lower lip, she rolled her mouse over the word processing icon and clicked.

The screen flashed, and a low chuckle emanated from the computer speakers. *"Not today,"* the voice whispered. *"There are portals yet to open."*

The star-studded home page appeared on the monitor, with

71

its tiny brass keyhole sparkling at the center. Vita gnawed at the inside of her cheek. Someone was playing games with her. She had put her feelings aside and convinced herself that she really did want to get back to work, and now this. A virus with an attitude.

"OK, OK," she muttered. "Let's just get this over with, all right?" She rolled her mouse over the keyhole, revealed the key, and inserted it into the lock. The invisible door in the sky swung open, just as it had when Vita had first entered Jacob Stillwater's workshop, and the same bright light blinded her.

But the scene that appeared on the screen was not Jacob's shop, or his house, or even the big oak tree where Sophie and Rachel had played. It was a village green surrounding a large, splashing fountain. For a split second the sound of the water brought back an image of little Sophie being carried down the rapids, and Vita felt a fist squeeze her lungs, cutting off her breathing.

But there was no river. No white water. No danger.

Just a placid village square, occupied by a young couple sitting together on a park bench, holding hands.

Vita looked closely at them. The man was handsome—impeccably dressed with sandy hair, a broad forehead, and a strong jaw line with a deep cleft at the chin. She didn't recognize him, but there was something familiar about the woman. She was pleasant-looking, though not striking, with long brown hair pulled back from her face and deep blue eyes. Around her neck, a sparkling silver oval caught the sunlight and reflected it back like a beacon.

Rachel Woodlea. All grown up, and with a beau of her very own.

~

"Oh, Derrick, it's beautiful!" Rachel fingered the locket. Her voice still bore a shy, whispery quality, as it had when she was a little girl. She lowered her eyes and ducked her head. "What a special gift."

"I searched everywhere to find one like your grandmother's, the one you gave to your little friend so long ago. What was her name? Sonya?"

"Sophie. I've told you a dozen times. Sophie."

Derrick shrugged. "Well, now you have a better one to replace it." He leaned his head down and peered into her eyes. "Happy birthday, dearest Rachel. Now, no more gloomy memories about Sonya. Your twentieth birthday is a day for celebration."

"I remember Sophie's last birthday," Rachel mused. "We had a wonderful party, and—"

"None of that." Derrick held up a warning finger. "You have to learn to let the past stay buried, Rachel. Think about the present, and about the future. *Our* future. The future with you as my wife. Mrs. Derrick Knight."

Rachel shook herself and forced a smile. "Yes. Our future."

"How long do you think we'll have to wait?" Derrick gave her an intense look, as if probing into the depths of her soul.

"Three months, maybe four. By early summer, at the latest.

I've been saving every shilling I can manage from my work at the tavern. Sometimes the fellows even tip me, especially when they win at the gambling tables, or when they're a bit too much in their cups." She shuddered. "It's horrid, Derrick. The noise, the smoke, the drunken brawls. Last week a married man twice my age tried to force me into the back room—"

"Just a little while longer," he interrupted. "I've been hoarding my pay, too, and pretty soon we'll be able to book passage on a ship and sail away to America." He raised an eyebrow and winked rakishly at her. "How much do you have?"

"Almost two hundred pounds, I think. I gave a bit to Mam to buy some things for Colin."

Derrick frowned. "Colin's your baby brother, not your son. It's not your responsibility to clothe him."

"He needed shoes and books for school, Derrick. He's shot up like a weed in the past few months and has outgrown every stitch he owns."

"All right, all right. Just don't get too generous. You'd give away your last pair of bloomers if you thought some other girl needed them."

Rachel blushed at the mention of her undergarments. "I would not, Derrick. Besides, that money's hidden safe away, locked in my Treasure Box—the one Sophie gave me before she died. I keep it out of sight under a loose floorboard in the barn."

"Good. The more we save, the sooner we'll be on our way to

America in proper style." He rose to his feet. "I must go. I have work to do."

Rachel stood and pressed her lips to his cheek. "All right, then. Will I see you later tonight?"

"Don't I always come to the tavern at closing time and walk you home? Until later, my love." He kissed her hand and made his way across the green. Rachel watched him go and smiled.

Vita sat back and sighed. Rachel, the sweet, faithful child, had grown up into a sweet, faithful woman. She was working hard at a job she abhorred so that she and her fiancé could make passage to America. Little Rachel, engaged—and to a very handsome fellow.

There was something about Derrick that bothered Vita, but she couldn't quite put her finger on anything specific. It was probably just her own prejudices. Ever since Gordon, she'd had difficulty trusting men. She had little use for the entire gender, the way most of them swaggered around shot full of testosterone, preening themselves like enormous peacocks, and then congratulating themselves on their sensitivity when they remembered to use the word "woman" instead of "girl."

But this wasn't about Vita. It was about Rachel. And Derrick Knight might not be so bad. He seemed to adore Rachel—buying her gifts, planning for their future together. Perhaps he was a bit full of himself, but weren't they all?

Not all. Not Jacob Stillwater. Vita wondered briefly how he was getting along in the ten years since his beloved Sophie died. Now *there* was a man Vita could approve of—compassionate, kind-hearted, hardworking, creative. If this Derrick fellow turned out to be anything at all like Jacob, Rachel Woodlea would have a very happy life.

And if anyone deserved a happy life, Rachel did.

8

DOWN BY THE RIVERSIDE

The afternoon brought rain—a downpour, splashing through the emerging leaf cover and rolling off the eaves of the roof in a solid sheet. The kind of rain that made Vita want to crawl under the covers and take a long nap—except that she had already slept half the day away.

She had brought a tuna sandwich and a glass of iced tea into the office with her, and ate a late lunch in front of the computer. But so far nothing had reappeared since the scene with Rachel and her fiancé.

Twice Vita had picked up the phone to call Bits 'n Bytes, and twice she had hung up on the first ring. She couldn't explain it, even to herself. Why was she so reluctant to have her hard drive reformatted and get back to her normal work schedule? What was she waiting for?

Vita didn't know. But still she waited. She spent the time—the better part of an hour—flipping idly through her file on Alaska.

Both Norwegian and Princess had good cruise packages, but Norwegian made a double loop through the Inside Passage, both beginning and ending at Vancouver. For a traveler who had round-trip airfare to consider, Norwegian's itinerary was more convenient and less expensive than ending in Anchorage or Seward.

She gazed at the brightly-colored cruise brochures and could almost hear the waves lapping at the sides of the ship. It took a minute or two for Vita's mind to register that she wasn't just imagining the sound. But it wasn't waves; it was more like running water, like the rain cascading off the roof into little pools at the edge of the house. Vita listened intently, then shook her head. No. Rain didn't make that whooshing, rippling noise. This was the sound of laughing, leaping waters. A river running downstream over rocks.

She swiveled around in her chair and stared at the computer monitor. Its flat black surface was fading, and from the speakers she could hear the sounds more clearly now. When the scene materialized, Vita knew exactly what she was seeing.

The river in the woods where Sophie had nearly drowned.

⁓

Rachel sat on the bank, her long skirts gathered around her ankles. She tossed a small stick into the water; it circled for a minute in the still, deep pool, then surrendered to the current and floated downstream on the rapids.

Above Rachel and to the right, a fallen tree extended far out over the water. Cathleen had taunted her sister and Sophie from the horizontal trunk of that very same tree before dropping Sophie's Treasure Box into the river. Rachel threw another stick into the stream. This time Vita saw not a small twig, but a terrified little girl, caught in the undertow and carried down the rapids.

She didn't know how Rachel could stand to be here, at the very spot where her best friend had been lost to her. But then Rachel had endured ten years coming to grips with Sophie's death; Vita had only faced it for the first time yesterday. Maybe time did heal such a wound, or at least scabbed over the infection so that you didn't think about it so much.

A noise behind Rachel startled her—footsteps approaching through the woods. She turned toward the noise, and Vita could see that she had been crying. So much for the "time healing wounds" theory. Rachel still missed Sophie desperately; Vita could see it in her red-rimmed eyes, feel it in the heaviness of her limbs.

The footsteps grew closer, and a second woman appeared. Ten years older, thinner, more stooped than before, but still recognizable. Rose Woodlea. Rachel's mother.

⌒

"Care for a bit of company?" she asked, sitting down on the bank beside her daughter.

Rachel forced a smile. "How did you know where to find me?"

"Where do you always go when you need to think?" Mam waved a hand in the direction of the river. "Is she here?"

"Sophie?" Rachel nodded. "I don't see her, of course, but she's here."

"People say you never get over losing your first love," Mam said quietly. "I suppose that holds for a best friend, too."

Rachel turned and looked at her. "What about you?"

"My first love, or my best friend?" She offered a pale imitation of a smile.

"Well, you didn't lose your first love—at least not for a very long time. I know you miss Papa, but you had twenty wonderful years together." Rachel peered intently into her mother's eyes. "Unless Papa *wasn't* your first love."

Mam patted Rachel's hand and gazed out over the rushing water. "Your father and I were well suited for one another," she said. "Sometimes we want something so much that we truly believe we might die if we don't get it. And then when we get something else instead, we're glad that life didn't give us what we wished for."

"So there *was* someone before Papa?" Rachel whispered. "Who?"

"It doesn't matter. What matters is that your Papa was exactly the right man for me. I grew to love him with all my heart."

Rachel shook her head. "I don't think I could marry someone I wasn't already in love with."

"Love takes different forms, child. Passion is only one aspect of it. In rare cases, you find someone who draws out all that you are—heart, soul, mind, and body. Someone whose very presence in your life helps you become a better person, nobler, truer, more faithful, more of the person you were created to be. But that kind of love is highly uncommon, and nurturing it is the work of a lifetime."

Silence stretched between them, broken only by the splashing of water against rock.

"And what about your young squire, the handsome Mr. Derrick Knight?" Mam said after a while. "Do you love him?"

"Yes." Rachel paused. "At least, I think I do. What little I've experienced of romance has mostly come from books and poems—or the bawdy ballads some of the fellows in the tavern sing. But of course I love Derrick. He's a strong man and very determined. He knows exactly what he wants out of life."

"And he wants you."

"So it seems." Rachel fingered the locket that hung at her throat. "It's probably the first time in the history of the civilized world that a man has chosen the homely sister over the pretty one."

Her mother frowned. "It pains me to hear you talk of yourself that way, Rachel. It's true, your sister has had more than her share of masculine attentions, but she flaunts herself disgracefully. You're not homely, not in the least—you're a lovely girl, in your own quiet way. Isn't it possible that Derrick has seen beyond the surface and discovered your inner beauty?"

Rachel smiled and ducked her head. "I'd like to believe so."

"But you're not certain?" Mam gazed out over the rapids.

"Being the object of adoration can weave a powerful enchantment around a soul. Especially when a girl hasn't been adored nearly enough in her life."

"He's good to me, Mam. Maybe that should be enough."

"Maybe." Mam sighed. "Only your heart can tell you."

"The only thing my heart is telling me right now is that I wish Sophie were here." Rachel got to her feet and went to sit on the fallen log. "I want to talk to her, to hear what she has to say. I can't imagine getting married without her there. And every time I come here, I think back to that day ten years ago when— because of my fight with Cathleen—Sophie went into the river and died of pneumonia."

"It wasn't your fault."

"I know that, Mam. And although I have tried to blame her, I suppose it wasn't really Cathleen's fault, either. It was just a stupid, childish argument that ended up in tragedy. Still, I can hardly help feeling responsible."

"You loved Sophie, didn't you?"

"Certainly."

"You went into the river to get the Treasure Box, because you knew it was precious to her?"

"Yes."

"And she went in the river to help you. Because you were precious to her, too. She loved you, Rachel. At the time, I don't suppose she realized she was risking her life for you, but even if she had known, I expect she would have done it anyway."

Rachel gazed at her mother, her blue eyes wide and somber. "I'd rather have died for Sophie than let her die for me."

Mam extended her arms, and Rachel slid off the tree trunk and sank down beside her on the bank, surrendering to the embrace. "There is no greater love on God's green earth," Mam said, stroking her daughter's hair, "than to lay down your life for a friend." She held Rachel tight and rocked gently back and forth. "I know you miss her, Rachel. And it's a noble sentiment, being willing to exchange your life for hers. But have you considered that there might be a hidden destiny in all this—some higher purpose?"

Rachel leaned back and frowned, scrutinizing her mother's face. "I can't accept that. What possible purpose could there be in Sophie's death?"

"Not in her death, child. In your *life*." Mam stood up and brushed her dress off. "I'd better be getting back to the house. Dinner won't cook itself."

"Wait!" Rachel grabbed at the hem of Mam's skirt. "If my life really does have a purpose, then what is it?"

Her mother smiled down at her. "That's a question only you can answer." She walked a few paces from the riverbank, then turned back. "Life rarely turns out as we expect, my girl. Just keep a sharp eye out, and adjust with the changes. You've got a good heart, a kind soul. You'll know what's right to do when the time comes."

9

THE JUDAS TREE

It was the first time Vita had seen the inside of the tavern where Rachel worked. On the dingy glass doors leading to the street, she could just make out the letters of the name, painted backwards, like da Vinci's secret diaries. Her mind translated: *The Judas Tree.*

An altogether disreputable-looking place, with an irregular stone floor, great gnarled beams overhead, and white stucco walls stained a dismal yellowish gray from decades of smoke and neglect. Spanning one end of the dimly lit room, a high bar stood like a fortress wall, separating the chairs and tables from the kitchen and the floor-to-ceiling shelves that held smudged glasses and steins and half-filled bottles of every conceivable brand of liquor. At the other end, a broad, soot-encrusted hearth contained an unattended fire, now burning itself to its last embers.

Vita didn't need a great deal of imagination to envision the place on a Friday or Saturday night. She could almost see the fire blazing high, with coarse men silhouetted against its light, pounding their ale mugs on the tables as they won—or lost—the last deal of the cards or throw of the dice. She could picture Rachel fending off advances as she served another round of beer or ale or whiskey.

But not tonight. Tonight the place was empty, except for one solitary figure.

Rachel looked around. Most of the lights were out, and all the chairs were upended on their respective tables. The Judas Tree had shut its doors for the evening. Even the manager had gone home, leaving her to clean up and close the place. Rachel had just taken a wet mop to the grimy floors when she heard the door creak open behind her.

"Sorry, we're closed," she said automatically and went back to her mopping.

"I beg to differ," a husky voice rumbled in her ear. Before she could turn, a hand grabbed her waist and jerked her into a rough embrace.

Rachel spun around, raising the mop handle as a weapon against the intruder. Then, just before she struck out at him, she aborted the blow. "Derrick!" She began to laugh, a high-pitched sound bordering on hysteria. "You frightened me near to death!"

He took the mop out of her hands and leaned it against a table. "You really should keep the door locked when you're here alone, my dear Miss Woodlea," he said. "Any man off the street could walk in here and have his way with you." As he spoke these last words, his voice dropped to a throaty, provocative whisper, and he leaned close to kiss her.

Their lips met briefly, and Rachel took a step back. "Derrick, I've got work to do."

"It can wait. Don't tell me that mopping the floor is more interesting than this—" He kissed her again, gathering her body close against his.

Rachel hesitated. "Of—of course not," she stammered. "But—"

"But nothing." He led her to the back corner of the room, where a long banquet-size table stood against the wall. Slowly, deliberately, never taking his eyes off Rachel for a second, he removed the chairs and set them one by one on the floor. Then he held out his hand to her. *"Had we but world enough and time,"* he quoted in a quiet, entreating voice, *"This coyness, lady, were no crime—"*

"Derrick—"

He captured her hand and drew her to him. *"But at my back I always hear Time's winged chariot hurrying near. And yonder all before us lie deserts of vast eternity."*

"Andrew Marvell," Rachel murmured as his lips moved insistently against her own. "It's a beautiful poem, but—"

He backed her against the table, and her knees gave way. *"Now, therefore, while the youthful hue sits on thy skin like morning*

86

dew, let us sport us while we may—" He pressed closer to her and slid the back of his fingers seductively down the curved line of her throat. "I want you, Rachel. Here. Now."

She tried to push him away and found herself trapped. "I know, Derrick. I—I feel the same way." She stumbled over the words. "But we should wait."

"Why should we?" He moved against her.

"It won't be long until our wedding. We are engaged, after all."

"Exactly my point." He ran his hand up into her hair and caressed her neck. "Engaged is practically married. What's the harm?"

"The doors—"

"I locked them behind me when I came in."

"What if someone comes—?"

"It's nearly midnight. The streets are deserted. No one's about."

"Oh." Rachel closed her eyes. She tried to think, but the tiny rivulets of liquid fire running up and down her nerve endings made reason impossible. No one had ever held her like this before, touched her, kissed her with so much passion, made her feel so . . . adored.

Adored. What had Mam said? That being adored can weave a powerful enchantment around the soul. It *was* a kind of spell; she could feel Derrick drawing her in with every kiss, every touch. Spinning with invisible threads a lush silk web, more sumptuous than the softest feather bed covered with satin sheets.

It would be so easy just to abandon propriety, to fall into his arms and stay there forever.

His kisses grew fiercer as his ardor increased. His hands grasped her waist and lifted her up onto the table. One kiss more, and there would be no turning back.

"Derrick, NO!" The protest rose up from some deep place inside of Rachel. She must have shouted, for he jerked back in surprise.

"What?" The single word came out harsh, accusing.

"I—I—" She sat up, her fingers moving nervously to tidy her hair and rearrange her dress. "Please. Let me go."

A fast-moving inner storm clouded his face. Rachel could see the vein in his neck throbbing as he clenched his jaw, and for a moment she feared he might strike her. But then the darkness blew past, and he smiled—at least with his lips. "Of course, my darling," he said, his voice tight with restraint. "I would never force you into something you don't want."

"I *do* want it!" Tears stung at Rachel's eyes. "But not now. Not here. Not until we're married." She shook her head and tried to clear her throat. "Please understand, Derrick. It's important to me to wait."

He helped her down and put the chairs back on the table. With his back to her, Rachel couldn't see his face, only the stiff set of his spine and shoulders. Her whole body ached for his touch, but she kept her distance.

At last, when he turned around, he gazed at her with an odd expression. "Let's get married," he said.

Rachel frowned at him. "Of course we will."

"No, I mean now. Immediately. This coming Saturday."

"Derrick, that's less than a week away."

"What's to stop us? We don't have to stand on ceremony. We can just put out the word to the village, contact the vicar, and do it." He grabbed both her hands and squeezed them. "I don't want to delay another minute"—he gave her a crooked grin—"but I suppose I can wait five days if I have to."

Rachel could barely breathe. "Are you sure?"

"We have enough money for our passage, don't we?"

"I think so. And some to spare."

"Then we're set. First thing tomorrow I'll arrange it with the priest and book two berths on the next ship to America. We'll have our honeymoon on board." He hugged her lightly and kissed her gently on the cheek. "Do you want me to stay with you until you're finished here?"

Rachel looked around the tavern. "It's not necessary. I've got about another thirty minutes of work to do, and I can get home by myself."

"As you wish." He moved to the door, threw the lock, and gave her a jaunty salute. "Until Saturday, my darling."

Then he opened the door and disappeared into the night.

~

Rachel should have been exhausted by the time she got to her mother's cottage, but instead she felt energized, exhilarated.

Bypassing the house, she walked the path to the barn, opened the door, and lit a single lamp.

In the corner pen, a sweet-faced Guernsey opened her eyes and gave a soft moo. "Biscuit, you dear old girl," Rachel said, coming over to stroke the animal's velvety nose. "I'm going to hate leaving you, you know. But there's no place for cows on a ship to America."

She slid to a sitting position in the hay outside Biscuit's stall and let the comforting scents of hay and udder balm and sweet feed envelop her. No matter how determined she was to build a new and better life in America with Derrick, Rachel's heart already ached with missing this place. The village. The cottage. This barn. Mam and Colin. Even Cathleen, if she were pressed to admit it. This was the only world she had ever known, and now, in less than a week, she would step onto the deck of a steamship and leave it behind forever.

And the memories! Would she leave them behind, too?

She scooted over toward the wall, pried up a loose board in the floor, and retrieved Sophie's Treasure Box from its hiding place. Even after ten years, she still thought of the box as Sophie's, not her own. And yet it held her treasures—Queen Titania, the ragged handkerchief doll. A tatted lace collar Mam had made for her birthday. A fragrant perfume sachet that had once belonged to her grandmother. A dog-eared likeness of the family Colin had drawn for her during his first year in school. A hammered brass heart Sophie's father Jacob had given to her on the first anniversary of her best friend's death.

These were her treasures—memories. Mementos from the people she loved. Not the two hundred pounds that lay in a small burlap bag at the bottom of the box.

Rachel closed the box and cradled it in her lap, stroking the little dragon at the edge of the sea, tracing with one finger the outline of America. The Land of Promise. And soon, her home.

She shut her eyes and leaned her head back against the barn wall, and Sophie's face materialized behind her eyelids. Sophie as she had been—before the river, before the pneumonia. The smile, the auburn curls, the laughing brown eyes.

Remember me, she had said right before she died. *Remember . . .*

Well, Rachel would remember. Until the day she herself walked into the embrace of the willow-woman and heard the green song, she would never let go of the Treasure Box, never forget the friend whose brief life had meant so much to her.

Never.

The computer screen was gray and shadowed, but Vita could make out movement in the pale light of a descending half-moon. Someone slipping behind the broad trunk of a big oak tree. The silhouette of a stone cottage with a thatched roof. The cottage door swinging open.

"Come on!" a voice hissed from behind the tree.

"It's late," a woman's voice whispered back. "Everyone's asleep."

"So much the better. Let's go!"

The figure moved from its hiding place and took a couple of steps toward the house. A man, shrouded in a dark overcoat, with his back toward Vita.

Vita raised an eyebrow. What was this—a midnight tryst, some secret rendezvous? Had Rachel changed her mind?

The woman closed the door behind her and tiptoed out into the clearing. It wasn't Rachel. Moonlight caught in a cascade of blonde curls, creating a reflected halo of spun silver around her head.

Vita squinted at the woman's face. The features were older, matured, but there was no mistaking that snobbish, superior expression. This was no angel. It was Cathleen. And apparently still up to the old tricks she had cultivated when she was thirteen and chasing after Rafe Dalton.

"I'd nearly decided you weren't coming," she said as she stepped into the man's embrace.

He tipped her head back and lowered his mouth to hers in a hungering kiss. "My sweet vixen," he murmured. "How could any man stay away from you?"

She laughed softly. "Before long, you won't have to."

10

THE UNMARKED WAY

All morning, while she showered, dressed, and prepared her breakfast, Vita couldn't get her mind to clear. She kept thinking about Sophie and Rachel and Derrick Knight. About Gordon and Hattie and Mary Kate. Time moved around her like a river of silt, a fluid, unpredictable motion that sometimes stood still and sometimes rushed by at an astonishing pace. Rationally Vita knew it had been five days since she first discovered the Treasure Box program, but based purely on perception, it could have been five minutes or five years. A flick of an eyelash or a lifetime.

For more than an hour now she had been sitting at the kitchen table, drifting, wandering in a maze of memories. Seeing Hattie's ruined face and Gordon's handsome one. The lost friend and the lost love.

But life is mostly about losses, isn't it? Vita thought. A single, seemingly insignificant choice, freely made or determined by another, inevitably eliminated a myriad of other options. Decisions made in a split second changed the course of destiny for all time. Two roads diverged in a yellow wood. Which one to take? The clear, well-traveled path or the overgrown and unmarked way?

Frost had elected "the one less traveled by" and claimed that his choice "made all the difference." But he *didn't* say, Vita noted with a perverse kind of pleasure, whether that difference was positive or negative. Perhaps he didn't know. Perhaps he was unable—or unwilling—to confront the alternatives. Maybe the great and insightful poet, like the rest of humanity, simply muddled along, taking what lay before him and haunted by a vague suspicion that once he had chosen—either way—it would forever alter the course of his life.

What would have happened, Vita wondered, if Hattie Parker had allowed that terrible accident to redirect her life—or never gotten into the car in the first place? Would Vita and Hattie still be best friends, sharing their grown-up secrets and struggles as they had shared their childhood fantasies? What if Gordon Locke hadn't looked into Mary Kate's eyes and discovered there what he found lacking in Vita? Would Vita now be Gordon's wife, mother to Gordy and Mary V—or children very much like them?

What if Vita herself had made different choices?

Vita shook her head and gazed out the kitchen window. Spring, with its abundant rains and sunshine, had resurrected the purple morning glories, and they spread with abandon up the old iron trellis and across the window sill. A few of them had even caught hold of the screen and continued their upward climb, like Jack's beanstalk, toward the sky. Vibrant, colorful show-offs in the morning, and by afternoon, retiring, antisocial hermits.

Maybe the best you could hope for in life, Vita mused, was to be like the morning glories. Latch onto whatever trellis will hold you, take the sun when you can get it, and don't expect the grandeur to last forever.

~

The starry night on Vita's computer monitor went through its now-familiar metamorphosis, transforming itself into a brilliant sunlit afternoon. The toll of a bell drifted on the bright air as dozens of villagers in their Sunday finery made their way toward a small parish church situated on a green knoll at the edge of town. A carriage drawn by two bay horses stood tethered at one side of the stone walkway. Over the carved wood lintel of the nave door, a festoon of white flowers nodded gently in the breeze.

Rachel's wedding day.

Ordinarily, Vita didn't care much for weddings; they brought out her cynical side and left her wondering how long the union would last. But this wedding was different. Rachel had lost so much in her young life—and now, finally, something good was happening for her. She and Derrick Knight would take vows of lifetime love and fidelity, surrounded by their friends and family, and then depart into the sunset toward a new life in a new land.

The clear blue sky with its scattering of tiny clouds made

Vita think of an ocean, studded with whitecaps and merging into the horizon. What an adventure it would be, to board that ship and sail past the curve of the earth on the crest of a surging wave. She could imagine herself standing at the prow of a great clipper ship with the wind at her back and the world spread out before her, watching as the massive carved figurehead sent a shower of mist over the bow. She could feel the rough wood of the deck rail, taste the salt spray, smell the briny tang of the sea, hear the raucous call of gray and white gulls circling above the mast.

The church bells kept tolling, and Vita brought her attention back to the screen. Rachel and her mother now positioned themselves near the door, with Colin, in knickers and a starched white shirt, tugging at Mam's skirt. Beside them stood an older, balder, paunchier Jacob Stillwater, beaming his radiant smile down on the bride.

Vita gazed at Rachel, resplendent in a simple white dress with lace outlining the neckline and cuffs—a dress designed to show off the gleaming silver locket she wore at her throat. Her brown hair, curled on top of her head with a meandering stream of white satin ribbon running through it, accentuated her blue eyes and high cheekbones. Little Rachel—the gangly, shy, rather homely duckling, had turned into an elegant swan.

⁓

"We'll need to go in soon," Mam said, taking Colin's hand.

"We'll be fine," Jacob assured her. "We'll just wait here at the door until we hear the music." He turned to Rachel. "It's a pure blessing to me, child, your asking me to walk you down the aisle. After Sophie—" He paused, and a somber look flashed across his face. "Well, you know, I never had the chance to play the proud Papa at *her* wedding. I think she'd be happy for both of us."

Rachel let out a little sigh. "It means the world to me, too, Jacob. With my own father gone these five years now, no one but you could have made this day complete. It's a shame Sophie can't be here."

Jacob put an arm around her. "She *is* here, Rachel. Wherever she is, she's watching."

Rachel nodded, then turned back to her mother. "Where's Cathleen?"

Mam raised an eyebrow. "Late, as usual. She'll be along whenever she's good and ready." She shook her head. "Like as not, she's a bit jealous, I'll wager. Her little sister marrying before herself. But don't worry about her, Rachel. This is your day; don't let your sister spoil it for you." She led Colin into the church.

The final peal of the parish bells echoed into silence. Inside the church, the organ sounded a solemn chord, and Jacob offered his arm to Rachel. Together they glided down the aisle toward the altar, where the rector stood with the *Book of Common Prayer* open in his hands. With perfect timing, Rachel and Jacob reached the front of the sanctuary just as the processional ended.

When the music stopped, all eyes turned toward the door at the right side of the nave that led to the vestry. This was Derrick's cue to come out of the vestry and stand before the priest next to his bride. Rachel fixed her attention on the door, anticipating her first glimpse of her husband-to-be's handsome face. How would he react when he saw her? Would he think her beautiful, the woman of his dreams? She could hardly wait to see the look in his eyes—that look of adoration, the one that never failed to kindle a flame in her.

Tonight there would be no more holding back. Tonight she would freely give herself to him, abandon herself to his desire and her own, let him discover that their love was worth waiting for. Tonight they would be husband and wife, joined together by God for all time.

Rachel held her breath. Time seemed to stand still, but that had to be just her imagination, a product of her nervousness and excitement. Then she began to hear rustling noises behind her. Hushed murmurs spread from pew to pew. The priest's face had gone white as his surplice. Jacob, still holding Rachel's arm, closed his eyes and moved his lips inaudibly. His usually ruddy skin took on a greenish tinge, and he looked as if he might be sick.

A minute passed. Then two. Finally Jacob pried Rachel's fingers from the sleeve of his coat, went to the vestry door, and knocked. In the quiet of the church, the sound fell on Rachel's nerves like physical blows, the ringing of hammer against spike, a crucifixion.

But no stone rolled away to reveal a resurrected bridegroom.

Jacob knocked again, then turned the handle and opened the

vestry door. From nearly anywhere in the sanctuary, you could see the entirety of the small room, with neatly-pressed clerical vestments and altar cloths hanging along the walls.

It was empty. Not a sign that Derrick Knight had ever been there. Or ever would be.

∾

Rachel lay facedown across her bed in the small anteroom of the cottage, her dress rumpled, her shoulders shaking. Clutched in her hand she held the silver locket, its chain broken. A thin red welt raised up on the back of her neck from the force of ripping it free.

"Rachel, Rachel," Rose said helplessly, stroking her back. "Maybe something happened to him—an accident, something . . ." But she didn't believe it herself, so how could she possibly convince her distraught daughter?

Rachel continued to weep. Rose continued to try to comfort her—with little effect. To be left standing at the altar without a groom on what should be the happiest day of her life was the ultimate humiliation for a woman. Held up to ridicule throughout the village, and beyond. The jilted girl. The poor shamed lass whose lover scorned and betrayed her and left her to the malice of the gossips.

Tongues would wag, that much was certain. It had already begun. No longer would she be Rachel, the hard worker, the faithful daughter, the quiet, sensitive one. From now till the end of her days, she would be Poor Rachel. Her tale to be told and retold, embroidered and elaborated, for the entertainment of a village that had little else to talk about.

And what of Derrick Knight? Rose Woodlea was not inclined, not in the least, to give him the benefit of the doubt. If he knew what was good for him, he'd be halfway to somewhere else by now. Somewhere far away, never to set foot in this county again.

At last Rachel's tears subsided a bit, and she sat up and swiped a hand across her face.

"Better?" Rose peered into her daughter's eyes.

Rachel nodded. "But why would he—how could he—" Her eyes filled up again. "I thought he loved me!"

Rose's words came out on a sigh. "Men can be unpredictable creatures, that's certain. But I do know one thing: Derrick Knight understands less about love than—than Biscuit the cow!"

Rachel smiled halfheartedly. "But why, then, does it hurt so?" She lay back across the bed and threw an arm over her eyes.

"Because you trusted him."

Outside the window, the afternoon light was fading, and the inside of the cottage had grown dark. Rose lit a lamp and set it by the bedside. "I'm going to put the kettle on. We'll have ourselves a nice tea, with poached eggs and buttered toast and"—she paused and chuckled—"cake. Lots and lots of cake."

Rachel raised up on one elbow. "I'll come and help you. But *no* cake!"

Rose shook her head vigorously. "No work for you tonight,

my girl. You stay here and rest. I'll call you when it's ready. I'll get your sister to—" Her scalp tightened with apprehension. She had never seen her elder daughter at the church, but then there had been so much commotion. She might still be in the village, or—

Rachel sat upright. Her eyes, brimming with unshed tears, glittered in the lamplight—the look of some innocent woodland animal with its leg in a trap. And then she asked the question they were both dreading:

"Where is she, Mam? Where is Cathleen?"

Vita knew it was coming. Still, the shock ran through her as though she'd grabbed a live power line. It had happened again—or, more precisely, before. The last time she had been confronted with these emotions, she had been too stunned to do anything but turn inward and grow cold. This time the full force of the abandonment crested over her in a roaring wave. She found herself gasping for air.

When her heart slowed to its normal pace, Vita tried to separate herself from Rachel's situation. True, Gordon had left her for Mary Kate, but he hadn't demeaned her by leaving her stranded at the altar. He had been as honest as he was capable of being—told her face to face that he had fallen in love with someone else, although he hadn't in that moment had the courage to tell her who.

Still, Vita understood all too well the fires of Rachel's hell. She knew the anguish, the misery, the torment, the self-doubt. But she knew something else, too—something Rachel had not yet discovered.

The liberating power of anger.

11

SAFE HAVENS

Outside Vita's office window, a fat brown sparrow flitted back and forth, building a nest in the high hedge that surrounded the sunroom. Mesmerized, she watched as the bird flew in and out of the dense thicket, carrying twigs and sprigs of dried grass and even a length of hemp twine, skillfully weaving the bits and pieces together to form a cozy sanctuary for its young.

A snatch of a tune drifted through Vita's consciousness—children's reedy voices, singing about God's eye being on the sparrow. Her mind latched onto the image. The bird, close against the glass, had no idea Vita was watching from the other side. Every instinct built into its tiny avian brain had guided the sparrow to the back of the bush; it had chosen this spot, the densest portion of the hedge, to guard its babies from predators and prying eyes. And yet, quite outside the realm of its awareness, the sparrow had positioned its safe haven in full view of Vita Kirk.

Did the Almighty see human beings the way Vita saw the

bird—instinctively attempting to shield against danger, desperately fluttering about, trying to create an illusion of security in a world full of peril? And did the Creator smile—indulgently, benevolently—at the creature's attempts to hide even from the gaze of one who meant them no harm?

No harm? Certainly Vita had no dark designs against the tiny sparrow, but how could anyone possibly say the same about God? For all that religious rhetoric about a loving, protective Deity, every sign Vita had seen pointed to the opposite conclusion. Hattie. Gordon and Mary Kate. Sophie. Rachel.

The reality was, bad things happened to good people. And infinitely more irksome, in Vita's mind, was the correlative truth: *good* things happened to *bad* people. Even the Bible said so, if Vita could trust a twenty-five-year-old memory dredged up from confirmation class: *Why do the wicked prosper, O God?*

"Not likely to get an answer for that dilemma," Vita murmured to herself as she punched the button to boot up the computer. People had been raising the question for millennia, but so far God—if such a Being existed—seemed to be taking a long sabbatical.

~

Apparently Rachel Woodlea was asking the same question.

When the familiar star-studded night sky on the computer screen gave way to a daylight scene, Vita saw Rachel, alone, walking along the river near the spot where Sophie had fallen in. The rush of the water and the song of birds overhead combined to create a placid, restful atmosphere, but Rachel seemed anything but peaceful.

"Why?" she fumed, pacing back and forth on the bank. "Why?"

Vita could feel the girl's turmoil in her own stomach. She hadn't yet figured out how, but sometimes when she went into the Treasure Box program, she could hear people's thoughts and share their feelings. Not always, and not with everyone, but often enough that she was becoming accustomed to the sensation.

It was rather like viewing a movie and reading the book simultaneously. On screen, she saw the action and heard the dialogue. But inside, on a deeper level, Vita could actually understand what the characters thought, how they felt. She could see the world from their perspective.

Like now. Vita had watched Rachel's aborted wedding only a few hours ago, and yet she knew that for Rachel, two agonizing weeks had passed—fourteen days of solitude in her tiny room. Knew that Rachel had quit her barmaid's job at The Judas Tree, and that Elisabeth Tyner, the dressmaker who had created her wedding gown, had offered her a position in her shop. The pay was adequate—better than what Rachel had earned at the tavern, and the working conditions were pleasant. Yet Rachel hadn't been able to bring herself to say yes. People in town were still gossiping about the wedding fiasco, and Rachel still felt unprepared to face their pity and disdain.

Vita watched as Rachel continued to pace.

"Won't someone answer me?" she shouted to the rushing river. "Sophie? Papa? God? Anyone? Please, I beg of you, won't someone tell me what to do?"

At last Rachel gave up pacing and seated herself on the riverbank. She gazed out over the tumbling rapids, listening intently for any interior voice. But no voice came, not a single word of comfort or advice or direction. She had come up with only one solution to her dilemma, one final recourse, and it was a last resort that made her insides ache with dread.

To leave home, to go to another village. To begin a new life.

She had more than enough money to start over. She would split the two hundred pounds with her mother to help with expenses and with Colin's schooling. Perhaps when she got settled Mam and Colin might want to join her.

But no. Rachel knew, deep in her heart, that Mam would never be able to leave this place. It had been her home for more than twenty-five years. As a newlywed, barely out of her teens, she had come to live in the cottage on the edge of the woods. Every living soul who knew her name walked the streets of this village. Here her children had been born, and her husband buried.

If Rachel were to do this, she would be doing it alone.

Alone. The word gashed into Rachel's heart like a dull knife, scattering bits and pieces all along its path. She should be a wife now, a new bride on her way to a new life, protected and cherished by a faithful husband. But Derrick was gone, and so was

Cathleen. To another village, another county? Perhaps even another country?

Of course, Rachel thought. *America.* Derrick had talked incessantly about the wonders of the land across the sea. Marble cities with brick-paved streets. Riverbeds lined with nuggets of gold. Vast emerald prairies, lakes of sapphire, and amethyst mountains jutting to the sky. Emigrating had been his dream for years, and Cathleen certainly would need no persuasion. She would do anything to get away.

"America," Rachel whispered, nodding to herself. "They've gone to America." And although she could not know for sure, she felt a sense of finality settle over her, as if she were rid of both of them forever. All that was left now was for Rachel to make her own decision—a choice for *her* life, for *her* future.

But could she do it? She could only begin to imagine the struggles she might face—finding work and a place to live, making new friends, carving out a space for herself in an unfamiliar town. Still, it could not possibly be worse than living for the rest of her days in a village where people turned their heads aside and whispered behind their hands as she walked by.

Rachel got to her feet, brushed off her skirt, and with one last longing gaze at the willow trees along the riverbank, turned and set off for home.

At last Mam's cottage came into view. She walked straight past the front door and headed down the path toward the barn. Now. It had to be done now, before her nerve failed her.

Once inside, Rachel pried up the loose board where Sophie's Treasure Box lay hidden and reached a hand inside the alcove. Nothing. She stretched her arm as far as it would reach, but her fingers grasped only dust and cobwebs. Had she pulled up the wrong board? She blinked, waiting for her eyes to adjust to the dim light. But there was no mistake.

It was gone. Not just the two hundred pounds, wrapped in its burlap cocoon, but everything. The lace collar. The handkerchief doll. Colin's picture. Everything that held Rachel's memories. Cathleen had taken it all.

Even the Treasure Box itself.

Vita shielded her eyes as the scene on her computer screen shifted. Bright afternoon sunlight glittered on the cresting waves. A pod of dolphins leaped playfully in the spray churned up by the prow of a massive Cunard liner with the name *Carmania I* on its side. On the foredeck, two figures stood leaning over the rail off the port bow, laughing and pointing. A man and a woman.

She grabbed his hand. "See, here come two more! And a baby! A little dolphin family."

But he wasn't watching. His eyes were fixed on the horizon. "Look."

She followed his gaze and squinted. "What am I looking at? A shadow? A cloud?"

"Can't you see it? The island? The harbor? The statue with her hand raised up?"

"How absurd. You can't see anything from here."

He laughed. "Use your imagination, darling, not just your eyes. I see a new world and a new life."

Gradually, as they watched, the smudge at the edge of the world took on clearer form, and she drew in a deep breath. "New York. At last. The Land of Opportunity."

The man turned, and Vita caught her first glimpse of his face. Derrick Knight. "Since I was fourteen years old, I've been counting the days until this moment. Waiting for my new life to begin."

Cathleen tossed her curls. "Don't you mean *our* new life?"

"Of course," he said absently, putting an arm around her waist and drawing her close. "Of course."

By the time the ship entered the harbor and drew up even with the Statue of Liberty, Derrick and Cathleen, along with all the other passengers, had retrieved their belongings and come back up on deck. Now they stood pressed shoulder to shoulder along the rail—some of them cheering, some gaping in silent awe at their first glimpse of their new country.

Derrick filled his lungs with the clean, fresh air. *"Give me your tired, your poor, Your huddled masses yearning to breathe free—"*

Cathleen turned up her nose as if she had caught a whiff of one of the passengers from steerage. "What on earth is that?"

"A poem. By Emma Lazarus. It's inscribed on a plaque in the base of the statue. I read about it." He grinned down at her. *"The wretched refuse of your teeming shores—"*

"You and your poetry," Cathleen scoffed. "Besides, I don't like it one bit. Tired? Poor? Huddled masses? Wretched refuse? How insulting!"

"Send these, your homeless, tempest-tossed to me," Derrick finished. *"I lift my lamp beside the golden door."*

"Well, I suppose that part's all right," she conceded. "What happens now?"

"According to the officer I talked to yesterday, we'll stop first at Hudson Pier. Doctors will come aboard and examine us to make sure we're not sick, and then—"

"You mean they think we're carrying some kind of *disease?*" Cathleen shuddered. "That's absolutely ridiculous. This isn't the Middle Ages—it's 1921! And we're perfectly respectable people."

"Just be thankful we were able to travel second class. The riffraff below decks are taken to Ellis Island. I hear *they* stand in line for hours for their medical exams and processing. A great many of them end up being quarantined for months—if they don't die first."

"But we'll be cleared to go ashore beforehand?" Cathleen persisted.

Derrick nodded. "And then we go through customs."

"How long will that take?"

"I have no idea how long it will take, my *dear,*" he responded

110

through gritted teeth. "Try to be patient, will you? You've got your whole life ahead of you."

~

The scene on the monitor faded to black and reappeared with Rachel seated before the hearth, staring into the fire. Flames licked the dry wood and sent sparks shooting up the blackened chimney. "It's gone," she said through clenched teeth. "The money. The box. Everything I worked for, dreamed of, cherished."

The longer she sat there, the more enraged she grew, until her own soul blazed with a white-hot fury.

Rachel Woodlea had finally found her anger. And she wasn't the only one.

"I've never been one to speak ill of my own children," Mam said, slamming bowls onto the table and sending spoons clattering against the rough wood. "But if I ever get my hands on that eldest daughter of mine, I'll teach her a lesson she'll not soon forget."

"Not if I get to her first." The words came out quiet, controlled.

Mam turned and stared at her daughter. "Rachel—"

Rachel narrowed her eyes. "Don't give me that reproving look of yours, Mam. I've taken Cathleen's abuse for years. She had no call to throw herself at Derrick. And then, to steal not only my hard-earned wages, but Sophie's Treasure Box?" She pounded a burning log with the poker until sparks shot out past the hearth and onto the floor. "I'll find her, and I'll get back what's mine if it's the last thing I do." She stomped at the embers with a vengeance.

"America's a big country," Mam said. "Without the money, how can you possibly get passage? And even if you did, how would you locate her?"

"I don't know." Rachel let out a sigh. "I'll work, I suppose, until I can save enough to pay my way. Mrs. Tyner will hire me at the dress shop. Perhaps Cathleen will write. Perhaps the government keeps records of immigrants. Perhaps—"

"I know where they've gone."

Colin had been sitting at the table, quiet, unobtrusive. Now Rachel turned on him, reaching the table in two steps and leaning close in to his face.

"What did you say?"

"I said, I know where they've gone."

"Cathleen's gone to America, Colin—at least we're almost certain she has."

"No. Listen." His face puckered up as if he were about to fly into a rage, and Rachel mollified her tone.

"All right." She patted his hand. "We're listening, Colin."

"Well—" He took a deep breath. "Late one night, maybe two or three weeks before your—your wedding—"

Rachel pulled back as if she had been slapped. "What happened?"

"I got up to go to the privy, and on my way there, I heard

112

noises in the barn. A lamp was lit in there. I saw them—Cathleen and that man—"

"Derrick?"

"Him, yes. They were all tangled up together in the hay. He had his shirt off. They were laughing. He was telling her about his plan. He said he had a—a 'contact,' I think the word was, in a place called Chi—Chicago. A man named Ben something."

Rachel held up a hand. "Could it have been a surname—Benedetti?"

Colin frowned. "Maybe. Something about a restaurant and work when he got there. Lots of money."

"Precisely the same rubbish he fed me."

Mam gripped Rachel's arm. "You know who this Benedetti is?"

"Derrick mentioned him once, when he was initially trying to persuade me to go with him to America. I didn't think much of it at the time. But if what Colin says is true—"

The lad pulled himself upright in as dignified a pose as an eleven-year-old could muster and crossed his arms defiantly. "I might sneak around a little, but I don't lie."

Mam came to the other side of the table and enveloped him in a hug, kissing him all over one cheek. "Colin, my precious boy!"

He swiped at his face. "You're not mad at me for spying?"

"Not this time." She held up a warning finger. "But I'd prefer you didn't make a habit of it."

Rachel peered at him. "Why didn't you tell us before now?"

113

Colin leaned back and shrugged. "I know how to keep a secret."

Rachel set her lips in a thin line. "Well," she muttered grimly, "it seems the secret is out now."

~

When the scene faded to black, Vita shut off the computer and slumped back in her chair. The image of Derrick and Cathleen laughing together on the deck of the ship haunted her, mocked her. How could they be so unfeeling, so callous? What kind of lover would do such a thing? What kind of sister?

Then she remembered Gordon leaving her for Mary Kate. But when Gordon walked away, all Vita had to do was raise the walls, shut the gate, and clamp the padlock in place. The solitary life was not, perhaps, the ideal, but it suited her. It made her feel safe. In a closed garden nothing could hurt her. No one could violate her own safe haven.

She swiveled around and peered into the hedge outside her window. Late afternoon was surrendering to dusk, and the little brown sparrow, blissfully unaware that anyone was watching, had curled itself into its newly built nest and settled in for the night.

Vita resisted the impulse to pound on the glass and startle the bird out of its complacency. Frightening the poor beast wouldn't accomplish anything, and in truth, the sparrow wasn't the real object of Vita's frustration.

What she really wanted to do was reach into the computer and shake some sense into Rachel Woodlea. Yes, Rachel had finally connected with the power of her anger, but she was about to use it in the wrong way entirely. Going after Derrick and Cathleen would accomplish nothing. She ought to leave them to whatever fate awaited them in Chicago and get on with her own life. To shore up her walls, protect herself—not go off on a harebrained chase across the ocean and make herself even more vulnerable.

In vain Vita wished for some way to communicate with Rachel, to make her understand that the world was a cruel and hazardous place, and the sooner she learned to protect herself, the better. There were no safe havens in this life, no place where prying eyes and predators could not reach. Not for the sparrow, not for Rachel Woodlea.

Vita resisted the thought even as the words formed unbidden in her mind: *Not even for Vita Kirk.*

But of course that wasn't true. Vita knew, from years of experience, that she could find a place of safety—in solitude.

If only you could build your nest high enough, far enough away . . .

12

GUARDIAN ANGELS

Of necessity, Vita spent the following morning in town, shopping for provisions to replenish her empty larder. No matter how compelling the Treasure Box story might be, she still had to eat. The leftovers were gone, as well as the last of the frozen dinners. One pathetic freezer-burnt toaster waffle and the makings for a mustard sandwich wouldn't go very far.

By eleven-fifteen, her cart was loaded with enough food for a month—staples such as bread, milk, cheese, and eggs, as well as chicken, pasta, ground chuck and garlic spaghetti sauce, assorted vegetables, and a half-gallon of chocolate chunk ice cream. She chose the shortest line, then stood glancing at her watch every ten seconds and tapping her foot as the old woman in front of her painstakingly unloaded her groceries onto the conveyer belt.

"Excuse me, dear," the woman told the cashier in a thin, wavery voice. "That broccoli was supposed to be ninety-nine cents, not a dollar twenty-nine."

The teenage cashier, who wore two gold eyebrow piercings and a tattoo bracelet, flipped a switch on the pole over the register. The light overhead began to flicker on and off. "Come on, come on," Vita muttered under her breath.

"Price check on line two," the cashier announced into the microphone, then waited, snapping her gum, for a manager to appear.

Finally a man in a white shirt and tie ambled over. "What's the problem?"

"Broccoli scans at one twenty-nine, but the lady says it's suppose to be ninety-nine."

The manager turned away and came back a few minutes later with a heavyset woman wearing a produce apron. "She's right," the woman said. "It's on special today for ninety-nine."

It took another five minutes for the lethargic teenager to cancel the sale and reenter the broccoli at the right price. "That'll be forty-three fifty."

The old woman's face crumpled, and she sent an apologetic glance in Vita's direction. Her face was webbed with wrinkles, and her eyes a pale, weak gray-green. "I only have"—she re-counted her food stamps—"thirty-eight dollars. We'll have to see what I can put back. Maybe the rice—I still have a little bit at home— it's two-seventy. And the peanut butter—I'll go back and get a smaller jar."

Vita caught the cashier's eye. "Look, can you just ring me up while she's exchanging that stuff? I'm kind of in a hurry."

The teenager shook her head. "No can do. Gotta finish this order before I can close the register."

"All right, then." Vita opened her purse and pulled out a five dollar bill and two quarters. "Here you go." She extended the money in the old woman's direction. "This'll make up the difference."

The elderly woman recoiled. "I couldn't possibly. It's very generous of you, I'm sure, but taking charity is completely out of the question. Now if you'll pardon me, I'll be right back."

She squeezed past Vita and made her way slowly down aisle six, carrying the peanut butter in one trembling hand.

The courthouse clock had already struck noon by the time Vita got home, and the round cardboard carton of ice cream was beginning to feel squishy. She put away the groceries, folded and stored the paper grocery bags in the pantry, then threw together a sandwich of cold cuts and cheese and hurried into her office.

Why she was feeling so impatient, Vita could not imagine. By now she was fairly confident that Rachel or Cathleen—or some other new twist in the story—would be waiting for her whenever she got around to turning her computer on. Still, she felt driven by a sense of urgency, as if her presence as an observer mattered in a way she could not fully comprehend.

The sparrow had temporarily vacated the hedge, and for a

moment Vita felt a sense of melancholy as she gazed at the forlorn empty nest. But when the computer booted up, revealing the night sky with its scattering of stars, she turned her attention away from the empty nest, back to the Treasure Box program.

From her research for a book she had written two years ago, Vita could easily identify the scene in front of her: Chicago, early 1920s. The city street, flanked on both sides by high buildings, was clogged with traffic. Streetcars rattled along on their tracks. Horse-drawn carriages weaved in and out, attempting to avoid the newer, noisier automobiles. A large mason's truck, loaded with bricks, blocked the intersection, and two mounted police-men drew their horses closer and attempted to give the driver directions.

Her view zoomed in on a bright yellow awning midway down the block, with black letters that read *Benedetti's*. In front of the door stood a man and a woman in intense conversation.

⌒

"Are you certain this is the right place?" Cathleen asked for the third time, staring up at the tall buildings that surrounded them.

"I told you already. This is it. And stop gaping." He closed his eyes and shook his head, then curbed his exasperation and pointed at the canvas awning. "Read the sign, for heaven's sake. Benedetti's. The proprietor's name is Angelo Benedetti, and he's expecting us."

A car backfired behind them, and Cathleen jumped. "This

119

place is awful, Derrick—so many people, so much noise! No trees, no birds. And the buildings—you can barely see the sky."

"Right," he snapped sarcastically. "You've always been such a nature lover." He grabbed her arm and squeezed it. "I didn't force you to come with me, Cathleen. But this is what you said you wanted, so get used to it. Else get on the boat and go home."

Just as Derrick put his hand to the door, an ancient white-haired woman approached him. A beggar, apparently, in dirty tattered clothes and a moth-eaten shawl. Her face was a road map of wrinkles, and she gazed at them with watery eyes an odd shade of greenish-gray.

"Spare a bit of change for an old woman down on her luck?" she pleaded, holding out a battered tin cup toward Derrick.

He frowned. "Everybody's down on their luck. You can't expect people to—"

"Have a heart, Derrick," Cathleen interrupted. "Can't we afford to give her *something?* Just a little—"

He pulled her aside. "When we left England, we had two hundred pounds," he whispered between gritted teeth. "That's one thousand American dollars. The passage cost us nearly half of that, plus the train fare to Chicago, and food, and what we've laid out to rent a flat. We've less than three hundred dollars left, and no idea how long that will last us. And you expect me to go giving our hard-earned money away to some vagrant?"

Cathleen glared at him. "If I recall correctly, it wasn't *your* hard-earned money."

"And if *I* recall correctly," he countered, "it wasn't *yours*, either. You want to go back to England and be hanged as a thief?"

She was about to respond when the door to Benedetti's opened and a dark-haired man stepped outside.

"Grace! What I told to you about panhandling in front of my place of business? *Accenda!*"

The old woman cowered and hid the tin cup under her shawl. "Mr. Benedetti, I was simply—"

"I know what you do—you drive paying customers away. You hungry, the trash bins in the alley are full of scraps from last night's dinner—if the rats not got them all. But you keep away from my front door, *capisca?* Or next time I set the *polizia* on you."

Grace nodded, limped down the sidewalk, and disappeared into an alley at the side of the building.

The man turned toward Derrick and Cathleen. "*Scuse*," he said with a deferential bow. "My apologies. I am Angelo, the owner of this fine *ristorante*. You come in for dinner, yes? I make finest pasta in all of Chicago." He blew a kiss off his fingertips and grinned.

Derrick stepped forward. "You're Angelo Benedetti?"

"*Sì.*" He narrowed his eyes. "I know you?"

"We have a mutual friend. My name is Derrick Knight, from England."

Benedetti's dark eyes lit up, and he hauled Derrick into a hug and kissed him on both cheeks. "Signore Knight!" He clapped Derrick on the back. "Mario told me you come, but I expect you much sooner."

"The passage takes two weeks," Derrick explained. "We—well, we started out a little later than expected, and then we had to come by train from New York."

"Well, you here now—that is what matters." Benedetti's eyes sought out Cathleen, and he put a hand over his heart. "Your wife, Rachel, yes? *Bella, bella.*" He captured Cathleen's fingers and planted a kiss on the back of her hand.

"This is Cathleen," Derrick corrected.

"Not Rachel?" Benedetti frowned, obviously confused.

"There must have been some—some miscommunication."

Benedetti's expression cleared. "You look for job, no?"

Derrick nodded. "I was told, Mr. Benedetti, that—"

"No, no! You must call me Angelo." He poked Derrick in the chest. "Any friend of Mario's is my friend, too."

"All right, ah, Angelo. About the job—"

But Angelo wasn't listening. "We go inside, yes? You like chicken? I cook you a Chicken Marsala like heaven itself—on the house. And *vino.*" He gave a broad wink. "For Angelo, there is no Prohibition, *capisca?*" He held out his arm to Cathleen. "Come, come. We eat; we get acquainted; we open a bottle of Chianti. Like friends. Later we talk about work."

He opened the door with a grand flourish. As they stepped

past him into the restaurant, Cathleen leaned close to Derrick. "Appropriate name, Angelo," she whispered. "The man is an absolute angel."

~

The scene in front of Benedetti's restaurant dissolved and the starry night sky reappeared on the monitor. Vita leaned back in her chair and let out a pent-up breath. "Why do the wicked prosper?" she muttered. Cathleen and Derrick deserved to be poor and miserable, not to have some "guardian angel" come to their rescue.

But that brand of justice only happened in maudlin movies. In the real world, it seemed, saints were vilified and sinners came out victorious. Villains landed on their feet while their victims lay broken and bleeding in the gutter.

Still, it would be nice if just once scoundrels like Derrick and Cathleen got paid back in kind. To be thoroughly wretched in their new paradise, or be thrown out of the garden altogether.

Vita herself would volunteer to stand at the gates with a flaming sword.

~

Rachel stood at the open door of the dress shop and stared out across the street into the gathering dusk. Behind her, she could hear the rhythmic pace of Elisabeth Tyner's new electric sewing machine as it hummed a counterpoint to the splashing of the fountain in the center of the village green. From her vantage point in the doorway, she could just make out a couple walking hand in hand toward the bench at the base of the fountain. A handsome, sandy-haired man and a woman with blonde curls. Like Derrick and Cathleen.

"I will never forgive them," she murmured under her breath. "Never." Taking the money was bad enough, but to steal Sophie's Treasure Box—that was an offense for which there could be no absolution. If she ever got to America, and if by some miracle she managed to find the two of them, she'd make them suffer. Precisely how, she didn't know—at least not yet. She would have to work out that part as she went along.

Mrs. Tyner's voice called to her from the back of the shop. "Rachel, dear, I believe it's time to close up. Do come have a cup of tea with me before you leave."

Rachel shut the door and pulled down the shade, then locked the day's proceeds in the safe underneath the counter.

"Kettle's boiling!"

Rachel went into the back and stood shifting from one foot to another.

"For heaven's sake, sit down, dear." Mrs. Tyner smiled at her. "There's no reason for you to be nervous around me."

"Yes ma'am." Rachel sat. "I want to thank you, Mrs. Tyner, for taking me on to work here. You've been so generous with me, paying me so well and teaching me to do tailoring. Mam calls you my guardian angel."

"Guardian angel?" Elisabeth Tyner laughed. "Hardly. But I am happy to see you doing so well."

Rachel nodded. It wouldn't do to tell her employer how she still had difficulty braving the curious stares and whispers of the villagers. As yet no one had been rude to her face, but she found it a challenge to ignore them and go on about her business.

Still, enduring such pain did have its redemptions. Rachel had learned an important lesson—that opening yourself to love and hope only opened you to heartache as well. A year ago—even a few months ago—she would have scoffed at this truth as pure cynicism, the pessimistic disbelief of a suspicious mind. But now she knew better. A hard shell, that's what life demanded. Stone walls around your heart, and stout bolts on the doors to your soul.

Mrs. Tyner might be a gracious, generous lady, but Mam was wrong. There were no guardian angels in this life. No heavenly protectors, no divine eye watching, no invisible hand leading.

Nobody else would look out for Rachel Woodlea, so she would look out for herself.

13

ANOTHER DAY IN PARADISE

Vita watched as for the second time that morning, Cathleen made a frantic dash for the bathroom. She knelt on the cold tile, her stomach churning, until the waves of nausea subsided. At last she got up, bathed her face with cool water, and returned to the kitchen.

"Good thing we have an indoor privy," Derrick grunted from behind his newspaper. "What's the matter with you, anyway?"

"I—I don't know." Cathleen sank into the chair opposite him. "My stomach's just upset, that's all. It'll pass."

He pulled his pocket watch from his vest, clicked open the case, and squinted at the dial. "I have to be at work in ten minutes."

"I'm all right—you go on."

"Don't forget we're invited to dinner downstairs at eight," he reminded her as he retrieved his suit jacket from the coat tree next to the door. "You can wear that blue dress—and do something with your hair, will you?"

She ran a hand through her disheveled curls. "The very mention of that blue dress makes me want to throw up again," she said. "I'm sick to death of it—I've been wearing it for three solid months, every time I need to dress up the least little bit."

"So wear something else."

"I have nothing else, Derrick. Nothing suitable for dinner with your bosses. And I've seen the way their wives look at me. I'm quite sure they gossip behind my back about how pathetically unfashionable I am." She turned her most entreating smile on him. "I was wondering if I might not go shopping for a new frock."

He waved away her concerns. "The blue one will do just fine. Put that lace collar on it or something—you know, the handmade one you *brought with you* from home."

Cathleen repressed a caustic reply. Derrick never missed an opportunity to remind her, however subtly, that she was a thief, in possession of her sister's stolen goods—including the lace collar Mam had made for Rachel's birthday.

She sank onto the moth-eaten sofa and looked around the room. "Don't you ever get tired of living this way?" she asked. "This place is so *dismal*."

Derrick frowned. "You should be grateful. If Angelo Benedetti didn't own the entire building, we might still be in that horrible flat we rented when we first arrived. As it is, we're saving money, and we're right above the restaurant, where I can keep an eye on things when Angelo's not around."

"I suppose," Cathleen conceded. "But how do we ever plan to

improve ourselves? When you accepted this job, I hardly thought you'd be employed as an errand boy."

Derrick folded the newspaper and slapped it down on the table. "Not errand boy. *Courier*. I deliver papers and contracts to Angelo's business partners. It's important work. And Angelo is already talking about moving me up in the business."

"We've nowhere to go *but* up," she muttered. "Have you seen the rats and smelled the rotting garbage in the alley below our bedroom window?"

He stood up and donned his suit coat, then stalked to the door and opened it. "When you start bringing in money, you'll have earned the right to criticize," he said. "In the meantime, I suggest you keep your mouth shut." He slammed the door behind him, and as she heard his boots clattering down the stairs, she realized he hadn't even kissed her good-bye.

When Derrick was gone, Cathleen washed up the breakfast dishes, cleaned up the kitchen, and picked up the newspaper and odd articles of clothing he had left scattered about. She had just begun to tidy the parlor when a thought struck her. "A blanket!" she murmured to herself. "I could tuck a colorful blanket—the bright blue one, perhaps—over the sofa. It would certainly cheer the place up a bit."

She went to the closet in the bedroom, where the blanket was stored for the summer on a high shelf. She could reach it, if she stretched—just the nearest corner.

The blanket slid off the shelf and into her arms, but when it came, it dragged something else along with it. Something that glanced off her head and dropped to the floor of the closet. She laid the blanket aside and looked down. A boot—one of a pair, Derrick's second-best boots, to be precise. But what were boots doing on the highest shelf, under the blanket?

She retrieved it and turned it upside down. A thick roll of bank notes fell into her palm.

Cathleen stared at the money.

"Someone's been keeping secrets," she whispered to herself. "Well, Derrick, dear, I think it's time for a new dress." She smiled. "Something smart and festive, I think. In a bright ruby red."

It was nearly noon, but Rachel had other things on her mind besides a midday meal. She left the dress shop and strode across the central green toward the road that led from the edge of town to the river.

"A plan," she muttered under her breath. "I need to come up with a plan."

In the distance, she could hear the rippling sound of the river as it cascaded over boulders and wound its way downstream. The river had brought her both sadness and succor over the years. It had taken Sophie from her, but it had also become her sanctuary, her thinking place. And she needed to think.

She had to get the Treasure Box back. This had become her mission in life, her obsession. To find Cathleen and make her pay for what she had done. Whether vindication would bring any kind of inner satisfaction, Rachel had no idea. It was simply the only option open to her.

Along the road, a myriad of summer flowers bloomed— yellow primroses and lady's slippers and bright thistles in the sun-washed ditches, nodding wild violets and lush ferns in the shade at the base of the trees. Rachel had always considered the village of her birth, with its sedate streets and surrounding woods, as quite the loveliest place on earth. A paradise. Every sunset brought a benediction, every sunrise the blessing of another day in Eden.

But no longer. Instead of stopping to touch the shy primroses at the edge of the road and watch the powdery gold at their center rub off on her fingers, she trampled them underfoot. She saw the sunset and the flowers and the lights on the water, but the connection between her eyes and her soul had been severed. The presence had left the garden. The voice of blessing had gone silent.

Rachel reached the bank and gazed unseeing out over the river. If she could just hold on another few months, she would have enough money saved to make the crossing. She no longer believed what Derrick had told her about America being a garden of delights, but it hardly mattered. For Rachel, there was no paradise.

Not here.

Not anywhere.

14

A Day of New Beginnings

Red. Everything was red. Wine poured out over a white linen tablecloth. A drift of sheer fabric, like the skirt of a dress made for dancing. Falling petals from a rose. A cardinal in the snow. Autumn leaves swirling on the wind, scarlet against a stark blue sky. A crimson sun sizzling into oblivion on the arc of a blood-red sea. Fireworks exploding against a black velvet sky.

Even before she awoke, Vita knew it was a dream. A crazy, mixed-up dream, full of nonsense images brought on by too much garlic in the spaghetti sauce—or, in old Ebenezer's words, "an undigested bit of beef, a blot of mustard, the fragment of an underdone potato."

She opened her eyes. Even the real world—her world—was washed in a translucent red, as if someone had photographed the room with a filter over the lens. The sun was just rising, and the lace curtains stirred on a breeze coming through the half-open window. A beautiful morning. One of those glorious, bracing spring days shot through with possibilities that even Vita Kirk could not ignore.

She stretched and smiled and finally abandoned the comfortable warmth of the bed. Raising the window higher, she leaned forward and inhaled the invigorating air. A remnant of Browning came back to her from a nineteenth-century poetry class ages ago: *God's in his heaven—All's right with the world.*

As uncertain as Vita might be that God was in heaven—or anywhere else, for that matter—she couldn't help agreeing that everything did seem right with the world this perfect day. Birds singing. The crisp green scent of grass on the air, and petals from ornamental fruit trees drifting like pink and white snowflakes across the lawn. A day of new beginnings.

A day when nothing could possibly go wrong.

⌒

Something was wrong.

Rachel pushed open the door and entered the dress shop. Usually the shop was filled with the ever-present noise of the sewing machine, beating out its familiar rhythms. But today, only silence.

"Hello?" she called. "Mrs. Tyner?"

"In the back!" a voice answered from behind the drape that separated the workroom from the front of the shop. "I'm making tea—come and join me."

Rachel entered the back room and let the curtain fall shut

behind her. Elisabeth Tyner stood with her gray head bent over the small two-burner hot plate, waiting for the kettle to boil. "Take a seat, dear. I'll have the pot steeping in no time."

Rachel settled into the single chair and folded her hands in her lap. At last a high-pitched whine emanated from the kettle, and Mrs. Tyner removed it from the burner and carefully poured the steaming water into the pink flowered teapot.

When the tea was brewing, the older woman turned and faced Rachel. Her eyes, crinkled at the corners by deep crow's-feet, seemed unnaturally bright. "I'm afraid I have some bad news for you, dear."

"Bad news?" Rachel parroted.

"Yes. I wanted to talk to you about it this morning, but I was waiting for confirmation, and just this noon—" She pointed to a yellow paper that lay unfolded on her worktable. A telegram. "I—well, you see, I've decided to sell the shop."

Like an incredibly slow child, Rachel responded, "Sell the shop?"

Mrs. Tyner poured the tea, handed a cup to Rachel, and tucked the tea cozy over the pot. "I fear it's true, dear. I'm simply getting too old to work so hard any longer. Out of the blue beyond, an offer came in. Entirely unsolicited. A very generous offer—" She shrugged and gave a wan smile. "Like a miracle."

But what about me—what about my miracle? Rachel wanted to scream. *This job was my only possibility of getting to America!* An image rose up in her mind of Saturday nights at The Judas Tree, fighting to repel the advances of drunken patrons, and something inside her froze into a cold, hard lump. She stifled back tears of anger and dejection.

"The new owner is taking over on Monday," Mrs. Tyner went on. "A woman from London, recently widowed, who wanted to get away from the noise and press of the city. Her daughter will come with her, so unfortunately she won't be needing a shopgirl. I would have let you know earlier, of course, but this has all taken place so suddenly."

Rachel nodded dully.

"You've been such a blessing to me," the woman continued. "And as this will be our last day together, I have a little surprise for you." She went to the corner, where she kept an adjustable fitting mannequin, and removed the sheet that covered it with a little flourish. "I had to guess at your size, but I'm fairly certain it will fit."

It was a coat of worsted wool, the rich dark hue of ripe cherries, with a notched collar and bright brass buttons down the front. Rachel had never owned such a fine garment, and despite her disappointment at losing her job, she took in a little gasp of pleasure.

"Mrs. Tyner, how exquisite! When did you—"

"I've been working on it for some time—rather a bonus for all your help, you know. I didn't realize when I started it that it would turn out to be a going-away present." She removed the coat from the mannequin and held it out. "I stayed late last night to finish it. Let's try it on, shall we?"

Rachel set her teacup aside and stood. She slipped her arms into the sleeves and gathered the folds of dark red fabric around her. The lining was made of quilted satin in a deep vermillion color, and the coat draped around her body as if it had been molded to her form. The collar against her cheek wasn't rough and scratchy like her old threadbare jacket, but exquisitely comfortable, soft as the fleece of a newborn lamb.

"Mrs. Tyner, I—well, I don't know quite what to say. It's absolutely beautiful." Then her employer's words registered in Rachel's brain. "A going-away present?"

Her employer nodded. "My son Neville has been after me for nigh onto a year now, wanting me to move to Southampton to live with his family. I've finally agreed to live out my final years as an indolent grandmother. He'll regret it; mark my words—I intend to spoil those children mercilessly." She refilled their teacups and smiled. "But the coat is also a going-away present for *you*. For America, you know."

Rachel ran her hands up and down the luxurious wool. "It may take me longer than I expected to get there," she managed around the lump in her throat. "I'll need to find another position."

Mrs. Tyner wasn't listening. She came over and put an arm around Rachel's shoulders. "I do love this fabric," she said, caressing the coat the way she might have stroked a beloved pet. "Feel the pockets—I lined them with the wool, too, to keep your hands warm."

Rachel slid her hands into the pockets, and her fingers closed around something thick and stiff. She carefully worked it free—it was an envelope, folded in half. She extended it in Mrs. Tyner's direction. "You must have left this in the pocket."

"Look at it."

Rachel unfolded the envelope and stared at the writing on the outside. *For Rachel*, it said. *Go with the blessing and grace of God.* "For me?"

Elisabeth Tyner's eyes brightened with unshed tears. "That's what it says. Open it."

Rachel broke the seal—a blue wax puddle with an ornate *T* stamped in the middle—and opened the envelope. Inside were thirty-five crisp, new ten-pound notes.

"Over three hundred pounds?"

"For America, my dear. For your passage, and then some. To get you started. And perhaps to replace a bit of what you've lost."

Rachel struggled to breathe. "Mrs. Tyner, it's a grand and generous gesture. And I can't accept it."

"Sit down, Rachel."

Rachel laid the envelope on the sewing table, removed the coat, and sank into the chair, grateful for the chance to get off her trembling legs. Her knees had gone weak, and she was shaking all over. When she tried to take a sip of the lukewarm tea, her cup rattled furiously against its saucer.

Mrs. Tyner took the cup from her hands and moved the sewing bench closer to Rachel's chair. "Rachel, you must listen carefully to what I have to say."

"Yes'm."

"All my adult life, it has been my habit—and my joy—to give back a portion of what I earn to God's work. Normally it goes to the church, or to other worthy causes—" She bit her lip, apparently groping for words. "When I decided to sell the shop, I felt a very strong leading that I should share some of the profits with you."

"You mean God *spoke* to you? God has never spoken to me, no matter how much I've tried to pray."

"Not audibly. In here—" Elisabeth Tyner laid a hand over her heart. "More like an inner nudging, deep in my soul."

"But why? I've worked for my wages, and you've paid me quite generously, more than I might have expected. I certainly don't deserve it."

"Sometimes we don't get what we deserve, if you take my meaning." Mrs. Tyner's gaze pierced into Rachel's. "To tell you the truth, I'm not altogether sure why. But I do feel very certain that you are intended to go to America as soon as possible—perhaps for some other purpose than you know." She picked up the envelope full of money, pressed it into Rachel's palm, and closed her fingers around it. "Take it, please."

Rachel swallowed hard. "I'll repay you, Mrs. Tyner, every single shilling."

"You'll do nothing of the sort," she responded. "This is not a loan. It's a gift. I have no doubt you'll use it for good. All I ask is that you listen for the Almighty's direction, and when you're given the opportunity, that you pass a bit of the blessing along to someone else."

Rachel felt the warmth of Elisabeth Tyner's small hands grasping hers, and her resolve faltered. She had been so sure of her purposes in going to America—to track down Derrick and Cathleen, to retrieve the Treasure Box, to make them pay for their betrayal and deception. Guilt began to gnaw at her, but she pushed it aside. This was her one opportunity to get to America, and she had no intention of passing it by.

"You're certain?" she said at last.

Mrs. Tyner smiled. "Absolutely." She stood up and drew Rachel to her feet, enveloping her in an earnest embrace. "Be true to yourself, my child," she whispered into Rachel's ear. "Be true to your Creator. Find your dreams. Listen closely, and you'll hear God's call."

She drew back and smiled, then retrieved the red woolen coat and placed it around Rachel's shoulders. "And stay warm."

Cathleen paused at the bright green door that stood just to the right of the front entrance to Benedetti's restaurant. The doorway opened directly onto a long flight of stairs leading up to the apartment. It was always kept locked, and even when her hands weren't full, she sometimes had trouble getting her key to work. She had to pull out a little on the doorknob and then turn the key—a task that demanded both hands. Today, juggling a small bag of groceries, the two sofa pillows she had purchased at Marshall Field's, and the big white box containing the red silk dress, she couldn't even seem to fit her key into the lock, much less get the door open.

"*Buona sera, Signora.* Having a little trouble?"

Cathleen turned to find Angelo Benedetti standing behind her.

"Allow me." He fished a key from his pocket, inserted it into the lock, and held the door open for her. "You do a little shopping, I see."

"Yes." Cathleen returned his smile. "Just a few things for the house—and a new dress for me."

"Ah. Your Derrick will be relieved. He was concerned for where you might be."

"He's *here?*"

"*Sì.*" Angelo rolled his eyes in the direction of the stairs. "Waiting for you." He stepped back and nodded. "I keep you no longer. You go. I see you at dinner, no?"

"N–no," Cathleen stammered. "I mean yes, of course. Eight o'clock."

"Until then." Angelo bowed slightly and escaped into the restaurant. Cathleen began to climb the stairs. This was not the way she had planned it, not at all. But perhaps if Derrick had finished work early, he would be in high spirits. She needed for him to be in a good mood, tonight of all nights.

She reached the landing, leaned the dress box against the wall in the corridor, and opened the door to the flat. Derrick sat in the armchair next to the front windows, staring out through the dusty, streaked glass.

"Where have you been?" he said without looking at her.

"We—well, we needed some food."

"It doesn't take all day to buy a few groceries."

"No." Cathleen hesitated. "I thought the place could use a little brightening up." She set the bags down and displayed the two pillows—a bold print, a background of blue and white with a floral design in yellow and green and red. Arranging them on the sofa, she stood back and smiled encouragingly at him. "I thought using the blue blanket would add some color to the room. Now, doesn't that look lovely?"

Derrick did not so much as glance at the sofa. "And what else?"

Cathleen took a deep breath. She reached around the corner into the hall, brought in the white box, and held it against her chest like a shield. "I bought a new dress. You'll love it, Derrick. I got it on sale."

At last he turned and looked at her. "Where exactly did you get the money?"

"I—I had a little put aside," she hedged.

"And you filched the rest from me."

The implication that she was a thief—and even more, the haughty superiority in his tone—set off a spark of anger in Cathleen that quickly flared to a full blaze. "Oh, it's *your* money, is it?"

"Isn't it?" He rose from the chair and reached her in two strides, and as soon as he drew close, she could smell the liquor on his breath. "How dare you steal from me!" He jerked the box out of her hands and threw it onto the floor, then grabbed her by the shoulders and shook her, hard. When he released her, the force threw her back onto the sofa.

Cathleen stared up at him. "I thought we were in this together, Derrick. I thought—"

"What? That you had a right to everything that was mine? Everything I worked for?"

"*Yours?* That's all you ever think about—yourself!" she shouted. "And just what is this important work you do? Delivering packages, like a common street urchin? From the smell of you, I'd wager you spend most of your time in the speakeasy on the corner!"

He jerked her to her feet. "For your information, Angelo will be announcing my promotion at dinner this evening."

The fire in Cathleen's belly sputtered down to mild annoyance, and a flash of hope streaked like lightning across her mind. "A promotion? Derrick, that's wonderful. That means we can—"

"What? Get married, buy a house, live happily ever after?"

"Well, yes. I just assumed—"

Derrick clenched his jaw. "If you have any notion of living off me for the rest of your life, you'd best think again."

"You can't mean it."

"I do mean it." He narrowed his eyes. "What makes you believe I would possibly *want* to marry you? I've got grander ambitions than you can begin to imagine—and better prospects."

"But you love me!" she protested. "You told me so, when—" Cathleen paused. "When we first—"

"You're a fool, Cathleen. In the heat of passion, a man always says such things to a woman. It means nothing except that he wants her—for the moment. Love you? Marry you? I can barely stand to look at you." He walked to the windows and stared out into the street.

"But what of all your promises, all your fine words about building a new life together in America? What about me? What about the baby?"

Derrick whirled around. "What did you say?"

"I said, we're going to have a baby, Derrick. I realized it just today."

"Since when?"

Cathleen fixed her eyes on the bleak tan rug. Her stomach churned, and she feared she might be sick. "About three months, I think. I believe it may have happened during the crossing, on the ship. I don't always keep very close track of my cycles, but when I counted backwards—"

"You're certain?"

"As certain as I can be without seeing a doctor. That's why I've been so sick in the mornings, Derrick. And so moody and depressed." Cathleen approached him and put her arms around his waist. "We're going to have a baby, darling. A new life, created from our love. Doesn't this change everything?"

For a moment he stared at her impassively, neither moving nor speaking. Then he took one step back and slapped her across the face, twice. The second blow split open her lip and drew blood, and she fell to the floor, shaking and sobbing.

"You're worse than a fool," he said in a menacing whisper. "You're a bloody imbecile! And you'll not blackmail me into this imaginary life you've dreamed up for the two of us." He wedged the toe of his boot against her throat and applied enough pressure that she began to choke.

"Derrick, please! You're hurting me."

"I'll hurt you a good deal worse if you don't do exactly as I say."

Cathleen closed her eyes and tried to breathe. "What—what do you want me to do?"

He glared down at her. "Angelo's expecting us for dinner. Do not embarrass me; do you understand? Make up some excuse for going away—your poor ailing mother back in England, who is dying and desperate to see her only daughter, perhaps. You can say you're leaving tomorrow for an indeterminate amount of time. Agreed?"

She nodded as best she could under the constraint of his boot.

"Fine." He removed his foot and stood over her with his hands on his hips. "Get up and get dressed. You can wear your new dress—the one *I* paid for. And cover up that cut. I do not want to see you again after tonight."

"But where will I go?"

"I have no opinion on that, my *dear*. To the nunnery, to the whorehouse, back to Merrie Olde England. It's entirely up to you."

∽

Vita watched the screen fade to black. Her shoulders knotted painfully, and her whole body was rigid with tension. In spite of herself, she whispered into the gathering darkness: "Poor Cathleen."

Poor Cathleen, indeed. Vita herself had wished misery upon the two of them, and she knew the girl was simply reaping the fruits of her own betrayal. She deserved whatever she got, but still Vita couldn't help but feel a little sorry for her. She could tell that Cathleen loved Derrick—at least to the degree that she was capable of loving—and hopelessly craved his love in return. And although Vita knew from experience that unrequited love could in the long run be a gift rather than a tragedy, a one-sided romance always left a wounded heart in its wake.

— For Cathleen, the price would be much higher.

It was always possible, of course, that she might learn some lesson from the pain. Some remorse, perhaps, for what she had done to Rachel. A modicum of contrition, a resolution to change her ways in the future. Repentance, as religious folks called it.

Exhausted and ravenous, Vita got up from her desk and went into the kitchen. But halfway through her leftover spaghetti, she realized she had left the light on in her office and hadn't turned off the computer for the night. She finished her dinner and went back to the sunroom, intending to shut everything down and then read or watch television for an hour or so—something that would help her relax. After a week of long nights and interrupted sleep, she really needed to go to bed early.

Just as Vita reached for the power button, however, the screen flickered back to life.

⁓

Cathleen stood in the bedroom twirling in front of the mirror to admire the graceful flow of her new dress, silken and sinuous, a vibrant shade of ruby red. Her traveling bag lay open on the bed, half-filled with the meager selection of clothes and personal items she had brought with her on the crossing.

It was a real bobby dazzler, this dress, with its daring neckline and swirling hem that came just below the knee. The color set off her blonde curls magnificently. All the men at dinner had gaped at her, speechless—all except Angelo, who had immediately taken Derrick to task. "Your *signora,* she is *bellissima,*" he said, wagging a finger in Derrick's face. "You marry at once, *capisca?* Have many *bambini.* Else I think you crazy in the head for letting her get away."

Then Angelo had kissed Cathleen on both hands and both cheeks, rambling about how beautiful she was, how elegant and luscious she looked in the divine red dress. And Derrick had smiled and nodded as if he had every intention of dragging her to the altar as soon as was humanly possible.

With a sigh Cathleen slipped the dress off and held it at

arm's length. In another month it wouldn't fit anymore, but she might as well keep it. Derrick couldn't return it, and she simply could not bear the thought of him giving it to any other woman.

She folded it carefully and laid it in the bag along with the other garments that were already too snug around the middle. Then she turned back to the mirror and smoothed her chemise over her rounded stomach and thickening waist. How could she not have known? She simply hadn't paid attention. And now she was about to be out on her own, without a husband, without work, without a place to live. And with a baby on the way.

Tears stung her eyelids. Derrick was right—she *had* been a fool. A fool to trust him, to believe his lies. A fool like thousands of other gullible women who somehow managed to convince themselves it couldn't possibly happen to them. Never mind that he had betrayed someone else. Never mind that he had left a broad swath of broken hearts and empty pocketbooks in his wake. Never mind that he sometimes struck her—after all, he only did it occasionally, and only when he was drunk or angry. Never mind all the evidence to the contrary: this time it would be different.

Fighting back tears, Cathleen moved the bag to Derrick's side of the bed and sank down onto the coverlet. What on earth was she going to do? How would she manage?

A wave of shame rolled over her, and for the first time in months Cathleen thought longingly of England—of Mam and little Colin and yes, even of Rachel. Of the quiet village where she had grown up, the fountain splashing in the center of the green, of the rushing, laughing river that provided a sweet and peaceful background music to their life in the little cottage at the edge of the woods. She had hated that life, had left it behind without a second thought. And now she wanted it back.

She got up, went to the closet, and pulled down Rachel's Treasure Box from the overhead shelf. Cradling it in her arms, she ran her fingers over the painted blue surface of the box, tracing the outline of the east coast of America, then dragging her finger across the Atlantic to the tiny island that was her home. Could she return? Did she have the strength, the courage, to face everyone—especially her sister—and ask to be forgiven?

From the restaurant below, she could still hear the sounds of music and laughter as Derrick celebrated his promotion with Angelo and his business partners. No doubt the illicit wine was flowing like a river, along with assorted other bootlegged libations. Prohibition might be the law of the land, but it had never seemed to affect Angelo and his *amici* much.

And finally Cathleen knew why. Tonight at dinner, Angelo announced that Derrick was, indeed, about to be promoted— from a courier to a runner. From the snatches of conversation around the table—half in English and half in Italian—she had put together a picture of what that meant. A courier shuttled messages back and forth about plans for the smuggling of illegal liquor. A runner made the deliveries. It was a position of importance, of responsibility, Angelo had said, a steppingstone to a future that held the promise of great riches. Tomorrow morning Derrick would be taken to meet the Don.

But by then Cathleen would be on a train to New York. To Hudson Pier. To a ship that would take her home. If she could come up with the fare, that is.

She nested the Treasure Box carefully into the corner of her bag, then returned to the closet and looked up at the shelf that held Derrick's second-best boots. It wasn't really stealing, she reasoned. Derrick owed her. And it was for a good cause. Passage back to England. The possibility of redemption and reconciliation. She dragged the boots down and reached inside. Her fingers closed around . . . nothing.

The money was gone.

Cathleen left the bedroom and wandered into the front parlor. Outside the double windows, she could look down into the street and see the traffic going by. Chicago never slept, it seemed—the noise and bustle and commotion never ended. What kind of paradise was this, where you never saw the stars, never heard a nightingale singing, never felt the soft loam of forest moss under your feet? Only gaslights and blaring horns and unforgiving pavement.

As she watched, three shiny black automobiles pulled up and stopped in front of the awning over the door of Benedetti's restaurant. A dozen men piled out—musicians for the party, no doubt, dressed in dark suits and carrying their instruments in cases.

Cathleen turned away from the window just as the noise began—a deafening clatter, like the backfiring of a hundred automobiles. Like a thousand sledgehammers breaking up the cobblestones. Like an endless string of firecrackers igniting to celebrate Independence Day.

Behind her, the windows exploded. Shards of glass and wood flew everywhere, and something hard and hot pierced into her flesh. She put a hand to the wound and felt the warm ooze of blood seeping through her fingers.

She dropped to the floor. Down below, in the *ristorante*, she could hear screaming and yelling and more fireworks. Then silence, followed by the screech of tires and the distant wail of sirens.

And everything went black.

15

MIDNIGHT IN THE GARDEN

A full hour after the monitor had gone dark, the smoke continued to hover in a shapeless cloud over Vita Kirk's soul. In her mind she still saw shattering glass and flying splinters and blood spattering against the walls. Her ears rattled with the gunfire, the screams, the squeal of tires, the wail of a policeman's siren come too late. She even tasted the acrid sting of gunpowder on the back of her tongue and smelled the lingering odor of violence, of death.

In a stupor of astonishment, Vita shut down the computer, took a sweater from the hall tree in the entryway, and went out into the backyard.

It wasn't a yard, really, but an enclosed garden, with walls made of the same rough limestone as the blocks that formed the foundation of the little Victorian house. Three stone walls encased the perimeter of the yard and butted up against the back of the house. A single gate opened to a walkway that meandered around to the front but Vita kept it padlocked except when Eddy the yardman came to mow the grass.

In the far corner, near the alley, a large weeping willow draped its graceful branches over the top of the wall, and bright purple and yellow irises bloomed against the mossy stones. Along one side, fragrant white lilies of the valley crowded into a bank of bleeding hearts. In the blue-gray dimness of the garden, Vita could not see their color, but she knew.

Red. Red like Cathleen's dancing dress. Red like the wine and blood that had mingled on the white linen tablecloths in Benedetti's restaurant.

Pushing the image from her mind, Vita settled herself in the swing, drew the sweater closer around her shoulders, and looked up into the night sky. A sliver of moon hung tangled in the upper branches of the willow, and here and there a star winked back at her. The only constellation visible from this angle was sturdy, muscular Orion, his silver sword hanging from his belt.

A fragment of a verse—or perhaps a poem, something— whispered inside Vita's head: *Those who live by the sword die by the sword*. She had seen *The Untouchables*. She knew what gangsters did. The hit was on Angelo and his associates. Cathleen was just a bystander caught in the cross fire.

Vita's mind conjured up images of the carnage in the upstairs flat. Downstairs, in the restaurant, it would have been worse. Mentally she tallied up the victims: Angelo Benedetti, who turned out to be no angel at all. Perhaps a dozen or more of Benedetti's *famiglia*—like Angelo, probably guilty of countless notorious crimes. They probably deserved to die by the sword, but at the moment Vita felt disinclined to render such a judgment. And what of Cathleen and Derrick? They, too, were guilty—of greed and deception, of theft and betrayal. Guilty of wanting too much and loving too little. But was death a just punishment for such offenses, when all of humanity labored under the same faults and frailties?

And one more. One unnamed, unformed Innocent, who had yet to experience firsthand any of life's joys or temptations. One who would now never have the chance to wrestle with the unanswerable questions of creation or delight in its simple pleasures. What had he or she done to merit a violent end to a life which had never begun? Where was the justice in that?

But just or not, the sentence had been served. They were dead. All dead.

Not so long ago Vita had thought, with the smallest twinge of self-righteousness, that given what she had done to Rachel, Cathleen Woodlea deserved whatever she got. Now Vita knew it wasn't true. No one deserved this. Not Cathleen, not Angelo and his mob buddies, not even the thoroughly despicable Derrick Knight.

Death was no answer. It solved nothing, only removed the last faint hope for the restoration of the soul.

Poor Cathleen. She had gotten what she wanted, and discovered in the end how quickly the sweet fulfillment of the heart's desires can curdle into sour disappointment. How often in life, Vita wondered, did a burden come wrapped up to look like a blessing? How often did the real blessing lie in *not* getting what you wished for?

Vita turned the idea over and over in her mind. When she was younger, what she had wanted was Gordon. A handsome husband, children, a circle of friends, a normal life. She wanted what Mary Kate had.

But did she?

Would she have been content to live in Gordon's shadow as her sister did, socializing with his friends, listening without participation in his academic discussions, heeling alongside like an obedient puppy in his footsteps?

The idea shocked her. Vita had never once looked closely at what Mary Kate had received when all her wishes had come true. She had been too closed in upon herself to see beyond the walls. Now suddenly, in a moment of startling clarity, she realized that marriage to the handsome, athletic, intellectual Gordon Locke would have been—for Vita, at least—an unmitigated disaster. Even assuming she could have mastered the role, which she thoroughly doubted, she would have hated playing the meek, obedient little wife. She would have come to despise and resent the overbearing self-confidence that had once so attracted her to Gordon.

And with that awareness came another question Vita had never asked herself: was her sister happy? Vita knew, without a doubt, what qualities in Mary Kate had captured Gordon's attention. She was pert, pretty, blonde, and malleable—or at least she had been when Gordon first married her. A trophy wife. The ideal hostess for the parties that could catapult him into the upper echelons of the academic pyramid. Not a wife who would argue with him or challenge his assertions, but one who would smooth his ruffled feathers, fetch his drink and slippers, and create a peaceful sanctuary on the home front when he returned from the scholastic wars.

Was that the life Mary Kate had anticipated? And now, years later, as her thirties crept by and middle age loomed on the horizon, did Mary Kate ever question her choices? Did she ever speculate about what kind of woman she might have become if she had married someone who treated her as an equal—or not married at all? Did she ever sit alone in that big ivy-covered house while the twins were away at school and wonder what on earth she was going to do with herself when they were grown and gone? What secret longings lay in the deep recesses of her heart and mind and soul, below the surface image of perfection she always projected?

Vita sat there in the swing, hugging herself against the chill of midnight, and a strange sensation crept over her. For the first time in years, she could think about Gordon Locke without anger. Without recalling the pain and humiliation she had felt when he left her for Mary Kate. Without despising herself for wanting something she couldn't have.

It felt like . . . like liberty.

No. She didn't want Mary Kate's life. She didn't want Gordon. She didn't even want vengeance.

What, then, did she want?

Rachel's face rose up in Vita's mind, the way she had looked when she thought about Cathleen. Angry and hurt and determined to track her sister down and make her pay for what she had done. Rachel didn't know—not yet, anyway—that Cathleen had already paid, had already sacrificed everything she possessed. A price far greater than anything Rachel, even in the hottest of rages, would wish on her.

It was too late for Rachel and Cathleen to make amends.

And suddenly the answer pierced through Vita's defenses like moonlight through the clouds. She knew what she wanted.

She wanted her sister back.

16

ANY PORT IN A STORM

It might have been springtime in the mountains of North Carolina, but in Chicago, it was the dead of winter. Mesmerized by the driving storm that raged across the screen, Vita suppressed a shiver. Hypnotic, the way the wind buffeted the snow and sent it flying in mad swirls around the corners of the tall buildings. A danse macabre, a ballet both menacing and magnificent, choreographed by nature to reflect the terrifying beauty of her disposition.

Vita exhaled a deep breath. Somewhere out there—in a pauper's grave, no doubt—lay Cathleen and her unborn child, covered but not warmed by a new blanket of snow.

The downtown streets, nearly obscured by the blizzard, lay empty. Not a single automobile braved the icy pavement. A solitary streetcar, caught in a drift, sat abandoned in the center of the intersection.

Then, out of the corner of her eye, Vita caught a flash of color, like a cardinal in the snow. A lone pedestrian, bent forward against the force of the gale, plowing along the sidewalk. A pedestrian in a red woolen coat.

Too late, Rachel Woodlea had found her way to the Windy City.

For the hundredth time in the five months since she had arrived in Chicago, Rachel blessed Elisabeth Tyner for the warmth of this coat. She shoved her hands into the pockets, ducked her head, and pressed on into the storm.

It was insane to be out on such a beastly afternoon, but Rachel seldom got an entire day to herself, and she wanted to make the most of it. Six days a week, she labored in the alterations department at Marshall Field's—a position she obtained on the strength of Mrs. Tyner's letter of recommendation. She enjoyed the work and had even begun to develop a friendship or two, but the job left her precious few daylight hours to conduct her search for Cathleen and Derrick and dear Sophie's Treasure Box.

Five months of scrabbling for bits and pieces of information, and Rachel had come up with next to nothing. There had once been a restaurant called Benedetti's, the alterations supervisor had told her—but she had heard it had shut down after the proprietor's death. She had no idea where Benedetti's had been located. No one knew anything at all of an Englishman named Derrick Knight.

And then, just last evening, the supervisor's husband had come in near quitting time, intending to escort his wife home. The snowstorm was already setting in, and word had gone out that the alterations department—perhaps even the entire store— would likely be closed the following day. To pass the time as he waited for his wife to complete her paperwork, the man struck up a casual conversation with Rachel.

"You're from England, right?" he asked in his flat Midwestern accent.

"Yes sir, from a small village in the Cotswolds."

Rachel hadn't intended to reveal any personal information to the gentleman, but like many Americans, he turned out to be the garrulous type, and before long she had told him—without discussing any of the less savory details—about the search for her sister, who had crossed several months before she herself had made the passage.

"And her husband had a job lined up?"

Rachel flinched inwardly at the word *husband*, but she kept her face expressionless. "Indeed, sir, at a restaurant, I believe—an establishment called Benedetti's."

"Angelo Benedetti?" A disapproving pall fell over the man's countenance.

"I couldn't rightly say, sir. Perhaps." With rising apprehension she watched the shifting shadows in his eyes.

"That restaurant closed down months ago."

"As your wife told me, sir. She said she believed Mr. Benedetti had died. But she didn't know where the place was. Still, perhaps if I could find it, someone in the neighborhood might be able to give me some information as to the whereabouts of my sister."

"Benedetti's dead, yes," he said curtly. He peered into her eyes. "You seem like a nice young lady, Miss—ah, Woodlea, right?" Rachel nodded. "Since you're looking for your sister, I'll tell you where the restaurant was. But don't go snooping around in that area after dark. And be careful." — —

Now Rachel stood on the sidewalk and looked from the scrap of paper in her hand to a number engraved into the keystone of the doorway. Above her head, shredded remnants of a weathered yellow awning partially shielded her from the ravages of the February storm.

It was the correct address, but the gentleman had to be wrong about the place. The building looked as if it had been lifted out of a war zone and set down in the middle of the city. All the windows and doorways were boarded up, and the brick facade of the building was riddled with bullet holes all the way up to the second story. Several paper signs, faded by the weather, warned off anyone who might come near: *KEEP OUT. NO TRESPASSING. PRIVATE PROPERTY.*

Rachel looked down. In the broken-up mosaic entryway that led to the door, she could make out a large elaborate *B* crafted from gold-colored tiles within an ornate circle. And below that, in smaller letters, *Ben__ det_ i's Rist_rante.*

The blustering wind had subsided, and the flakes now fell steadily, drifting down to cover the streets and sidewalks with an ever-deepening layer of white. She took a shaky step backward and watched, trembling, as the snow filled in the broken spaces in the tile. There was something wrong about this place. Something terrible had happened here. In the marrow of her bones, she could feel the chill of death. Violent death.

One could hardly be in Chicago for a fortnight without hearing the stories: the bootleggers and rumrunners, the wealthy mob bosses with their powerful cars and fast women and ill-gotten gains. Feuds between rival families and shoot-outs in the streets.

But now those blood-splattered images had a face. Her sister's face. Had Cathleen been here, in this building, when—

"Spare a bit of change for an old woman down on her luck?"

The cracked, raspy voice came so unexpectedly, and so close behind her, that Rachel jumped and whirled around, poised for a confrontation.

"Easy there, deary. A frail old bird like me ain't likely to do much harm."

Rachel let out the breath she had been holding and surveyed the woman. She wore layer upon layer of oddly-assorted clothing: a man's tattered overcoat, so long it nearly reached her ankles; a pair of mismatched shoes; black woolen mittens with the fingertips cut out. Wisps of frizzy white hair escaped from the moth-eaten gray shawl that covered her head.

A beggar. An impoverished old woman who kept body and

soul together by panhandling on the city streets. A derelict. Rachel had been warned to keep her distance from the city's indigent. They could be unpredictable. Crazy. Even dangerous.

But this old woman hardly looked like a threat. Aside from her rather unorthodox approach to fashion, she might be someone's granny. Her ancient face, cobwebbed with lines and flushed from the wind and cold, bore an expression of benign amusement. Her watery gray-green eyes held just a hint of merriment, as if she were on the verge of laughing.

Still, one could never tell.

Rachel thrust her gloved hands into the pockets of her coat. Deep in the left pocket, her fingers closed around a small change purse which contained twelve American dollars and four streetcar tokens. Her rent on the flat was paid up for the month, and there was plenty to eat in the pantry. She could easily give the woman a dollar or two—even a fiver—and still make it to Friday, when she would receive another week's wages.

Give her the money, an inner voice entreated. *Even without it, you've far more than she will ever own.*

But then she wouldn't be able to afford those nice kid gloves from the accessories department at Marshall Field's.

You have a pair of gloves. Open your hand, the voice urged.

Rachel resisted the thought. Besides, what would the old woman do with the money? Waste it, probably, on a pint of bathtub gin from some back-alley bootlegger.

Pass a bit of the blessing along. Open your heart.

The final phrase struck a nerve, and Rachel bristled inwardly. She had opened her heart before—to her best friend, to her fiancé—even, it might be argued, to her sister. Sophie had died. Derrick had betrayed her. Cathleen had stolen everything she held dear. Opening your heart left you weak and vulnerable. She had learned that lesson through hard experience and wasn't inclined to repeat it.

Snow sifted down, covering the gray shawl over the beggar's head with a layer of white, like the small arced halo on a Byzantine Madonna. "Sorry, I—" Rachel shrugged and dragged her eyes away, back to the brick building with its boarded-up windows and bullet holes. Cathleen's face swam across her mind in a wash of red, and a shot of panic darted through her veins.

"Quite all right, deary." The woman smiled, showing a mouthful of crooked teeth. "Think nothing of it. We've all of us had bad times. You can't give what you don't got."

She reached out to pat Rachel on the arm, but Rachel recoiled from the touch. She jerked her hands out of her pockets, pushed the woman aside, and turned to flee. She had to get away—away from this horrible place, away from the woman's piercing eyes, away from the boarded up windows and bullet holes.

Blindly she bolted, sliding on the icy pavement. Through drifts of snow, past a wooden barricade, toward the streetcar stalled in the intersection.

"Stop! Deary, wait! Come back!"

Rachel threw a glance over her shoulder. It was the old crone, waving, shouting at her, following her. If she could just get to the corner—

Then her foot came down on a broken cobblestone, hidden under the snow. Her right ankle twisted under her, and she tumbled headlong into the street. She could hear the beggar woman wheezing, running, trying to catch up. She struggled to her feet, but the ankle wouldn't hold her weight. The pain of the effort brought tears to her eyes. She took one step and pitched forward again.

Something caught her before she fell. Rachel could smell the odor of wet wool and grease and unwashed body. She looked up to see two pale greenish eyes peering down at her, like a baby bird peeking out from a nest of grizzled hair and gray wool shawl.

"Let's get you up, now," the old beggar said, clasping Rachel under the armpits. She was surprisingly strong for one so old and seemed to have no trouble helping Rachel to her feet and supporting her as they limped over to the broken-down streetcar. "Set yourself right there on the step, and rest for a minute. Catch your breath."

Rachel obeyed, wincing at the throbbing pain. It had stopped snowing, but the sky was growing dark. What was the old hag intending to do? Rob her, perhaps, or worse?

The woman held up a small leather change purse. "You dropped your pocketbook when you ran off."

Rachel jammed her hands into her pockets and came up

empty. She stared at the wrinkled face. "Why didn't you just keep it?"

"Don't take what's not mine." She extended the purse in Rachel's direction. "What people throw out or give freely, I take. Like the birds of the air and the lilies of the field. I get by just fine without stealing."

Reluctantly, Rachel accepted the change purse and slid it into her pocket. "Do you have a name?

"Everyone has a name," the old woman replied. "Even those whose names are only known to God. Mine's Grace."

"I'm Rachel. Rachel Woodlea."

The rheumy old eyes filled with an inscrutable expression, almost like recognition. "Pleased to make your acquaintance, Rachel Woodlea. How's that ankle feeling?"

"It hurts," Rachel admitted, "but I don't think it's broken."

"That's a blessing, now isn't it?" Grace got to her feet and held out a hand. "We'd better get a move on."

"Where are we going?"

The old woman eyed the clouds. "It'll be dark soon, with more snow coming. You're in no shape to walk anywhere, and it's not likely there'll be any cabs or streetcars running until they get the streets cleared. Better come home with me for the night."

Rachel gazed at Grace's outstretched hand and saw that her fingers, protruding from the cutoff mittens, were gnarled and bony, the fingernails dirty and chipped. She wondered idly what "home" might be like for a woman like this—a splintered packing crate in a dark alley, a sheltered doorway, the damp and musty corner of an abandoned warehouse? But it didn't matter. She no longer saw a crone, a hag, a derelict. This beggar was not a threat.

She was just a sweet old woman named Grace.

17

WHERE THE WORLD ENDS

Her mind consumed by the increasing pain in her right ankle, Rachel paid little attention to where Grace was taking her. She had enough to concentrate on just keeping her feet under her. It was a slow and treacherous journey, one wobbling step at a time, but after several turns along the shadowed streets and alleyways, they stopped in front of a mountainous pile of old wooden packing crates.

"Welcome to my humble abode," Grace said with a cackling little chuckle.

Rachel stared at her. "What—I mean, how—?"

"Watch." She put a hand to one of the crates and shifted it to one side, revealing a doorknob and part of an old metal door.

Night was approaching, and dusk had drained the world of color, leaving the alley filled with eerie shapes in shades of black and white and gray. A scrabbling sound caught Rachel's attention. She looked down just in time to see the shadow of a large creature with a pointed snout and naked tail scuttle past her leg and vanish into the pile of crates. She jumped, landing on her injured ankle, and almost fell. "Rats!"

"Don't mind them, deary." Grace laughed. "They're my watchdogs—and right good at their job, too." She pointed toward the end of the alley, where a beast the size of a small cat was nosing through a pile of garbage. "That's Bruiser. The one who just went under the crates I call Rex. Anybody snooping around takes one look at them and runs the other way."

Rachel suppressed a shudder. "I can't imagine why."

Grace opened the door and motioned Rachel through the small crevice. When both of them were inside, she pulled the crate back into its place and shut the door behind them. "Clever, isn't it? If you didn't know a door was there—"

"You'd never find it." Rachel smiled in the direction of Grace's voice. She had no idea where they were, only that they were totally encompassed in darkness. Claustrophobia began to creep over her, but before full-blown panic could set in, Grace began to lead her forward.

They rounded a corner, and somewhere in the distance—it seemed miles away—Rachel could just make out a faint glimmer. Biting her lip, she leaned against Grace and limped resolutely toward the light. The throbbing in her ankle was steadily worsening, and she was afraid she might pass out. But just when she thought she could walk no farther, she found herself in a large room with a single candle burning on a low table.

"Sit, and prop that leg up," Grace said, motioning to a worn but still serviceable easy chair with a matching ottoman. "I'll get a fire going."

Rachel eased down into the chair and gingerly lifted her foot onto the ottoman. In the dim light, she could see Grace's silhouette moving back and forth, and a few minutes later, a fire blazed to life in a large brick hearth. The heat seeped into her bones and she began to relax.

Grace removed her overcoat, hung it on a peg in the corner, and went about the task of lighting additional candles. Rachel's eyes followed the old woman around the room, her wild white hair stuck up in all directions like an insubordinate halo. An angel? Rachel wasn't certain. Mam would have thought so, that much was sure. But if not an angel, certainly not the crazed lunatic Rachel had first assumed her to be.

At last, when the room was bathed in a warm golden glow, Grace came to stand over Rachel. "So, what do you think of my home?"

Rachel looked around. On the far side of the room lay a sleeping pallet, two or three crates, and a large and lumpy pile of something with a dark blanket thrown on top. In a semicircle around the fireplace sat the chair she currently occupied, a stained sofa riddled with holes, and a second easy chair. Just to the right of the doorway was a scarred wooden table surrounded by four chairs.

"Where are we?"

"In the back room of Benedetti's, what used to be Angelo's private office." She grinned, showing every one of her large crooked teeth. "Angelo used to let me eat scraps out of the cans in the alley. Guess he never figured I'd inherit the place."

"You *knew* Angelo Benedetti?"

Grace shrugged. "As much as a beggar on the street can ever know a wealthy gangster."

Rachel felt her insides clench. "He *was* part of the mob, then."

"The restaurant was a front; everybody knew it. Fine food, if the leftovers I scrounged from the heap were any indication. But this place wasn't Angelo's primary moneymaking venture." She pulled off her mittens and tossed them onto the table. "He ran a bootlegging operation."

"What happened?"

"I wasn't around here that night, but I reckoned Angelo had been conniving to take over somebody else's territory." She shook her head. "Not an honorable thing to do, even by Mafia standards. One of the other families sent him a message."

"You mean they killed him?"

"Him and his cronies, plus a whole bunch of other people. Shot up everything on two floors. Wrecked the place, too." She went over to the fireplace and picked up a small log from a pile stacked neatly against the wall. When she brought it back, Rachel could see that it was not a log at all, but the splintered leg from a wooden chair. "Left me lots of good firewood, though."

"So you simply moved in?"

"That's about the size of it. When the dust settled and the cops

169

were gone, they boarded the place up. I found my way in, scavenged up what I needed, and have been here ever since." Grace chuckled. "Now, let's take a look at that ankle."

She removed Rachel's boot and inspected the ankle in the firelight. "It's a bad sprain, but the cold—and your boot—kept it from swelling too much. I'll wrap it up for you."

Rachel closed her eyes and leaned her head back against the chair as Grace went to collect whatever supplies she needed to treat the sprain. When she opened her eyes, the old woman was standing in front of her holding out a glass bottle full of clear liquid.

"Drink some," she said. "It'll make you feel better."

Rachel balked. "Is it—?"

"It's *water*." Grace rolled her eyes. "I have a little tea, but I was saving it to go with dinner."

Rachel hadn't realized how thirsty she was until the bottle was half gone. Apologetically, she turned to Grace, who was sitting on the floor at her feet sorting through a little box, pulling out pins and needles, some long pieces of fabric torn into bandages, and a half-empty bottle of Doctor Tarwell's Miracle Liniment.

"I found enough bandage to tie it up good and tight," Grace was saying. "When you live on the street, you got to be prepared for the worst."

Rachel heard her speaking, but the words didn't register. All her attention was focused on the box.

A small tin box, painted a soft blue.

With brass corners and handles.

And a map of the world on all four sides.

Rachel sat in her chair, still as death, while Grace continued to sort through her supplies as if nothing had changed, as if the earth hadn't suddenly stopped rotating on its axis.

"Let's put on a bit of this liniment first—that should help ease the—" She turned toward Rachel. "Lord save us, deary! What's the matter? You look like you've seen a ghost."

Rachel recoiled. A ghost. Yes. Sophie's ghost. Cathleen's ghost. "The . . . the box," she stammered.

"Pretty little thing, isn't it?"

Grace shut the lid and approached Rachel with the bottle of liniment and wrapping cloths in her hands. But Rachel lunged forward, trying to reach the box, and her injured foot slipped off the ottoman and fell onto the floor with an agonizing thud. She clenched her jaw and cried out in pain.

"Easy, there," Grace warned.

"The box! Please, let me see the box!"

"All right, all right." Grace handed the box to her and began anointing her foot with the liniment and wrapping it with the lengths of bandage.

Rachel sat in silence and allowed Grace to doctor her ankle, all the time cradling the Treasure Box in both arms. There could be no mistake, even though it looked a bit the worse for wear, with a scrape or two here and there and some scratches in the paint. It was Sophie's box. There were the little sea lions lounging on the beach, and the smiling dragon in the waters at the edge of the world.

The presence of the Treasure Box here, in this place, could mean only one thing—Cathleen and Derrick had found their way to Angelo Benedetti's *ristorante*. Rachel desperately wanted to believe they hadn't been here when the unthinkable happened. But the evidence she held in her hands contradicted any shred of hope her heart could muster. The box was here. Cathleen wasn't.

Her eyes stung, and her sister's face surfaced in her mind, as if Rachel were looking at a body submerged in shallow water. Before she had left on the steamship to America, and throughout these long months of searching, she had been driven by the need to find Cathleen and make her pay for her betrayal and deception. Now guilt settled over the other emotions that layered like silt in Rachel's soul—not adult responsibility, but a guilt founded in childish fears: *I wished something bad to happen, and it did. It's all my fault.* The weight of it pressed all the air from her lungs, and she gasped for breath.

Adult reason, of course, told her that she couldn't bear the burden of her sister's death; she hadn't been here, and even if she had, what could she have done to stop it? But she could not forget all those years of enmity between herself and Cathleen—the hostility and envy, the rivalry, the animosity. The reality was, she had never really had a sister—she'd had an adversary, a nemesis. Even now, as an adult, Rachel had followed Cathleen to America not because of any sense of love or family loyalty, but for retribution.

Suddenly it all seemed so foolish, so senseless. What had Rachel hoped to gain in coming here, in tracking down the two of them? A relationship with her sister had been the furthest thing from Rachel's mind. She had no prayer of getting her money back, and she certainly didn't want Derrick.

That left only one reason: to regain possession of Sophie's Treasure Box. The one evidence Rachel had that life held out some promise, however slim, of hope. The memory of a friendship that had endured even beyond this life, bringing a measure of peace to her soul.

She opened the lid and read once more the familiar words: *Love Is the Key That Unlocks Every Portal.* She traced her finger around the edges of the little smiling dragon. What was it the old charts said, at the end of the known world where the seas dropped off into the void? *There Be Dragons Here.*

Well, the mapmakers were right. Childhood fantasies and innocent faith could only carry you so far. Rachel had sailed to the end of the world and discovered it to be a perilous place, fraught not with smiling dragons but real ones who breathed fire; not with placid blue seas but dangerous maelstroms that sucked you down to oblivion. A place where sisters died and dreams shattered and you were left with nothing but memories and remorse and the specter of what might have been.

Grace finished tying off the bandages, gave Rachel's foot a motherly pat, and leaned back. "There. All done. You'll want to take it easy for a while, though. Stay off it as much as possible."

"Where did you get the box?" Rachel whispered.

"Oh, it ain't mine. It's hers." She pointed toward the back of the room. "She just lets me use it."

Rachel's eyes went to the far wall. No one was there—only Grace's sleeping pallet and a jumbled collection of odd possessions.

Grace got to her feet and went to stoke up the fire. "I'll get some dinner on; you must be hungry." She went to the peg where her overcoat hung, reached into the pocket, and pulled out something wrapped in wrinkled butcher paper. "Got a real good ham hock," she said, holding up the joint for inspection. "And a few carrots and potatoes from what the green grocer over on the next block threw out. Make a tasty soup, I'd think."

"Grace, about the box—"

"You're right taken with that little box, aren't you, deary? I have to admit I was, too, when I first laid eyes on it. Don't reckon she'd care to sell it, but you never know. You'd have to ask her about that."

Rachel set the Treasure Box on the table next to her chair and leaned forward. "Grace," she said with a determined effort to keep her voice calm, "who are you talking about?"

"Why, *her,* of course." Again she pointed toward the back wall. "Come on, honey," she called, raising her voice. "It's time to get up. I'll have dinner ready pretty soon."

174

Rachel strained her eyes in that direction again but saw nothing.

"I found her in the building after the cops had gone—hiding in a pantry. Hurt pretty bad, and scared out of her mind. I take care of her."

Rachel closed her eyes and made an effort to compose herself.

"Here she comes. Be gentle with her. She's—well, not quite right, if you get my meaning."

Rachel heard a noise behind her and turned. The lumpy pile in the corner, the one covered by a blanket, began to move.

The lump rose upright and assembled itself into a more or less human form—a woman, with straggly, filthy hair and multiple layers of castoff clothing. As she limped across the room, dragging her left leg, Rachel noted that her entire left side seemed to be crippled or paralyzed—the left shoulder drooped, and the left arm swung uselessly at her side.

"Come sit by the fire, deary," Grace was saying. "We've got ourselves a visitor."

The woman eased herself into the chair opposite Rachel and shrugged the dirty blanket from her shoulders. She kept her head down, and hanks of unwashed hair hid most of her face from view.

But Rachel wasn't looking at her face. Her attention was fastened on the woman's midsection, which swelled outward like an overinflated beachball and threatened to burst the buttons of a ragged sweater already stretched to its limit.

The only phrase that came to Rachel's mind was "great with

child." This woman, this indigent, looked as if she might deliver at any moment. But what then? What would happen to the baby? How could she possibly care for a child in these surroundings? Where would she find—

"Rachel?"

The voice interrupted her thoughts, and Rachel looked up, her eyes going immediately to Grace, who stood next to the fire stirring the kettle of soup. But Grace's back was turned, and she gave no indication of having spoken.

"Rachel?" repeated the voice, raspy and uncertain, rusted from disuse. Something in the sound of it snagged at a rough place in Rachel's mind. She turned—slowly, unwillingly—and forced herself to look at the beggar woman's face for the first time.

The long stringy hair, dangling in matted strands, might have once been blonde, but now bore the greenish brown color of tarnished brass. The eyes, what Rachel could see of them through the half-open lids, were blue, and the pallid skin was smudged with dirt and soot. But the most prominent feature of the face by far was the puckered scar that ran in a ragged line from the outer edge of the left eyebrow to the corner of the woman's mouth. As Rachel watched, the woman's lips moved, and that side of her face drew up in a grimace. "Rachel?" she said a third time.

Something in Rachel's stomach jerked with a sickening lurch, an unsought and unwelcome recognition. "Yes," she responded hesitantly. "My name is Rachel."

Grace rose from the fire and came to stand next to the woman.

She reached out a hand and stroked the filthy hair with all the gentleness of a mother comforting a very young child. "Lord help us, deary! She spoke to you! She's never said a blessed word in all these months. I don't even know her name." – –

"Cathleen," Rachel said, her voice cracking. She tried to drag her eyes away from the filthy, haunted countenance, but she could not. "Her name is Cathleen and she—" She paused, summoning the courage to finish. "She is my sister."

The scarred face twisted in a pitiful contortion, the grotesque imitation of a smile. Then, with great effort, she slid the Treasure Box from the table, balancing it precariously between her good right hand and her crippled left. She struggled halfway to her feet, deposited the box into Rachel's lap, and sank into the chair again. "It's yours," she said, the words slurring together. "I kep' it for you." She pointed. "See? The lil' dragon with the smiling face?"

Rachel looked down at the box, then up at the once-familiar countenance, now so ravaged and filled with despair that it was barely recognizable. A single tear leaked from her sister's left eye, following the jagged path of the scar until it dropped onto her bulging abdomen.

Yes, Rachel thought as she gazed at the ruined image of what was once her sister, *there be dragons here.* Here, in this place of peril, you could have your beautiful face mutilated by fire from the dragon's breath, your dreams charred to ashes. Here, where the world ends, you could slip off the edge without warning and be lost forever.

18

A CRY IN THE NIGHT

Vita never had trouble sleeping, and she had little patience for those who complained of insomnia. The minute her head hit the pillow, she was gone, into a deep and usually dreamless slumber. It was, she always said, the gift of an unburdened conscience.

In the past week or so, however, she had begun to appreciate the problems brought on by sleeplessness. Her normal routine—in bed by ten-thirty, awake with the dawn—didn't seem to be working any longer. She couldn't manage to get her brain to shut down so that her body could rest, and when she did sleep, her overactive imagination conjured up strange and disquieting dreams. She would awaken in the middle of the night or the middle of the morning, dazed and disoriented, haunted by troubling images that came to her in the darkness.

Tonight she couldn't get her mind off Rachel and Cathleen. She dozed a bit, but her subconscious reeled. Rats scrabbling in the alley. Something red, moving inexorably toward her like the molten flow from a volcanic eruption. Grace's bright beady eyes peering out from a nest in the hedge outside her office window.

The dream shifted. She was in a dark, cold place, fettered hand and foot. She couldn't move, couldn't escape. And above her, staring down at her, a woman with a scarred face and a swollen belly and dirty blonde hair. Cathleen, at first, but subtly transforming into someone else. Someone familiar. Mary Kate, with Cathleen's scar.

Suddenly she heard it: a sound in the night, like the reedy cry of an infant. Vita bolted upright in bed, but her arms and legs were caught in a tangle of sheets and blankets, and for a minute she couldn't move. She kicked and thrashed violently until the blankets pulled free, and then sat panting on the side of the bed, clutching the clock and staring at it stupidly until its numbers registered in her brain: three-fifteen.

Vita willed her heart to slow its painful throbbing. She was awake now. Back in the real world. It was only a dream. Everything would be all right.

The sound came again, a feeble wailing noise. A cat, probably, prowling around the back of the house. She shoved her feet into her slippers, threw on her robe, and went to the open window, but the only noises outside were the chirping of crickets and the distant echo of a dog's bark.

Then she heard it a third time—not out in the yard, but inside the house. She started downstairs, belting her robe around her as she went. The sound came from her office—faint, but very clear. Vita reached the doorway of the sunroom and stopped. There it was again, emanating from the computer speakers on the shelf above her desk. Not the cry of an animal, but of a human. A person.

A person in pain.

~

Rachel lurched up from the sofa as the cry startled her to wakefulness. For a moment she sat there, squinting into the darkness, trying to identify what she had heard. Where was she? And what was that noise?

Her eyes focused on the hearth, where a fire had burned down to glowing embers, and she remembered. Grace's place. The back room of Benedetti's restaurant.

A gust of wind moaned around the corner of the building. Rachel shivered. It must have been the wind; that was all. Just the howling of the storm that raged outside. She drew the ragged blanket closer around her shoulders, limped over to the fireplace, and added more wood.

With a little coaxing, the fire blazed up, and she stood there for a moment or two, letting the warmth soak into her. Then the cry came again, from behind her—a muted wail. Not the wind outside, but something inside, a sound almost human, like an animal caught in a trap.

She turned, and in the flickering firelight she could see movement—on the floor a few feet to the right of Grace's pallet, a jerking under the blanket. Cathleen.

Wincing as the pain from her sprained ankle shot up into her calf, Rachel hobbled to the corner of the room and knelt beside her sister. "Cathleen," she whispered, putting a hand on her shoulder. "Cathleen, wake up."

Cathleen rolled over and jerked upright. Her eyes, wild and white in the firelight, did indeed look like the eyes of a frightened animal, and her whole body tensed in terror.

"Hush," Rachel soothed. "It's all right. It's Rachel, remember? You were having a nightmare. I heard you call out." She stroked her sister's back and felt a shudder run through her. "Are you cold?"

Cathleen nodded.

"Come over near the fire, then. Come on, I'll help you."—

Getting an expectant woman up from the floor was no easy task, but at last Rachel managed to put an arm around her and help her to her feet. Together they lumbered over to the sofa and sank down in front of the hearth.

"Here, take some water," Rachel urged, retrieving the bottle from the table next to the sofa and putting it to her sister's lips. Cathleen upended the bottle and drank deeply. "Better?"

Cathleen nodded again. "The dream—it was—" Her shoulders twitched violently, and she shut her eyes. "Shooting. Blood everywhere, an ocean of it. I was trying to get away, but—"

181

"But you couldn't."

She hung her head. "I—I should have died. I'd be better off." She laid a grimy hand over her swelling midsection. "We'd both be better off."

"Cathleen, you don't mean that!"

Her head shot up, and her eyes bored into Rachel's. "Didn't you wish me dead, after what I did?"

Rachel hesitated. For just a moment, all the old anger came flooding back—the memory of Cathleen's deception and selfishness, the shame of standing at the altar waiting for Derrick, that horrible moment when she pulled up the loose board in the barn floor to find that everything she cherished was gone. A hot stab of resentment knifed through her. She shouldn't have to be here, in this hideous place, trying to comfort the sister who had betrayed her so terribly.

Then her eyes rested on the scarred and filthy face. Cathleen had never possessed Rachel's intelligence or abilities or likable nature. She'd never had a friend like Sophie or a mentor like Elisabeth Tyner. All she ever had was her beauty. She had always depended upon her looks, upon her ability to attract the lads and manipulate them into doing what she wanted. Her only hope for a secure future had been to find a man, get married, and be taken care of. Even if she had to steal her sister's fiancé and life's savings in the process.

Poor Cathleen. She had chosen so unwisely. And now, scarred and broken, she would bear the guilt of what she had done—to her sister, to herself, to her unborn baby. Was it so much to ask that Rachel should now give her the benefit of the truth, and a little compassion?

"I was angry with you, yes," Rachel admitted. "Running away with Derrick was a terrible thing to do, although I suppose you got the worst end of that bargain."

Cathleen acknowledged Rachel's words with a crooked smile.

"And stealing the money I had worked for—well, I was furious about that, even though I was fairly certain Derrick had put you up to it. But it was taking Sophie's Treasure Box that was the last straw. You knew how much I valued it—how important her memory was to me."

"I know." Cathleen averted her eyes.

"So yes, I was angry. I wanted not just to get the Treasure Box back, but to get revenge—or at the very least, retribution. To hurt you the way you had hurt me." She paused, fumbling for words. "But—but I never wished you dead, Cathleen. I never hated you."

Cathleen peered through her hair at Rachel. "Never?"

Rachel thought about the question for a moment, and at last forced out a half-truth, the words she knew she ought to say but did not feel. "For a while I thought I did. But no, I don't hate you. You're my sister. I could never hate you." She got up and went to the hearth, laying on more wood and poking at the embers with a broken chair leg. "Tell me about Derrick." She kept her back turned toward Cathleen. "I want to know what happened."

"I loved him," Cathleen answered miserably. "At least, I thought I did. He told me he loved me—oh, Rachel, I was so stupid to believe him!"

"Until I was forced not to, I believed him, too," Rachel said quietly. She faced Cathleen and raised an eyebrow. "So which one of us was more stupid for believing him?"

"That would be me." Cathleen let out a pent-up breath. "He never even promised me the altar."

"He didn't marry you?" Rachel's eyes went to her sister's protruding abdomen. "I assumed—"

"I assumed a great deal, too." She shifted on the sofa, trying to get more comfortable. "We honeymooned on board ship during the crossing. We just never got around to the wedding."

Rachel looked around at the room, then back at her sister's face. "Cathleen, what happened here?"

Cathleen shrugged. "The only thing I remember clearly was the front windows shattering. Upstairs, in our flat."

"And Derrick was killed."

"He was down here at dinner. Everybody downstairs was killed." Cathleen turned and looked toward the back of the room, where Grace still slept on her pallet. "They shot up the second floor just for good measure. Two bullets hit me—one in the shoulder and one in the knee. The first one went all the way through; the second one Grace removed after she found me. I suppose I kept hidden; I don't recall. I do remember falling." She raised a hand to her face and traced the puckered scar that ran down the length of her cheek. "I may have struck something when I went down, or been hit by flying glass."

Rachel bit back tears—not only at the account of her sister's ordeal, but at the matter-of-fact way Cathleen spoke about it. "But you survived."

"Grace says it's a miracle." Cathleen frowned. "I'm not so certain of that myself." She drilled her forefinger viciously into a hole in the sofa—a perfectly round hole, Rachel noted for the first time, a hole that might have been left by a stray bullet.

"And you never spoke about it—even to Grace?" Rachel fixed her eyes on Cathleen's finger as it ground into the bullet hole.

"When I first came to, I was out of my skull with the pain," she said, her voice barely more than a whisper. "Even talking—or attempting to—hurt. Then, as my body healed, I couldn't bear to think about what had happened, and—" She cleared her throat. "After a while, it just seemed easier to keep silent."

Cathleen laid her head back against the sofa. Clearly, talking had depleted her, and Rachel felt the exhaustion in her own body as well. For a while neither of them spoke. They sat side by side, staring into the fire until finally Cathleen's voice broke the silence.

"Rachel, I'm—I'm sorry. Can you ever forgive me?"

Without looking at her, Rachel reached out and patted her sister's hand. "It's all right. I understand."

"It's not all right, and you do not understand!" Cathleen snatched her hand away and lurched awkwardly to her feet. "Rachel, look at me. Perhaps I deserve what I've gotten, to be living this way—" She waved a hand to indicate the darkened room. "Whatever I may have suffered doesn't begin to make amends for what I did to you. I may not deserve your forgiveness, but—" She sank back onto the sofa. "But I don't want your pity."

The barb hit home, and Rachel closed her eyes against the sting of truth. She did pity Cathleen, but she had not even begun to forgive her. The anger she had harbored for so long had instead melted into a righteous condescension, allowing her to feel noble and compassionate toward her sister without really facing the hard work of forgiveness.

"All my life, I've been jealous of you," Cathleen said in a more subdued tone. "Even when we were children, I envied your friendship with Sophie. I wanted someone to love me that much. It was my fault she died—that prank I pulled with the Treasure Box. But even knowing that, I wasn't sorry she was gone. I wanted something like the Treasure Box, something of my own—something I could look at and say, 'This is a sign that someone really cares for me.' But I never could manage to find it—not in friendship, not even in romance. The next best thing for me was to take what you had."

A soul-deep weariness washed over Rachel as Cathleen was speaking—not just the exhaustion of being awake in the early hours of the morning, but the fatigue that comes with months, even years, of carrying a heavy burden. For over a decade, she had blamed her sister for Sophie's death, and for so many other things that had caused enmity between them. But Cathleen hadn't forced Sophie to go into the river when Rachel had fallen. Cathleen hadn't forced Derrick to abandon her. Cathleen wouldn't have even known where the Treasure Box and Rachel's money were hidden if Derrick hadn't told her.

Cathleen had changed. In more than twenty years, Rachel had never once heard her sister say, "I'm sorry." Now she was not only apologizing, but taking responsibility for what she had done to hurt others. Perhaps the bitter disappointments she had faced had brought her to an understanding of other people's pain. Or maybe she simply needed to unburden herself, to confess and find a measure of absolution. Whatever her motives, it hardly mattered anymore. What mattered was that she had asked a question, a question that still hung unanswered between them: *Will you forgive me?*

Her sister had already faced the truth—now it was time for Rachel to do the same. Time for her to acknowledge the pain Cathleen had caused and release it. Time for her to stop mouthing facile platitudes and speak the words that would liberate her from the bondage of anger and vengeance. She needed to forgive, not for the sake of Cathleen's freedom, but her own.

She never got the chance.

When she turned back toward Cathleen, Rachel found her sister doubled up in silent agony, her arms clutched around her stomach. Her cheeks had gone pale, and the ugly puckered scar stood out vividly against the ashen skin. Despite the chilliness of the room, a sheen of sweat covered her face. On the seat between them, something warm and wet oozed into the fabric of the sofa.

"The baby!" Cathleen gasped, reaching a hand toward Rachel.

"But it's not time. Didn't you say—"

"Whether it's time or not, this baby is coming."

Vita stared at the screen while dawn crept over the horizon and pierced through the high privet hedge, painting the sunroom in watercolor hues of pink and gold. Memories layered one upon the other like transparencies. Scenes from the past: Hattie Parker's scarred face turning away for the last time. Rain pounding against the raw mound of earth at Mama's grave. Gordon's voice on the telephone, telling her that Mary Kate was in labor and was asking for her to come.

And other, more recent memories: Sophie lying in the shallows of the river. The weeping willow tree in the back garden, draping its branches over the wall. The little brown bird nesting in the hedge. Red wine flowing across a white linen tablecloth.

She closed her eyes, trying to shut off the images, but they wouldn't go away. They pressed into her brain as if etched there with acid. Even more images came. Hap Reardon's laugh. Jacob Stillwater in his workshop. The strange dark man in Pastimes. The Treasure Box, with its delicately painted maps and the little smiling dragon in the waters.

Then Cathleen's voice came through the computer speakers again, screaming, and Vita opened her eyes.

⌒

"Bring all the candles over here," Grace ordered, taking command of the situation. "We'll need as much light as we can get. And in that crate next to my bed you'll find some clean towels and a pair of scissors."

At Rachel's questioning look, she gave a little shrug and a grin. "I found them in Angelo's bathroom. I knew we'd need them eventually."

Rachel ran for the crate and came back with the towels.

"Just take it easy, deary," Grace was saying. "Breathe—that's it, deep, relaxing breaths. First babies sometimes take a while in getting here. You're going to be fine."

Grace had dragged Cathleen's pallet over next to the fire, and Cathleen lay with a rolled-up blanket under her head. Another contraction came, and another shriek.

Rachel stifled down a rush of panic. "Shouldn't we—call someone?"

"Go outside and see if anyone's about. A policeman, maybe."

Pulling on her coat and boots, Rachel limped down the long dark hall. She fumbled with the latch and finally managed to get the door open and the crate pushed aside. At last she stepped out into the alley.

The city was silent as a tomb.

Snow was falling thick and fast. The drifts came almost to her knees. Even the rats were gone, taking cover from the storm.

Clutching the red coat around her, Rachel waded through the snow down the alley, around the corner, and out into the street. It was still dark, but the reflection of the snow provided enough illumination for her to see a little. The abandoned streetcar was now only a huge gray lump in the center of the intersection. Beyond that, half a block in either direction, all was a blur of bluish white.

"Help!" she called, her voice dissipating on the wind. "Someone please, help!"

No answer. No movement.

"Help!" Rachel screamed again, but only a muffled echo came back to her. Tears stung her eyes and froze on her cheeks before they fell. And then, like a miracle, she saw something: a faint, dusky figure, immensely large. She ran, limping, in its direction. "Help! Please, help!"

At last it materialized out of the dark and the storm—a horse and rider, both covered with a thick layer of wet snow. A man in a dark blue coat and cap, with some kind of medallion on his chest. A mounted policeman.

"You ought not to be out in this weather, ma'am," he said, looking down on her from a great height. The horse snorted and stamped, and Rachel backed up a step or two. "Are you lost?"

Rachel shook her head. "No, I—" She gasped for breath. "We need help. Come on, Constable, please!"

She retreated into the alley, and the man followed. When she got to the back door of Benedetti's restaurant, opened it, and indicated he should enter, he just sat there astride his mount, scratching his head. "Well, I never—"

"This way! Hurry!" Rachel practically dragged him down from the horse and pushed him through the doorway. Once inside, she took his gloved hand and led him forward until they stood in the back room, illuminated by fire and candlelight, where Grace knelt between Cathleen's legs.

The policeman took one quick look around the room. He shook off the snow, shed his coat and gloves, and knelt beside Grace.

"You know anything about midwifing?" she asked curtly.

"A little." He shook his head and grinned up at Rachel. "Delivered a few calves, at least, back on the farm when I was a lad."

Rachel could see him more clearly now—a young man, not more than a year or two older than herself. He was clean-shaven, with a ruddy Irish complexion and sandy red hair. She wondered what good he'd be in a situation like this, but she kept quiet.

"I'm Michael," he said, hunkering down to get a better view of what was transpiring with Cathleen. "Michael McCall."

Grace grunted. "I'm Grace. The mother here is Cathleen, and the one who brought you in is her sister Rachel."

"And you're all *living* here? But that's against the—"

Cathleen let out a moan, and Grace lifted her head and stared at him as if he were the stupidest boy on the face of the earth. "I reckon arresting us will have to wait. We've got more important business on our hands right now."

～

An hour passed. Then two. Then three. Rachel lost all track of time as her sister's labor continued, stretching through the night and on toward dawn. She paced around the room, bathed Cathleen's face with a cold compress, fed her sips of water from a spoon.

Then, finally, when it seemed Cathleen could bear no more, the contractions quickened.

"Looks like this wee one has decided to come into the world after all," Michael said. He focused his attention on Cathleen. "It's all right, lass. You'll be just fine. The most natural thing in the—" He stopped suddenly, and his rosy face went white.

"What's wrong?" Rachel stepped closer.

"She's bleeding. I'll need an extra pair of hands."

"She won't die—promise me she won't die." Rachel heard her voice jump an octave, and she fought for control. "I can't lose her, not now—"

"Come down here," Michael said. "I need help."

Rachel's stomach shifted. "No, I can't, I—"

"Yes you can, deary." Grace's voice was gentle, entreating. "Come on, now."

Rachel took a deep breath and awkwardly lowered herself to the floor beside Michael. Grace moved up to Cathleen's head and held onto her hand.

"Cathleen, try not to push until I tell you," Michael said.

In place between Cathleen's knees, Rachel took in a deep breath, but the stench filled her lungs and nearly made her gag. Whoever had come up with this method of reproduction clearly hadn't thought the matter through very carefully. She had often heard women talk about the miracle of childbirth, and wondered briefly how anyone could claim this barbarism as a miracle. It was a nasty, bloody, horrible mess.

Then her heart began to pound, and she forgot all about the mess. "I can see it! It's coming! I see its head!"

Michael leaned over her. "Let me look. Yes! Push, now," he coaxed Cathleen. "When the next contraction comes, push hard!"

Cathleen pushed. A cry emanated from the depths of her soul, a horrible, agonizing, primal scream. The next moment, something small and slippery slid out into Rachel's hands.

"Hand me a towel." Michael's voice was terse, clipped. He took the baby from Rachel, wiped its face and cleared out its mouth, then upended it and smacked its bottom soundly. There was a hiccup, followed by a hearty, indignant wail—the loveliest music Rachel had ever heard in her entire life. This *was* a miracle. A bloody, barbaric miracle, but a miracle nevertheless.

"A girl." Michael wrapped the baby in a clean towel and laid the wrinkled, purplish infant, still attached by the umbilical cord, on Cathleen's chest.

In an instant Rachel was at her sister's side, pushing the matted hair away from her eyes, stroking her face, feeling the long puckered scar underneath her fingertips. "She's beautiful, Cathleen." Rachel battled against the rising tide of tears. "Beautiful. Just like you."

Cathleen opened her eyes and tried to speak, but her mouth twisted in a grimace instead. "It hurts—"

"Of course it hurts, deary," Grace soothed. "But it'll soon be better, you'll see. And this little one here will all be worth it."

The policeman still knelt at Cathleen's feet. "Please, God, no," he whispered.

Rachel jumped up, forgetting about her injured ankle, and nearly fell. She hobbled over to Michael, and when she saw it, her legs turned to jelly and her head began to reel.

Blood. There was so much blood. Soaking the blanket, seeping everywhere.

"Should it be like that?" she whispered.

Michael shook his head. "She's hemorrhaging. I can't seem to stop it, but if I don't—".

"Rachel."

Rachel turned. Cathleen had raised her head, and her face was as gray as the ashes in the grate. "Rachel . . . come here."

Rachel returned to the head of the pallet and took Cathleen's hand.

"Remember what you told me about Sophie? How she heard the song of the willow-woman?"

"Cathleen, no—"

"Listen to me," Cathleen grated. "The child—my baby.

194

Name her—" She closed her eyes, and Rachel could see she was summoning every ounce of strength she had just to speak. "Name her Sophia. Sophia Rose." A tear slid down her scarred cheek, and Rachel gently wiped it away.

"Yes." Rachel forced a smile. "Sophia for Sophie, and Rose for Mam. I understand."

"I want you to—to take care of her. Raise her to be . . . good. Like you. Like Sophie."

Rachel bit back a sob. "Cathleen, stop this. You will raise her yourself. You will get through this. You will recover. And you and Sophia Rose will come to live with me, and—"

"Promise!" she interrupted. "Promise you'll take care of her. Treat her as . . . your daughter."

Rachel did not answer, and Cathleen grabbed her hand with a fierce grip. "Promise! I owe you everything. But she's all I have to give you."

"You don't—you don't owe me anything."

Peace filled Cathleen's expression as she laid the baby in Rachel's arms. "And you've . . . forgiven . . . me?"

"Yes," Rachel whispered. "Yes, I've—"

Tears choked off the words before she could finish. But it didn't matter. Her sister couldn't hear her anymore. The last breath had gone out of Cathleen's ravaged body. Rachel still bent over her, trying in vain to formulate a prayer, but all she could manage was a silent inner scream: *Why?*

When Rachel finally gave up praying and raised her eyes, she could see the blurred, watery image of Michael McCall wiping a tear from his eye.

And in her arms, Sophia Rose Woodlea reached out with a tiny fist, grabbed her Aunt Rachel's finger, and held on.

19

WHAT CHILD IS THIS?

The screen went dark. Vita turned off her computer and sat staring into the distance.

Human existence was such an inexplicable, chaotic, disordered business. One dies while another lives, with no apparent reason for the choices Fate makes. A deal of the cards, a spin of the wheel. Just another game of chance. Sophie or Rachel, Cathleen or her baby. Which one lives, and which dies? And does the outcome really matter in the long run?

But while Vita's mind shifted into its old mode of conjuring up all the cynical arguments and pessimistic logic that had kept her safe behind her fortress walls for most of her adult life, her heart seemed to be taking a first tentative step through a small, unobtrusive, unlocked door. Maybe there *was* a reason.

Through Sophie's sacrifice, Rachel had lived. She had endured great heartache, but her pain had led her to America to find her sister and her infant niece, to find herself—even, Vita thought, to begin the process of forgiveness. Perhaps the struggle had a reason. A purpose.

Vita could hardly believe she was even considering such a radical idea.

For one thing, entertaining the premise that there was a purpose to these events meant Vita must inevitably wrap her mind around the concept of a *Purposer.* Some sentient Being, some Creator who, if not manipulating the marionette strings from afar, certainly exercised a measure of involvement in the lives of those it had created.

For Vita, this was a rocky, difficult path to negotiate. If she looked into the lives of Sophie and Rachel and Cathleen and discerned even the possibility of some larger design, she might have to concede—eventually, if not immediately—that her life, too, was subject to some meaning or mission outside the realm of her comprehension. She would have to give up the idea of being in control.

It was too much to contemplate—especially now, when she had been up all night and wasn't thinking clearly. At the moment she had enough to deal with just sorting out her emotional responses to witnessing Cathleen's death and the birth of Baby Sophia.

Later. She'd think about it later. Right now, all she wanted to do was drag herself upstairs, crawl into bed, and sleep.

~

It was her garden, and not her garden. The willow tree was there, in the back corner, draping its branches over the limestone wall, and the lilies of the valley crowded against the bleeding hearts in the bed on the west side. But everything had a surrealistic radiance, a depth of color and dimension unknown in the everyday world. As if the filmy coating of human experience had been stripped away to reveal the pristine, unpolluted beauty beneath.

The space was bigger. The walls were higher. And the garden had no gate.

Vita sat on the ground inside, happily tending to the flower beds. She felt the dark loam between her fingers. Her nostrils filled with the rich brown odor of the dirt, the floating fragrance of the blossoms, the scent of living things. She was safe here, in the garden. No one could touch her.

And then she heard it—an animal noise, a low insistent whine. Not a cry of pain, but a little moan of despair. Vita tried to ignore it, but it persisted, calling up from within her some ancient sadness, a weary, world-deep sorrow. She abandoned the flower beds and began walking the perimeter of the garden, trying to locate where it was coming from.

The whining intensified, stopped, and began again. Finally Vita dragged a garden bench over to one side, stepped up onto it, and looked over the wall into the world beyond.

It was a dog. A beautiful dog, with long silken hair in a dark sable color, and a snowy white ruff and paws. Like a collie, only smaller. It possessed an intelligent face and haunting dark eyes. Vita's mind dredged up an identification: Shetland sheepdog. The breed people called a Sheltie.

Vita had never owned such a dog—indeed, had never owned any pet at all. But as soon as she laid eyes on the animal, she knew he was her dog, and she loved him. Loved him with an unquestioned and unqualified devotion.

Apparently the dog felt the same way about Vita. The instant he saw her, he stopped whining and began wagging his tail, jumping and barking and dancing about in an attitude of pure joy. He pawed at the ground, dug at the base of the stones, even tried to leap to the top of the wall. But to no avail. Somehow Vita had left him outside. She had come into the garden without bringing the dog, and now there was no way to get to him. No gate.

How could she have forgotten him? She loved him; she wanted him with her, and yet she had left him behind without a second thought. Guilt pressed its invisible fingers against her throat and squeezed. A painful lump lodged there, cutting off her breathing. She sank down to the grass and began to cry.

The scene shifted, and, in the manner of dreams, Vita found herself suddenly and without explanation in a different place. In her office, at the computer. The sun had set and night was coming on; her eyes were tired and her back ached. She had the sense that she had been here all day, working.

She left the office, meandering aimlessly through the dim-lit rooms and down the hall until she came to a doorway she didn't recognize. There she paused and looked to the right.

Inside the room, in the half-light of dusk, was a baby's crib.

And in the crib a young child, not more than a year old, standing behind the bars, peering out at her.

Vita didn't know who the baby was, or who it belonged to. Yet by some instinct she knew that caring for the child had been her responsibility. She had promised; and yet she had spent all day in her office working, completely oblivious to the baby's needs. She hadn't fed it or given it water or changed its diaper, had not even checked to see if it was still alive.

The baby was not crying. It made no sound, did not even raise its arms to be picked up. It just stood there, staring at her with dull, vacant eyes. But Vita read reproach in its gaze, and suddenly she felt ashamed, panicked lest anyone should discover her irresponsibility. She had to do something, anything—quickly, before anyone found out.

But she had not the faintest idea what to do.

Vita awoke to a roaring noise, an insistent *vroom,* like the idling of a motorcycle without a muffler. A filtered afternoon sunlight reflecting across the bed. For a second or two she couldn't quite identify where she was. And then she remembered: she had been up all night and had gone back to bed shortly after dawn.

But what on earth was that infernal noise?

She went to the window and looked down. Eddy, the workman who mowed her lawn, was out in the yard with a chain saw, cutting up the huge limb that had fallen from the oak tree the night of the storm. The mower stood beside him on the grass.

Vita returned to her bed and sat on the edge, pressing her fingers to her throbbing temples. There was something—just before she awakened. Something important. A dream.

Then it came to her: not one dream, but two. The dog and the baby. One she had abandoned, and the other she had neglected.

Ordinarily Vita didn't put much stock in the interpretation of dreams. That kind of nonsense was better left to quacks and shrinks and hypochondriacs. And yet she was overcome with the unshakable sensation that these particular dreams were trying to tell her something. Some kind of message from her subconscious. Something she needed to know.

The images had to be connected to what she had just seen in the Treasure Box program. Rachel finding Cathleen. The birth of the infant Sophia Rose. Cathleen's death.

But what did any of that have to do with Vita? And why a dog shut outside a gateless garden and a baby left alone in a darkened room?

She thought first of the dog—his joyous bark, his dancing delight when he first caught sight of her. This was something that belonged to her, something she loved. And yet she had closed herself off from it—whatever *it* was—in favor of the safety of a place surrounded by high walls.

And the baby. Not crying, not making a sound. Just staring at her. What had she learned long ago in a psychology class?

When a child's needs have not been met for a very long time, it ceases to reach out. It stops crying, and simply waits to die.

The whole idea was ridiculous. It was just a dream. Vita hadn't abandoned or neglected anything important. She had a perfectly acceptable life, full and productive.

Or did she? –

Ever since the storm, when her computer had been taken over by the Treasure Box program, nagging doubts and long-buried memories had been working their way into her mind. Hattie Parker. Mary Kate and Gordon. The twins. Unwittingly, she had made the mistake of visiting the cemetery, and the ghosts had begun to follow her home.

Even ghosts that belonged to someone else's past. Sophie and Rachel. Cathleen and Derrick. The newborn Sophia Rose.

And now the joyful dog and the silent, staring child.

Who were they? Why were they haunting her? And what child was this?

After a quick shower, Vita dressed, retrieved her keys from the rack next to the front door, and went out into the yard. Eddy had piled the wood in a neat stack against the garden wall and was starting to load his lawn care equipment into his battered pickup truck.

"Afternoon, Miss Vita," he said politely, touching a fore-finger to the bill of a baseball cap which carried the logo of the minor league *Asheville Tourists.* "Great day, isn't it? I was just finishing up here."

Vita fished on the key ring for the small silver key that fit the padlock on the gate. "I came to unlock the gate so you could do the backyard."

Eddy removed the Tourists cap and scratched his head. "Already done it. The gate was open."

"Open?" Vita turned and stared at the garden gate. Sure enough, it was hanging wide open on its hinges. She could even see a glimpse of the lilies of the valley through the aperture. "Did somebody break in?"

"Don't look like it," Eddy said. "Nothing's broke; the padlock's just gone. You sure you didn't leave it that way?"

"I'm sure." Vita jingled her keys. "At least I think I'm sure." She went over to the gate and inspected the hasp. Just as Eddy said, the padlock had disappeared, but there were no scratches on the hasp or gouges in the wooden gateway—no sign of anyone trying to force the lock. It was simply . . . gone.

"Never mind," she said, half to herself. "I'll get another padlock for it."

Eddy shrugged. "OK. I'll finish packing up here and be on my way."

Vita left him to his loading and went back into the house. She put a pot of coffee on to brew and then proceeded to the sunroom to boot up the computer.

Everything was just as she had left it shortly after dawn: the desk neatly arranged with her files for the Alaska project on one side; the office chair in front of the computer; the Treasure Box on a table under the windows.

But something was different. Nothing had been moved, nothing was out of place, but still the room felt strange, wrong, as if someone had been in here, skulking about, touching her things. No lamp was on, and yet the room was bright, suffused in a sur-realistic light.

Her gaze went to the windows. Beyond the glass she could see Eddy at the curb, heaving his lawn mower up into the bed of the truck.

The awareness crept into her consciousness, like Sandburg's fog, on silent cat feet. She could see *Eddy*. Not a faint movement through the crevices of the hedge, but *everything*. The yard. The hundred-year-old oak tree. A portion of the garden wall, and the open gate. The mailbox on the corner. A kid on a bicycle half a block away.

The hedge outside her office window—the one that gave her protection and privacy—was gone.

She dashed out the front door, letting the screen slam shut behind her, and bolted across the yard. "Eddy, wait!"

He closed the tailgate of the truck and turned. "Yes'm?"

"Eddy—the privet hedge—there, in front of the sunroom—"

"Yes'm?"

"Did you—did you cut it?"

"No ma'am."

Vita felt her breath coming in short gasps. "What do you mean, 'No, ma'am'?"

"I—well, I know it needs trimming, but my electric shears are in the shop. I could do it by hand if you want, but I reckoned it'd wait another week or so—"

Vita grabbed him roughly by the arm and dragged him over to the hedge. Now that she was outside, she could see that the privet hedge was cut even with the window sill, with a few stray shoots poking up this way and that.

"You're telling me you didn't cut this hedge, right now, today."

"No ma'am." He gave her a curious look. "You always said you wanted it just this high, right at a level with the windows. I can trim back that new growth next week." He grinned and pointed toward the back of the hedge. "But you oughta know there's a bird nesting in there. I didn't think you'd want her disturbed."

Vita's eyes followed the direction of Eddy's point. Far back in the hedge, toward the wall of the house, she could see the sparrow's nest, with two bright beady eyes staring out from between the leaves.

"I was going to talk to you about it," Eddy went on as if this conversation were the most natural thing in Vita's world. "See if maybe you'd want me to leave the hedge alone until the babies hatched and flew away."

"Yes, but—" Vita paused. "I knew the bird was there—I could see it from my office. But the nest was—" She extended her arm above her head and pointed. "It was higher, way up there, almost to the middle of the window."

Eddy gazed at her. "'Scuse me for asking, ma'am, but are you all right?"

"I'm perfectly fine," she snapped. "I just don't understand about the hedge—"

"Miss Vita," he said slowly, carefully, "that hedge ain't been up over these windows in years. You always tell me to keep it cut down to the window sill. Always."

Vita could see that he was telling the truth. There was no sign of recent cutting—no severed branches, none of that 'new-haircut' look that shrubs have after they've just been trimmed.

"Whatever you say," she whispered, turning away. "Thank you, Eddy. Just send me a bill, all right?"

"Yes'm. You want me to leave it be—the hedge, that is—til summer, when the birds are gone? It'll get a little scruffy looking by then, but—"

"Yes, Eddy," she murmured. "By all means, let's leave the birds in peace."

Eddy grunted an assent, said he'd see her in a week or two, and trudged off in the direction of his truck. Without looking back, Vita fled for the sanctuary of the house and locked the door behind her.

20

BREAKDOWN

Vita sat trembling in her office chair and watched through the window as Eddy's battered blue pickup drove away. By the time he was around the corner and out of sight, she had broken out in a cold sweat.

What was happening to her? She had lived in this house for years, and never once had Eddy trimmed the privet hedge against her office window. She wouldn't allow it. That hedge had been her protection, her shield against the world's insistent infringement. She must still be asleep, still dreaming. But if this was a dream, it was the most realistic one Vita had ever experienced.

She pinched herself on the tender flesh inside her elbow, so hard that tears came to her eyes and a red welt raised up on the spot. Not asleep. Not dreaming. A nervous breakdown, then, caused by a lack of rest and overtaxed emotions.

She closed her eyes, took in a deep breath, and looked again.

No hedge. She could see all the way to the corner, and beyond. This was real. She wasn't imagining it.

But her mind had to be playing tricks on her, because she could remember . . . *both*. The privet hedge high above the windows, cutting off the sights and sounds outside, and that same hedge at its present height, neatly trimmed just to the edge of the window sill. Both memories went back years, and each seemed equally true.

And there were other overlapping memories, too. She remembered the sparrow's nest being both above and below eye level, from the vantage point of her desk. She recalled watching through the window as the huge limb from the oak tree came down during the storm; but she also could remember simply hearing the crash, and going out to the porch to see what had happened.

Anyone else in this situation, Vita knew, would go straight to the liquor cabinet for a good stiff drink. But Vita never touched alcohol, never kept a drop of anything stronger than cider in the house. She had never liked the stuff and had always deplored the way people like Gordon and his university friends acted as if liquor were an absolute necessity of life—enhancing one's celebration of the good times or medicating one's senses against the bad.

To Vita's way of thinking, that logic had always seemed a truckload of nonsense. If you were enjoying yourself, why anesthetize your senses to life's small pleasures? And if you were despondent, an additional dose of chemical depressant wasn't likely to make anything look better in the morning.

Still, she needed something to steel her nerves against this confusing and debilitating turn of events. Coffee. Good, strong coffee, that was the ticket. It would clear her mind and enable her to consider her situation more rationally.

Relieved to be liberated from the disturbing long-range views in her office, she went into the kitchen and poured a decanter of cold water into the coffee maker.

Think, she ordered her mind. She had to sort this out. There must be a rational explanation.

But the only rational explanations Vita could come up with were the most irrational of all: either both situations were true, or she was losing her mind.

⁓

Vita poured a second cup of coffee and resumed her seat at the kitchen table. For a while she stared out the window at the morning glories. They didn't seem so glorious at this time of day, curled up against the afternoon sun.

Vita could sympathize. All she wanted to do at the moment was crawl into bed, pull the covers up over her head, and escape. But she was neither a morning glory nor a pouting child, and as a reasonable, intelligent adult, she needed to confront the dilemma head-on.

Her mind went back to the beginning—or what she identified as the beginning. The evening of the storm, when her computer locked up and the Treasure Box program first appeared. She could recall the rain, the wind, the thunder and lightning, the crash of the oak limb as it severed itself from the trunk and fell to earth, the power blackout. That much, she knew, was real. But her mind still held the dual memories—of seeing the limb fall, and of not being able to see it because of the hedge that surrounded her office windows.

She forced herself forward in time. The insidious virus that wouldn't let her back into her own computer. The voice from the speakers: *"Love is the key that unlocks every portal."* And her first glimpse into Jacob's tiny hovel of a shop. What had the voice said then? *"Watch and learn."*

Where had she heard that voice before—low and entreating, dark and a little mysterious? She couldn't remember—or, more precisely, couldn't get her mind to retrieve the memory. It was there, Vita was certain. But it wouldn't come to the surface.

She pushed that problem aside and focused on the words. *Watch and learn*. Clearly, she was meant to learn something from the images on the screen. But what? And from whom?

Without warning Vita's cynicism kicked in, that sneering little voice in the back of her mind, mocking her, dragging her back to objective reality. Did she really think there was some intelligent presence at work in this program, some larger mind that could see her reactions and judge whether or not she was learning her lessons? Computers had advanced rapidly in the past few years, but Vita was pretty sure that the techno-geeks in Silicon Valley had not yet come up with a computer that truly interacted with its owner and thought for itself—or if they had, such a machine was not in Vita Kirk's price range.

Still, the voice had been clear—the Treasure Box program had been intended to teach her something. Tabling for the moment the question of who the Teacher was, Vita turned her attention to the possible "lessons" inherent in the program. She would evaluate this rationally, one step at a time, and a logical answer would undoubtedly materialize.

First there was Sophie—open, loving, vulnerable Sophie, who had sacrificed her young life to save her best friend. Vita tried to consider what she might learn from Sophie. *That loving someone could get you killed?* No, that was just her cynical voice interjecting its negative perspective. Vita tried to remember how she had felt when she had watched Sophie lying battered and bruised in the shallows of the river—and later, when the child exhaled her last breath and floated peacefully into the arms of her willow-mother. There must be some message here—

But Vita found that her memories wouldn't stay still long enough for her to get a firm grasp on them. Images from the Treasure Box program kept getting mixed up with images from her own life. Jacob Stillwater's laughing eyes overlapping with Hap Reardon's gentle expression and genuine smile. Sophie and Rachel sharing secrets, and Hattie Parker walking away. Cathleen looking and sounding remarkably like Mary Kate. The infant Sophia Rose and the abandoned baby of her most recent dream.

Vita closed her eyes and shook her head violently. She had to get this straight, had to separate what was real from what was not real. That was one test of sanity, wasn't it—the ability to distinguish reality from fantasy?

And yet it all seemed real—all of it. The Treasure Box program. The jumbled memories from her own past. The high hedge and the low one. The gateless garden of her dream and the actual garden, the one with the missing padlock.

In the midst of her confusion and despair, an idea occurred to Vita—a tiny glimmer of light in the darkness. Maybe she hadn't gone far enough in the Treasure Box program to discover what its images meant for her. Maybe there was more she needed to see before the pieces would all fall into place.

She swallowed down the last of the lukewarm coffee, dashed through the living room into her office, and clicked on the computer.

Even before Vita saw the scene that materialized on the screen, she found herself tense with apprehension. The voice, low and entreating, emanated from the speakers.

"Love, dear friends," it said, "is the key that unlocks every portal."

The starry background dissolved to reveal a tall, dark man in a black suit with a white clerical collar. He was holding a prayer book, and in front of him, with their backs to Vita, stood a man with curly reddish-blond hair and a woman in white, with long dark tresses that flowed down her back like a waterfall.

A wedding.

The groom turned to face his bride, and the bride, holding something in her arms, moved toward him for a kiss. Then Vita saw the face.

Rachel Woodlea. The squirming bundle in her arms had to be Sophia Rose. And the groom? Vita looked more closely at him. Michael McCall, the Chicago mounted policeman who had delivered Cathleen's baby the night she died.

A surge of pleasure rose up in Vita. Rachel deserved a happy ending.

But the elation didn't last long. The tall dark man—a minister, evidently—was speaking again.

"Take care," he said. "You hold in your hands—and in your hearts—something more rare and valuable than you can possibly comprehend—"

Vita's mouth went dry. She had heard those words before, coming from that very same voice. And she had seen that face—older, much older, but with the same bright brown eyes and intense expression.

The minister went on talking for a moment or two about the joys and commitments of marriage, and the additional responsibility of raising a child. Then he looked up from his prayer book and turned his attention outward, beyond the wedding couple, so that Vita felt as if his eyes were fixed directly upon her. "Walk the path God sets before you," he said in that same low, entreating voice. "And hold to this one unshakable certainty: it will lead you where you are meant to be."

Vita sat immobilized, speared to her seat by the man's intense gaze. The ceremony was over; the newlywed couple turned in Vita's direction and, as if she were standing at the end of the aisle, walked hand in hand toward her until they disappeared from view.

Somewhere outside her range of vision, an organ played the recessional. The dark-clad minister reached behind the pulpit, retrieved a cane, and leaned on it as he came down the aisle.

She studied his face as he drew closer, replaying his words in her mind, trying to place where she had seen him before. And then, just before he vanished off the screen, he paused and raised his cane to the tip of an imaginary hat brim.

An ebony cane, with the figure of a bird worked in brass on the handle.

see pg. 15

215

21

THE ROAD NOT TAKEN

By the next morning Vita knew she must, indeed, be on the slippery slope toward a total breakdown. Her brain would not shut down to let her sleep. All night long her mind kept replaying the same tape over and over: The minister at Rachel and Michael's wedding. The stranger who had approached her in Pastimes the day she purchased the Treasure Box. The voice on the computer program. All one and the same.

Impossible, her logical mind insisted. Even if by some incredible chance it was the same man, he couldn't have been younger than twenty-five on the day of the wedding.

She did some quick mental calculations. Derrick and Cathleen emigrated to America in 1921. If Cathleen conceived during the crossing, Sophia Rose would have been born in February 1922. And since Cathleen's child had still been a babe in arms at the time, Michael and Rachel's wedding had to have occurred in 1922 or, at the very latest, early 1923.

Thus the man she met in Pastimes—assuming he was, indeed, the same person—would have to have been more than a hundred years old.

None of it made sense. None of it. Vita felt as if her whole life—past, present, and future—were spinning out of control. And there was nothing she could do to stop it.

She was in the kitchen, spooning grounds into the coffee filter, when a voice startled her from her thoughts.

"Vita?"

The voice sounded vaguely familiar.

She turned to find her sister, flanked by the twins, standing in the doorway of the kitchen. Her hand went slack, and the coffee scoop fell to the floor, scattering black grounds all over the white vinyl tile at her feet.

"Vita, are you all right?"

"Yes, I'm fine. I just—" She blinked hard and shook her head. "How did you get in here?"

Mary Kate held up a ring crowded with an abundance of keys. "I used my key, of course. I rang the doorbell and knocked, but when you didn't answer, I figured you had gone to run some errands, so I let myself in."

She went to the pantry, pulled out a small electric broom, and with a brisk efficiency vacuumed up the spilled coffee grounds. Vita started to object, but her attention was diverted by her niece and nephew, who had her trapped in a rambunctious sandwich hug.

Little Gordy, the micro-image of his father, with blond hair and magnificent blue eyes. Mary Vita, her namesake, with darker curls and brown eyes. Vita hadn't seen them since Mother's funeral, when the children were toddlers . . . and yet here they were, nearly grown, nearly teenagers, hugging her as if they not only knew her but adored her.

Vita's mind began to lurch backward as a crack opened in her memory. They *did* know her, and she knew them. They *had* been together—often. She could remember their early years, Christmases and birthdays; their first day of school; the baseball game where Gordy broke his arm; searching for Mary Vita's favorite ice cream—Moose Tracks—when she had her tonsils out. But she could also remember those same years as one long stretch of silence in which she had no contact at all with her sister's family. Years of alienation, isolation, and solitude.

"Aunt Vita," Little Gordon was saying as he tugged on her arm, "Mary V says we're going to bake cookies. But I want to play catch." He knelt on the floor, unzipped a small overnight bag, and came up with a ball and two mitts. "Can we, huh? I've been working on that curve ball you showed me."

"She promised we'd make sugar cakes with frosting," Mary Vita objected from the other side. "Didn't you, Aunt Vita?"

Mary Kate settled herself at the table and smiled indulgently. "Hey, you two. If you don't stop bickering, your Aunt Vita will send you both home with me. Now settle down."

The twins grumbled a bit, but they stopped arguing and

came to hang on the back of their mother's chair. "I can't thank you enough, Sis, for taking them for a few days. Gordon and I really need the time—" She ended abruptly and turned to the children. "Why don't the two of you get your stuff to your rooms and then go out and play in the yard for a while? I want to talk to Aunt Vita for a few minutes before I leave."

"Well, I—" Vita stammered, trying in vain to get her brain to work. "I guess I'd better show them the upstairs, and—"

"We can do it ourselves." Mary V retrieved her bag from the doorway and grinned at her brother. "Come on, Gordy. I'll play catch with you until Mama and Aunt Vita are done."

The two of them dashed through the doorway, and Vita could hear them running up the stairs. Yes, they had been here before. Gordy slept in the upstairs den, and Mary Vita in the guest room. But Vita knew that they had never set foot in her house. Didn't she? She closed her eyes and tried to get her mind to latch onto what was real. In a minute or two, the footsteps came back downstairs and out the door, and the front screen slammed shut behind them.

"Whew!" Mary Kate sighed, leaning back in her chair. "They're usually not quite this wired. They're just excited about staying with you—as usual." She shook her head. "I ought to be jealous, Sis—they definitely like their Aunt Vita more than they like their Mama."

Vita stared at Mary Kate, who sat leaning her elbows on the kitchen table. Her sister had barely changed since the day she competed in the Miss North Carolina pageant. Still stunning, even in blue jeans, with a flawless complexion, natural blonde hair, and eyes the color of chocolate. Another dual memory flashed across her mind, a kind of déjà vu: Mary Kate had been here before, a hundred times, chatting with Vita at this very kitchen table.

And then again, she hadn't. They had never really been sisters, certainly not intimate friends. And yet they were.

Vita turned her back for a minute or two, busying herself with finishing the coffee while she got her bearings. Apparently the twins were staying for a few days. But when had that happened? What had Mary Kate said about needing time with Gordon? And since when did Mary Kate call her "Sis"?

A voice echoed in her head: *"Walk the path God sets before you . . . it will lead you where you are meant to go."*

All right, Vita decided, gathering up every shred of determination she had ever possessed. If she couldn't discern what was real and what was not, she would simply play the part that unfolded to her. She had no conviction that it would lead her anywhere meaningful, but what else could she do?

She kept her back turned and waited for the coffee to brew. By the time it was done, she had composed herself a little, and she poured two cups and brought them to the table. "How is Gordon?" she forced herself to ask. "When you called the other day, you said he was in the hospital?"

Mary Kate gave Vita a puzzled frown. "I didn't say *in* the hospital. I said *at* the hospital. He's fine—he's just, well—" She put her coffee cup down and rested her forehead on one hand. "I simply don't know what to do. He says he still loves me, but he keeps on seeing this doctor—"

"How sick is he, exactly?" Vita interrupted.

Mary Kate let out a caustic laugh. "Stay with me, Vita. Focus. I know it's terribly confusing, but—"

Vita sat down at the table. "I've had an exhausting few days. Refresh my memory, please."

"He met her at a party—Dr. Alison Atwell. Some name, huh? He swears they're not having an affair. He says she's 'helping him with his research'—something about the evolution of human physiology from prehistoric to modern times—and he meets her at the hospital four or five times a week to 'assimilate their findings.' Right. I'm neither blind nor stupid. I can guess what they're 'assimilating.' And given the problems we've been having—" She shook her head. "He's doing an academic paper on this Iceman— you know, the prehistoric guy they dug up from the snow? I don't understand it all—the only thing I know is that his relationship with Dr. Alison Atwell, whatever it is, isn't helping our problems one bit."

Vita sipped her coffee and kept silent. She felt as if she were watching her sister from a long way away, through the wrong end of a telescope. Time seemed to stand still.

"I should have known," Mary Kate was saying when Vita's attention returned, "that if he could leave you for me so easily, it might happen again. I just wanted so desperately to believe—"

Cathleen Woodlea's face rose up in Vita's mind. "That it would be different with you."

Mary Kate nodded. "Exactly." She reached out and grasped Vita's hand. "You've never held it against me, marrying Gordon the way I did, without a second thought about how much pain it would cause you."

"Gordon and I weren't right for each other." Vita heard herself say the words as if someone else, someone outside her own body, had spoken them. "I would have been miserable if I had married him." It was true, and yet Vita was acutely aware that she hadn't always felt this way—that she *had* harbored resentment against her sister. It was one problem among many which had driven them apart.

"Sometimes I wonder if *I* should have married him," Mary Kate went on. "I would give anything for the twins, of course, and I do love him. It's just that he can't seem to understand that I need my own life. I'm not the same naive girl he married. I need more than just being an adjunct to his career, a pretty little trophy hostess for his parties and academic conferences. I may not be pretty anymore, but I'm not brainless, either. I've changed. But he hasn't."

Vita gazed at her sister's face. "I think you're pretty," she said, meaning it. "I've always envied your looks."

"And I've always envied your brains." Mary Kate laughed. "So I guess that makes us even."

"You said you needed time with Gordon?" Vita prodded.

"Yes. He's finally agreed to counseling. For starters, we're going on this couples retreat—the counselor calls it 'Boot Camp.' It's at a lodge up near Grandfather Mountain. Six couples for three days of group and individual therapy."

"Sounds intense."

"It will be. But I'm hoping it will give us a chance to talk—really talk—about the future of our relationship." Her eyes fixed on some middle distance, and she sighed. "I've been seeing this counselor individually for a while, trying to sort out my own issues. Something she said the other day really struck me, and I want to know what you think about it."

"You want *my* opinion?"

Mary Kate stared at her. "I always want your perspective. You think more deeply than I do about things, and I trust that. I always have."

Her sister trusted her judgment? Vita's mind careened around this foreign concept. "OK," Vita conceded at last. "Let's hear it."

"She said that when people talk about finding God's will for their lives and relationships, they're often under the mistaken impression that there is only one path, one future. And that leaves them with only two mutually exclusive options: free will or Divine control. If you believe in free will, you shoulder the unbearable burden of finding the one 'right way.' If you believe in Divine control, you become fatalistic, assuming that whatever happens, happens—and you can't do anything to change it."

Vita leaned forward, gripping her hands around her coffee

cup until her knuckles turned white. "And this counselor has another idea?"

Mary Kate's eyes caught Vita's gaze and held it. "Yes. She suggested that there might be many futures, many possibilities for a life, but not all of them will come true. Like a computer program that takes you different places depending upon what links you pick. Being outside of linear time, God sees all the options, all the possible outcomes. For humans, limited by time, the actual events of our lives result from the choices and decisions we make. And yet God is in the midst of it all, with challenges and blessings and resolutions we can only guess at." She looked up, and her eyes blazed with passion. "So both could be true— free will and Divine intervention. They seem mutually exclusive, contradictory, but they're not."

Vita's mind flashed to Rachel and Cathleen. To Sophie's untimely death, Cathleen's betrayal, Rachel's obsession with finding the Treasure Box, the birth of little Sophia Rose, Rachel's marriage to Michael McCall. All the sad and tragic turns of their lives, leading them on to a place they couldn't possibly begin to imagine. *Challenges and blessings and resolutions we can only guess at,* Mary Kate had said. And for the first time in years, maybe the first time in her adult life, Vita caught a glimpse of the possibility that a power beyond herself—God, perhaps—might be present and involved in human existence without manipulating people like a menacing puppeteer.

"Many futures," she mused, "not all of which will come true."

"It's an interesting concept, isn't it?" Mary Kate said. "I'm not sure I fully understand it, but I think I like it."

Vita's thoughts lingered for a moment on the idea of many futures, and then moved to the more immediate question of Mary Kate. The woman was—well, transformed. No longer a flighty, shallow airhead, but a contemplative, thoughtful person. Someone Vita could sit down and have a productive conversation with. She was actually . . . likable. But just what had changed, Vita wondered—her sister's personality, or her own perspectives?

Mary Kate glanced at her watch and jumped to her feet "It's two-thirty. I have to go, or I'll be late picking up Gordon." She retrieved her purse and keys from the kitchen counter and headed for the door.

Vita followed her to the front porch. Out in the garden, through the open gate, she caught a glimpse of Gordy and Mary V in the backyard.

"Thanks for taking care of the kids, Sis. You're a wonder, as always." Mary Kate gave her a brief, one-armed hug. "I'll pick them up on Sunday evening around six, if that's all right." She waved to the twins and made a dash for the silver Volvo station wagon parked against the curb. Just before she got into the driver's seat, she leaned over the top of the car and shouted, "Bye, Vita. Love you!"

"I—I love you, too," Vita stammered.

But Mary Kate didn't hear. She had already revved the engine and pulled out into the street, leaving Vita to stare at the departing taillights and wonder if she was wrong about having a complete nervous breakdown.

At the moment, it felt more like a second chance.

22

BEHIND THE WALLS

The children had finally turned off the TV and gone to bed, and the house itself seemed to exhale a sigh of relief. Vita sat at the kitchen table with a glass of skim milk and a plateful of left-over cookies, letting her mind take in the events of the afternoon.

She bit into one of the frosted teacakes. They were surprisingly good—not too sweet, with a nice buttery texture. She hadn't remembered ever owning what Mary V called "Grandma Kirk's secret recipe," but sure enough, the girl knew exactly where to find it and every ingredient it called for. Even Gordy finally broke down and joined in the fun, cutting his portion of the dough into robots and spaceships and frosting several of the plain round cookies to resemble black-and-white soccer balls and orange basketballs and little white baseballs stitched with red.

She picked up one of the baseball cookies and held it with her thumb and two fingers. Where on earth had she learned to throw a curve? Vita hadn't the foggiest idea, yet she could not only do it, but teach little Gordy the finer points of the technique as well. While the cookies were cooling, the three of them had played ball in the backyard until Vita slammed a home run over the garden wall, across the alley, and into the neighbor's flower bed. The man came out into the yard, yelling about his prize-winning begonias, and the three of them had run giggling into the house and sworn each other to secrecy.

Vita couldn't remember the last time she'd had so much fun. Or, to be more precise, the last time she'd had any fun at all. She felt like a sleepwalker, an amnesiac, a female version of Rip Van Winkle awakening to a world which looked familiar but was entirely different from anything she had ever known.

Once or twice during the weekend, she had struggled with a compulsion to leave the twins to their own devices and spend a few hours in the office with the Treasure Box program. For one thing, she was eager to find out what had happened to Rachel and Michael and little Sophia Rose. Their lives had become such an intrinsic part of her own that she felt a little guilty abandoning them.

But when she took a step back and regarded herself with a critical eye, Vita immediately concluded that reality—in this case, her time with the twins—was infinitely more important than a story, no matter how captivating. She would not become like one of those bored housewives who never let anything divert them from their soap operas. The Treasure Box program could wait.

And it had waited—until now. She glanced at the clock; it was 9:30, still early. She ate one more cookie, one of Gordy's spaceships, and drained the glass of milk, then went into her office, intending to turn on the computer. Instead, she picked up the Treasure Box from the table by the windows and dropped into her desk chair.

Moonlight dappled the expanse of yard in shades of gray and blue, and one silver ray crept through the glass and lighted on the box Vita held in her hands. She lifted the lid and ran one finger across the inscription underneath: *Love Is the Key That Unlocks Every Portal.*

Mary Kate had called her "Sis" and said "Love you" instead of "Good-bye."

And Vita had responded, "I love you, too."

For a long time, while the moon shifted and the shadows deepened, she sat there—alone, and yet not alone. Wondering, wondering . . .

⌒

"Vita, I can't tell you what a wonderful weekend this was." Mary Kate settled herself at the kitchen table, accepted a glass of iced tea, and took one of the remaining sugar cookies from the plate.

"Does that mean—" Vita looked around to make sure the twins weren't within earshot, then lowered her voice. "Does that mean you and Gordon are on the road to recovery?"

Mary Kate let out a little laugh. "Gordon? I don't know what's going to happen with Gordon, to tell you the truth. But we did have some profitable conversations during Boot Camp, and he said he'd think about continuing with couples counseling after this weekend."

"That sounds promising." Vita sat in the chair at right angles to her sister and wrestled with conflicting emotions. On the one hand, she was happy to see Mary Kate and realized that for two days she had been eagerly anticipating her sister's return. On the other hand, Mary Kate's arrival meant that her time with the twins was coming to an end, and Vita felt an unaccountable twinge of regret over the prospect of saying good-bye to them.

All weekend, as she had "walked the road set before her," Vita had been aware of two conflicting realities—the isolation she had always thought of as her "real" past, and the "new" memories that assailed her, memories that included a close and loving relationship with her sister and niece and nephew.

Mary Kate was talking, responding to Vita's comment. "Promising, yes. But it remains to be seen what happens now that we're back in the real world, whether he'll decide this relationship is worth the time and effort to work on it. In the meantime, I'm going to work on myself."

Vita regarded her sister with intense curiosity. "What exactly does that mean?"

"It means that I made a decision this weekend, Vita. An important one." She leaned forward. "I'm going to graduate school."

"Really."

"Yes, really. And I have you to thank for it. You've always

inspired me, Sis. I told you I envied your brains, just as you envied my looks. But looks fade with age. Brains just keep getting stronger. It may be a bit late for me to start exercising mine, but better late than never. I'm going for a master's in social work, to become a counselor. If my studies end up making me more interesting to my husband, so much the better. But I'm not doing it for him—I'm doing it for myself."

"You want to be a counselor?"

Mary Kate nodded and bit into another cookie. "Yep. Ever since I started going to counseling, I've been fascinated with the process. We've done family genograms, childhood memories, dream analysis—"

Vita moved her chair closer. "Dream analysis?"

"Yes, it's amazing what dreams can reveal. Not all of them, of course—some dreams are just leftover images from a day's experience, or the result of—"

"'An undigested bit of beef, a blot of mustard, the fragment of an underdone potato'?"

"Exactly. That's from Scrooge, right?" Mary Kate laughed. "Yes, some are just bad pizza, but some are pretty significant. Call it your subconscious trying to get a message through, or God trying to communicate some truth about your life."

Vita opened her mouth to lodge an automatic protest against the idea that God might speak through a person's dreams. But before she could say a word, her mind began to call up memories from her own recent dreams—Sophie in the meadow, her mother becoming a willow tree; the images of red that preceded the midnight slaughter at Benedetti's restaurant. And the most disturbing ones of all: the joyful dog and the somber, silent baby.

She raised her head to find Mary Kate's eyes boring into hers. "Did I touch a nerve?"

"No, no." Vita tried to dismiss the idea. "Just some recent dreams I've had—they don't mean anything."

"Come on, spill it." Mary Kate crossed her arms and waited.

Vita hesitated, unsure whether she really wanted to pour out her innermost thoughts in her sister's presence. But at last she took a deep breath, and in a rush described the Sheltie she had left outside the garden wall and the infant in the crib she had neglected. "They're just silly dreams," she concluded. "Probably subconscious echoes from a computer program I've been using lately."

Mary Kate looked at her. "How did you feel when you woke up? Did you sense that these dream images were important?"

"Yes," Vita admitted reluctantly. "I got the impression that— well, that somebody was trying to tell me something."

Her sister nodded. "And you felt—"

"Guilty. As if I had failed to take care of something entrusted to me, something I ought to have . . . loved."

"Tell me about the dog."

Vita frowned. "What about the dog? I was inside the garden, he was outside the wall, and there was no gate. I knew I was safe behind the walls, but had forgotten him, left him outside, and I couldn't get to him." She focused on the memory of the Sheltie—

exuberant, joyous. The word stuck in her mind. "Could he represent joy?"

Mary Kate raised an eyebrow. "Maybe."

"OK." Vita took a deep breath. "So I've created this safe enclosure, this life with high walls and no gate. I'm protected from being hurt, but I don't have joy." –

"Does that feel right?" –

Vita felt tears sting her eyes. "Yes. But how can I let him in when there's no gate?" –

"I don't know," Mary Kate said. "But keep it on the back burner, and you'll come up with a solution." – –

The answer presented itself to Vita's mind in an instant: *Knock down a wall.* She thought of the missing padlock on her own garden gate, and shivered.

"Now, what about the child in the darkened room?" Mary Kate prodded.

"Something I'm supposed to care for, that I've neglected?" Vita shook her head. "I'm not sure."

"What did the child look like?" –

"Dark hair, huge brown eyes, a thin little face—"

"Like anyone you know?" –

Vita felt a small twinge of recognition clutch at her heart. "Like me."

"And what was she doing?"

"Nothing. She was just standing there, not crying, not making a sound. Just waiting."

"Waiting for you to come and take care of her."

Vita nodded. "Is it true that a child who is left uncared for finally ceases to cry and simply waits to die?"

"That can happen, yes. You might want to consider, Sis, if there could be something in your life—something important—that you've neglected over a long period of time."

The answer came unbidden, as if dropped whole into her mind. "My inner self," Vita murmured. "My soul. I've neglected my soul and shut joy out of my life."

"By George, I think she's got it." Mary Kate smiled.

Vita shifted uncomfortably in her chair. "Now I have to figure out what to do with it."

"That will come. Give it a while."

Vita gazed at her sister as if seeing her for the very first time. "It seems you've found your calling. You have a gift for this."

Mary Kate patted her arm. "You're an easy case, Sis. It was all right there, waiting for you to see it." She drained the last of her iced tea and stood up. "I'd better round up my brood and get home."

Vita stood on the porch watching as the last light faded and the twins piled into the car. Everybody waved good-bye, and Mary Kate promised to call her in a day or so. At last the Volvo's taillights twinkled out of sight around the corner.

After a while Vita wandered into her office and turned on the desk lamp. Light puddled in a golden oval, illuminating the rich oak finish of the desktop and the stacks of research in her neglected Alaska files. The office felt so peaceful, so quieting. With a sigh of deep satisfaction she leaned back in her leather swivel chair and surveyed her domain. Her eyes swept over the windows facing out into the yard, the bookshelves along two walls, the bulletin board filled with postcards from the places she had written about—

Vita stopped. Something about the board had caught her eye. It looked . . . different. Maybe it was just the light.

She got up and turned on another lamp, then went and stood in front of the framed corkboard that held her collection of postcards. There was the Eiffel Tower, the cottage in the English Cotswolds, and yes, the *Biergarten* in Munich. But these weren't just postcards—they were *photographs*. With actual human beings in the foreground.

She pulled one down and held it closer to the light. It was a scene from Castle Combe, in England—that lovely little riverside village where Rex Harrison's version of *Dr. Doolittle* had been filmed. A cottage on the riverbank, built from golden Cotswold stone, with a brilliant swag of pink roses over the door, all set against a backdrop of rolling green hills. Quite a lovely scene, and quite familiar.

She peered at the faces in the photograph. Two women, one with a thin face, brown eyes, long dark hair pulled back at the nape of her neck. The other, shorter and rounder, with sandy hair and a strange puckered look around her mouth. Not unattractive, just distinctive, as if she had suffered scarring acne as a teenager. Like best friends out for a holiday, they were both smiling broadly, each with an arm draped over the other's shoulder.

Recognition pummeled the air from Vita's lungs with all the force of a physical blow.

She was looking at herself. Herself, with one arm around the shoulder of . . .

Hattie Parker.

23

THE LABYRINTH

Vita scrutinized the photograph until her vision began to blur. It was Hattie, all right. Upon closer inspection with a magnifying glass, Vita could see faint distortions of the scars from the automobile accident—thin white lines crisscrossing the forehead and cheeks, a slight upward lift at the corner of the right eyebrow, a crook in the nose.

She hadn't laid eyes on Hattie since that day long ago in the high school parking lot. Hattie had been wearing that hideous black motorcycle jacket with the name "Scarface" embroidered above a skull and crossbones. And yet she could also remember them as friends. Best friends. Both single and unattached, they had traveled together on research trips for Vita's books. The journey to England had been the first, and one of the best.

She remembered the little place they had rented in the Cotswolds, a thatch-roofed cottage renovated from an old tithe barn. The fourteenth-century pub where they had dined every night on steak and kidney pie and pasty-type sandwiches called baps. The walking trips through the English countryside. The morning they had stumbled upon the ruins of an old Norman church in the verge where a cow pasture met the woods. The energetic rendition of *Twelfth Night* performed by a local troupe of players at the castle outside the village.

Every minute detail of that holiday came back to Vita in a breathtaking rush. She and Hattie had motored into Wales and spent a rainy afternoon at the ruins of Tintern Abbey, quoting Wordsworth to one another. They had walked along the Avon River from Salisbury Cathedral to the little church in Bemerton where metaphysical poet George Herbert had served as vicar. During their two days in Stratford, they had made rubbings of Shakespeare's epitaph and visited Ann Hathaway's cottage. Later, in London, they had spent three days taking in the British Museum, the Tower, and Westminster Cathedral. They had even managed to get first-row balcony seats for a rousing production of *Singing in the Rain* starring Tommy Steele.

Vita could remember it all. Most vividly, she could still hear the laughter they had shared, all those chilly nights by the small coal fire in the cottage as they played Scrabble and swapped dreams. And yet, in the midst of such clear and unnerving recollections, Vita could also remember empty, vacant years, years of missing Hattie and wondering whatever happened to her. Years of not knowing if she were dead or alive.

It was as if the fabric of her mind had been ripped at the seam, revealing another reality hidden behind the curtain—a reality, if anything, more real than what she had always known to be true. Her cynical mind, like the Wizard of Oz vainly attempting to reassert his authority, kept shouting, "Pay no attention to what's behind the curtain!" But the damage had been done. The curtain had been torn, and Vita couldn't stop herself from looking.

And there was something else about Hattie . . . what was it? Letters. Yes. Letters from Atlanta, where Hattie had gone to work for the Centers for Disease Control after college. Dozens of them, wonderful letters full of interesting tales about her career as a researcher.

Vita dropped the photograph into the oval of lamplight on her desk and pressed her fingertips to her temples. If there *had* been letters—if she and Hattie *were* still best friends—she might have saved them. Some of them, anyway. The ones which held the most significance for her. Maybe they could help her sort all this out, help her discern what was real. If she could only find them.

She rolled her chair back from the desk and began rummaging in drawers, pulling out file folders and manila envelopes. Nothing. She went through the small oak cabinet in the corner, and then made her way across the room, systematically searching every cubbyhole and drawer. Nothing there. The only place left to look was in the box on the far bookshelf, where she kept a will and her life insurance policy and other important papers. Vita turned, and as she brushed by the table under the window, the hem of her sweater snagged on the corner of the Treasure Box.

She caught it, upside down, just before it hit the floor. The lid jarred open, and she gritted her teeth, anticipating a nerve-rattling clatter as CDs and computer disks hit the hardwood floor. Instead, a small packet secured with a rubber band fell out at her feet.

Vita set the Treasure Box back in its place and gave it a nervous little pat, then gathered up the packet and returned to her desk.

Her fingers were shaking, and she couldn't get her eyes to focus. The rubber band broke in her hands as she pulled it off. There were six envelopes, legal size, in a soft cream color, with her name and address typed neatly on each one. In the upper left-hand corner, in a flourish of raised-ink black lettering, the name: Harriet E. Parker.

Vita had never seen these letters before . . . and yet she had. She recognized them, knew—without knowing how she knew—that Hattie's given name was Harriet, that her middle name was Eleanor, that in her adult professional life everyone called her Harry. But how had the letters come to be here, in her office, in the Treasure Box? She had a vague, transparent, dreamlike memory of putting them there herself, except that—

She closed her eyes and exhaled forcefully. If she wasn't already crazy, she'd drive herself over the edge by trying to figure all of this out. Better just to read the letters, to find out what she'd been missing all these years.

Vita looked at the first one, bearing the earliest postmark, June 3, 1988. Her mind cast back to the late eighties. She would have been twenty-five, just out of graduate school. Mother and Daddy were both still alive. In 1988 Gordon and Mary Kate had been married two years, but he was still writing his dissertation, and she was finishing a B.A. and working as a secretary part-time. They were planning their family carefully. It would be another two years before the twins came.

Vita opened the letter, smoothed out the pages across the top of her desk, and began to read.

Dear Vita,

By now you've probably decided I'd dropped off the face of the earth, and I wouldn't blame you a bit if you trashed this letter without even reading it. But please don't. You were always my best friend, and so for the sake of that friendship, please keep on reading.

After my accident in seventh grade, we drifted apart. All my fault, I admit. I was a mess. I wanted to die, and nearly did manage to kill myself on that Harley a couple of times. But I finally grew up, got my act together, and did well in college, although I felt pretty alone and isolated during those years. I ended up in medical research, got a master's degree in chemistry, and managed to land an entry-level research job at the CDC in Atlanta. I'm now living in a suburb called Stone Mountain—which is a joke to anyone who grew up in the REAL mountains the way we did. Stone Mountain is one big old rock sticking up in the middle of nowhere.

Anyway, I'm writing to let you know that, despite our separation, the memory of your friendship has sustained me for a very long time. You said (or intended to say) that you would always be my friend, and when times got difficult, I remembered that—remembered how much we cared about each other once, and remembering gave me hope.

We're both grown now, and maybe we've gone in different directions, but your name is still the one that comes to mind whenever I hear the words "best friend." I'd like to renew that friendship, if you're willing—to find out whether or not we have anything in common after all these years. I promise I'll never turn my back on you again.

Love,

Hattie

The letter began to blur in front of Vita's face, and she laid it aside and rubbed at her eyes with the heel of her hand. She had the unsettling sensation of holding two contradictory memories. On the one hand, she felt as if she were reading this letter for the very first time, getting her first faint glimpse of hope that reconciliation with her best friend from childhood might be possible. On the other hand, she was aware that the reconciliation had already been accomplished ages ago. Theoretically, Vita believed in the existence of paradox, but she had never faced it except on the safe jousting ground of philosophical discussion. Now the abstract idea confronted her in a much more immediate, more threatening form. Both could not be real—could they?

The curtain inside her head ripped open a little wider, and she recalled how she had debated for three weeks whether or not to answer the letter. But she did answer it, and discovered that the friendship she had cherished as a child was recoverable in adulthood. Although she and Hattie had, indeed, gone in different directions, they still shared vital interests and values in common. In the end, Vita's best friend had been returned to her.

As Vita scanned the other letters, additional memories arranged themselves in her mind. The argument that had ensued, years after Mary Kate and Gordon were married, when Hattie confronted Vita with the anger that still seethed under the surface and told her bluntly that she needed to let go of it. The pain Vita felt when she believed her best friend couldn't understand her. The emotional tension resulting from that fight, and the intense relief Vita had experienced when they finally made up. Discussions—sometimes quite passionate ones—about life and death, about God and the nature of the universe, about music and art and literature, about ethics and integrity and ambition.

It felt good, this sensation of not being alone, of having someone in her life who had known her for years, seen more than the public face, the image of independence and strength she had worked hard to project. Here was someone who knew her—really knew her—and still loved her.

And Hattie wasn't the only one. Vita thought of Mary Kate and the twins, and her mind called up fragments of other recollections—times she had been impatient with Gordy and Mary V, occasions when she had let her sister down, and when her sister had been insensitive with her. Squabbles over insignificant differences of opinion, and silly quarrels based in pride or self-centeredness or insecurity. All the various dimensions of family love and dissension. They knew her, too—knew her perhaps even better than she knew herself.

Vita's mind drifted to the discussion she had just had with Mary Kate—the possibility that there are many potential futures for any one life, not all of which would come true. And it occurred to her that if there were many futures, it stood to reason that there might also be many pasts, many "roads not taken."

Anyone else in Vita's situation might have asked, "What if Hattie hadn't written that first letter? What if Vita hadn't responded to it?" But Vita knew the answers to those questions, and hundreds like them. She had already experienced what her days would be like without a best friend, without a sister, without two energetic children in her life. She had lived that reality for most of her adult life and was beginning to realize that she didn't like it as much as she had always assumed.

Granted, there were disadvantages to being involved with other human beings. Personality conflicts, differences of opinion, vulnerability, the opportunity for experiencing pain and heartbreak as well as love and belonging. Vita had long been aware of these risks—the danger of being burned, the internal warnings about getting too close to the fire. But she hadn't realized, not until now, how cold life had been. How very, very cold.

~

Vita awoke at six the next morning from a strange dream. She had been in a high hedge maze, and—

No, not a maze, Vita corrected herself. *A labyrinth.*

Another new memory needled its way into her consciousness—her first glimpse of the famous thirteenth-century pavement labyrinth in Chartres Cathedral, when she and Hattie had journeyed to Paris years ago. During the Crusades, when travel was dangerous, devout believers could not often make the journey to Jerusalem, the Holy City, without fear for their lives. And so the medieval eleven-circuit labyrinth provided an opportunity for pilgrimage without peril. Those seeking repentance would often walk on their knees; others took on the quest of the labyrinth as an exercise in reflection and prayer, with the hope of becoming closer to God.

A maze, the tour guide had informed Vita, was a puzzle to be solved, with dead ends and wrong turns. A labyrinth had no wrong turns, needed no map—it was an experience, not a test. The point of a maze was to find one's way out as quickly and efficiently as possible; the objective of a labyrinth was to stay inside, to walk the path slowly and meditatively—to wait, to listen, to open yourself to new spiritual perspectives with each turn. If you just kept walking and listening and trusting, the labyrinth would lead you to the center and out again.

Vita propped her pillows against the headboard and settled back, thinking about the dream. There had been hedges all around, blocking her view—that must have been why she mistakenly identified it as a maze. At first she had experienced fear, and a bit of claustrophobia. But then she realized she was not alone. A small Sheltie was with her, nipping playfully at her heels, bounding back and forth, herding her down the path. And tugging on her hand, a child toddled along beside her—a small girl with dark hair and brown eyes and a intense, determined expression.

Someone else was in the dream, too—someone Vita could not see. From high above, she heard the voice speaking to her, encouraging her: *"Walk the path God sets before you. It will lead you where you are meant to be."*

Images confronted each other in Vita's mind: the dual, paradoxical memories of being alone, as she had always been, and being here, in the "new" reality, which included Mary Kate and the twins and, apparently, even Hattie Parker. This new world was much less orderly, much less controllable, subject to other people's whims and idiosyncrasies, marked with anguish as well as joy, with hurt as well as healing. In this new reality she had to deal with the painful rasp of heart against heart, mind against mind, soul against soul, as the people she loved sandpapered away her rough edges.

Yet even amid the pain and vulnerability, joy bounced at her side and nipped at her heels, urging her onward. Her own soul tugged her forward, that forgotten little spirit who had already grown from a neglected, silent baby to a determined toddler with a will of her own.

But what was behind this strange and inexplicable sea change?

Vita knew. For years she had ignored, denied, refused to accept the truth. But she could no longer turn away from it—she had seen it too clearly in the events spread out before her in the Treasure Box program, in Sophie and Cathleen and Rachel and tiny infant Sophia Rose. And she had to admit that even now she saw it in her own life, the new life, the one she urgently wanted to hang onto, despite all its complications and inherent difficulties. There was a Power beyond herself at work here—outside of her, and yet within her. Something she never wanted to face before, and now desperately longed to understand.

God.

She tried the word aloud, even though it felt foreign on her tongue. "God."

It was an acknowledgment, an act of contrition, a prayer. And no sooner had the word been uttered than Vita began to see something—not a vision, strictly speaking. More like footlights rising on the stage of her consciousness, a dawning awareness.

With her mind's eye she could see the labyrinth from high above, outside the confines of space and time—could see all the paths, all the steps, as if the whole process had already been completed. The journey held many switchbacks and turns, but because it was a labyrinth and not a maze, it was impossible for a pilgrim to take the wrong road. Every portion of the path was a unity, part of the whole, folding in on the unbroken design. All who started on the path, all who sought the truth—sought God—with a heart of integrity and a will to discover the Divine, inevitably found what they were seeking.

Vita leaned back, closed her eyes, and surrendered herself to the moment. She no longer feared that she was losing her mind, no longer wondered if the miracle of the new reality would vanish as suddenly as it had appeared.

The unvoiced prayer—the forgotten longing of her deepest soul, the tacit cry of the neglected infant in the darkened room—had been answered.

Someone had heard.

Someone had cared.

Someone had responded, when she didn't even know enough to ask.

24

JACOB'S PRAYER

By eight o'clock, Vita had showered and dressed and made her way to the swing in the back garden. She sipped at her second cup of coffee and watched two squirrels chasing up and down an oak tree, chittering to each other and making grand swooping jumps from limb to limb, almost as if they could fly.

The morning sun cast an ethereal light over the grass, the willow tree, the purple irises in the flower bed against the far wall. The sight stirred something in Vita. She had the sensation of being lighter, younger, more agile, as if freed from some invisible burden, and she was finally able to put words to a perception that had been working its way into her mind. Saint Francis had been right—all creation was kin. Brother squirrel, sister iris, father sunlight, mother willow—a family.

And Vita Kirk belonged.

She wasn't certain how to categorize this new perspective

that had come upon her. Metamorphosis? Transfiguration? Resurrection? None of the words quite fit, yet Vita knew she was changed. Everything looked different, felt different. The fragrance of spring blossoms seemed sharper, the colors more vibrant, her vision more focused. As if she had stumbled through life in a nearsighted blur and just received her first pair of glasses.

She leaned back in the swing, relishing the warmth of sunlight on her face, and shut her eyes. For a long time she sat there, as the light through her eyelids created a road map of blood vessels against her retina. Then a shadow stepped between Vita and the sun. She looked up, raised a hand to shade her eyes. A man. She couldn't see his face clearly, silhouetted as he was against the light, but his blondish-brown hair ruffled in the breeze, and he was smiling.

Maybe it was just a trick of the light. Maybe it was his smile, or the unassuming way he stood there, waiting for her to speak. But for a split second, Vita was convinced that the man who stood before her was—

Jacob Stillwater, in the flesh.

The figure moved out of the sunlight and stuck his hands in his pockets. "Good morning, Vita. Beautiful day, isn't it?"

Hap Reardon. Vita stared at him as he settled himself into the swing next to her and stretched his legs out. He was wearing neatly pressed khaki slacks, a white oxford shirt, and brown loafers with tassels on the tops. She had never noticed before what a nice smile he had, or the faint hint of a dimple in his left cheek. She had always been too eager to get away from him to observe much about him at all, in fact. Now she saw that he had clear blue eyes and little crow's-feet, and just the beginnings of a receding hairline. He looked almost . . . attractive, in a soft, middle-aged sort of way. And he did indeed bear a resemblance to Jacob Stillwater.

She met his gaze and discovered a curious expression on his face.

"Is something wrong, Vita? You're looking at me as if I just beamed down from another planet."

Vita blinked. "Sorry, Hap. I was just, well, thinking." She gathered herself together and tried to remember her manners. "Would you like a cup of coffee?"

He glanced at his watch. "I'd love one, but I don't think we have time. We ought to be going."

"Going?" she stammered. "Going where?"

He threw back his head and laughed—a hearty, melodic sound. "You haven't listened to your messages, have you?" Hap ran a finger down the crease of his trousers. "I should have guessed. I knew you were busy this week, trying to get some work done on the Alaska project, and with keeping Gordy and Mary V on top of everything else, well—"

Vita's mind raced. How on earth could Hap Reardon know about her deadline for the Alaska book? She had never spoken the first word to him about her writing projects, not that she could recall. And the twins? He spoke their names as if he knew them, as if they were all old friends.

"I left a couple of messages, and even came by the other day. But when I saw Mary Kate's Volvo parked out front, I figured you had your hands full. And I kept getting your machine, so it was clear you had the phone turned off. I know how forgetful you become when you're working, honey, but you really ought to check your messages once in a while." He took her hand and squeezed it. "You promised to go with me to the estate auction in Brevard, remember? And then afterward we're scheduled to have dinner with my mother. She's really looking forward to meeting you." He smiled into her eyes. "If you're too swamped to go, I'll understand, but—"

Vita shook her head. *Honey?* Memories began to crowd in upon her, misty images of time spent with him—a drive to Black Mountain to scout out antique stores, a candlelight dinner, a walk in the rain.

She pulled herself together and managed to stammer, "No, no. Of course not. I—" Vita looked down at what she was wearing—blue jeans and a burgundy turtleneck sweater with tennis shoes. "Just give me a couple of minutes to change—"

"I'd never dream of asking you to change." Hap stood to his feet, extended a hand in her direction, and chuckled. "Although you might want to work on that absent-mindedness thing."

Walk the path God sets before you, a voice whispered in the back of her mind. Vita smiled up at him and took his hand. "OK, let me just get my purse and keys," she said, "and we'll be on our way."

⌒

They chose the scenic route, a twenty-five mile trip that wound along Crab Creek Road from Flat Rock to the picturesque little college town of Brevard, sheltered at the edge of the Pisgah National Forest. Hap drove, skillfully maneuvering the big white van with *Pastimes* painted in purple on both sides. Vita was grateful not to be behind the wheel; if it had been up to her, they probably would have ended up lost in the Great Smoky Mountains National Park, or stranded in some holler right out of *Deliverance,* where the locals still made moonshine and ran off the "furriners" with a double-barreled shotgun.

Freed from having to give her attention to the road before them, Vita spent most of the drive in silence, listening to Hap talk about his work and sorting through fresh memories that continued to work their way into her consciousness.

"The wonderful thing about antiques," he was saying, "is not only their appreciating monetary value, but their intrinsic worth as icons of history. Sometimes I wish antiques could talk. What valuable lessons we might learn from them! I like to think that each one has its own story—a tale of ordinary people, maybe, finding their way to extraordinary courage and faith."

"Like the Treasure Box," Vita murmured.

"Exactly like the Treasure Box. Now, there's a piece that has a story to tell."

If you only knew, she thought to herself.

Hap turned in her direction and grinned. "It's virtually a miracle, the way some of these things endure—passed from hand to hand, coming down from one generation to the next, carrying decades, sometimes even centuries of history along with them. Don't you think the fellow who made that box—probably in England, over a hundred years ago—would be fascinated to find out how it came to rest in the mountains of western North Carolina?" He let out a wistful sigh. "Just proves that we never know how far our influence might travel, or who our lives will touch."

Vita gazed at his profile—a broad forehead, a nose turned up slightly at the tip, just the hint of a weakening chin. A clean-shaven, boyish face, not devastatingly handsome by conventional standards, and yet there was something intensely likable about him.

The answer came to her in the present and was called up from the past simultaneously: his imagination, his creativity. Yes, that was it. Hap Reardon had a wonderful way of . . . of *thinking*. A way of embracing the magic and mystery—the *wonder*—of everyday life. Vita paused in thought, distracted by a momentary image of Hap walking with her, hand in hand, through the woods, stopping every step or two to bend over and examine a wildflower, or to identify the song of some invisible bird in the trees. He was—her mental thesaurus struggled for the right adjective, but all she could come up with was *good*. A *good* man. An uncomplicated man, sensitive, compassionate, self-aware. A man at peace with himself and his life. A man who found delight in simple things. A man of faithfulness and integrity.

And a man she would never get bored with.

Vita's rational brain put on the brakes so hard she could feel the whiplash inside her skull. Wait a minute. Was she actually thinking of a *future* with Hap Reardon? Impossible. Ridiculous. Utterly unthinkable, and yet—

Yet it was true. Like a file photograph slowly downloading into her memory, the picture materialized: the two of them, at an overlook up on the Blue Ridge Parkway, on a blanket under the stars. Chilled to the bone and shivering in the night air, laughing about the insanity of a midnight picnic at this time of year. Hap taking her hand, gazing into her eyes.

Vita took in a ragged breath, and from somewhere deep within her she felt it. *Love*. Welling up in her so that she could barely contain it, battering at her in powerful waves, drowning her in its liquid warmth. She panicked, and went under.

It felt like death, like birth. Every nerve ending in Vita's body flamed with an incendiary sweetness, a phoenix-fire that conceived new life in the ashes even as it incinerated the old in a molten blaze of glory. The rational part of her brain cautioned her to stay back, to keep her distance; this conflagration could sear the soul and char the heart into a molten lump of lead. But the warning came too late. The heat was too intense, too compelling. Shrugging off the final layers of her carefully crafted armor, Vita Kirk reached out toward the fire.

Hap turned when her hand touched his arm, and their eyes met. "What?"

Vita stalled. "I—I—" She managed a wan smile. "I love you, that's all."

His grin widened, and he stroked her cheek with his thumb. "I love you, too, sweetheart."

That was it. Nothing remarkable or earth-shattering. Simply the most natural, most comfortable of interchanges between two people in love.

By the time they pulled away from the auction site and headed for Hap's mother's house, the big white panel van was full. Vita had claimed a small inlaid walnut table for herself; the rest would go to the shop.

Vita had no idea how Hap intended to cram all he had bought into that crowded little space, but she had to admit he was good at his chosen profession. He had spent less than a thousand dollars, and the carved cherry rice bed alone—a double-size fourposter—was worth more than that. All told, he would probably quadruple his investment on the haul he had made today.

She had watched him, fascinated, as he prowled up and down the aisles examining various items at the estate auction. The old woman who had died had evidently been something of a pack rat; in addition to the usual assortment of furniture, tools, and household appliances, there were a dozen or more flatbed trailers piled with boxes. On one flat, they found cheap stainless steel tableware alongside priceless sterling silver; on another, a hideous lamp—a buffalo with a clock in its belly, topped with a cowhide shade—in the same box with an unobtrusive but elegant little Tiffany.

Hap knew his business. He went around pulling out drawers, checking dovetails, examining hardware, explaining to Vita why this piece was authentic and valuable, while that one was a reproduction. By the time the auction started, he had made a list of what he wanted and the maximum price he would pay. Vita had a hard time keeping up with the rapid-fire pace of the bidding, but twice Hap caught the auctioneer pulling bids out of the trees— pretending to acknowledge a bidder in the back of the crowd and then upping the price on the basis of that phantom bid. Very graciously, and without malice, Hap asked for an identification of the competitor, and the auctioneer apologized, saving face by saying he mistakenly interpreted a movement in the back as a valid bid.

By the time the last item was sold, Hap had acquired several fine pieces of furniture, and a truckload of stuff Vita thought worthless until he explained their value to her. Things like old comic books, a Betty Boop clock, a collection of advertising signs, and a contraption called a Whizzer Bike, which turned out to be a motorized bicycle, the earliest ancestor of the moped.

And if Vita thought she was impressed with Hap's expertise in antiques, she found herself even more amazed with the way he dealt with people. There had been a little girl at the auction— eight or nine years old, perhaps—who was bidding against Hap on a box of assorted knickknacks. Hap won the bid at six dollars, but once he had the box in his possession, he motioned to Vita and sidled over to where the little girl was standing with her father.

"Hi," he said gently. "My name's Hap. Was there something particular in this box you were interested in?"

The girl was obviously fighting tears, but she bravely swallowed back her despondency. "Yes, sir. The little horse."

Hap reached into the box and came up with a small bronze statue. "This one?"

"Yes, sir. But you got it fair and square." She looked up at her father, who winked at her and nodded. "My dad taught me how to bid. And I couldn't go over five dollars."

"Yeah," Hap said. "Your dad's right; we all have to set limits on what we're willing to spend. I'm an antique dealer, and I've been outbid on things I wanted lots of times." He scratched his head. "This was going to go in my shop, but I'll tell you what— I've got a lot of stuff to drag home, and this little horse is just weighing me down. You wouldn't be interested in buying it, by any chance?"

Briefly the girl's eyes lit up with anticipation, but then her face fell and she shook her head. "Like I said, I only have five dollars. It's worth more than that."

"It is," Hap agreed. "But I've got other things to consider, such as space limitations and transportation costs and my over-head in the store. It might pay me just to go ahead and unload it while I've got a buyer." He gave the girl a serious look. "How does three dollars sound?"

She cut a glance at her father, then nodded vigorously. "You've got a deal."

The girl dug in her pockets and came up with two rumpled bills, three quarters, and a fistful of pennies. She handed the money over, took the little horse, and shook his hand, all business.

As Vita and Hap turned to leave, the girl's father caught him by the sleeve. "Thank you," he said.

"My pleasure." Hap grinned at him. "It's the most fun I've had all day."

As Vita recalled the incident, she turned to Hap, who had just pulled the van into the driveway of a little white house. "How much was that statue worth—the horse you gave to the little girl?"

"Not gave—*sold*," he corrected with a chuckle. "I might have gotten forty or fifty dollars for it." He gave a self-deprecating shrug. "Don't tell my mother, OK? She already thinks I'm a miserable soft touch."

"Soft touch, yes," Vita answered. "Miserable, no." She unbuckled her seat belt, leaned over, and kissed him on the cheek. "You're quite a man."

"I'm just a sucker for a pretty girl, that's all." Hap's ears reddened, and he ducked his head sheepishly.

Vita laughed. "Do we need to have a discussion about flirting?"

"I don't think so." He reached across the space between the bucket seats, took her hand, and stroked it lightly, tenderly. Vita's rational mind set off an alarm that she was on dangerous ground, that she could get her heart broken, that it had happened before and could happen again. But she had never felt safer, or happier, or more loved than she felt at this moment.

He leaned forward. Vita shut her eyes, waiting for the kiss. Five seconds. Ten. Nothing. *Maybe he's trying to work up his nerve,* Vita thought. She kept her eyes closed and waited some more. After about twenty seconds, she could stand it no longer. She slit one eyelid open and peeked.

Hap was snared sideways in the bucket seat, his left hip wedged under the steering wheel and his right pocket hung on the floorboard gearshift. He had been caught halfway to the kiss and was laughing so hard he could barely breathe.

"That's what I get for trying to be romantic," he said when he had regained his breath. "We'd better go in, or Mama will accuse us of necking in the car, and we'll never hear the end of it."

～

Hap's mother's home was one of those small, compact Grandma houses—white, with dark green shutters and a postage-stamp yard filled with multicolored annuals. As soon as she stepped across the threshold, Vita had the sensation of being transported back in time. The living room was furnished with maroon velvet furniture festooned with lace doilies and antimacassars. A large ornate candelabra dominated a baby grand piano crowded into the corner, and the dining room, an alcove separated from the living room by an oval archway, was pure Duncan Phyfe—a mahogany claw-foot table with six lyre-back chairs.

"You can see I come by my love of antiques honestly," Hap whispered as he ushered her into the room. "Mother just doesn't realize this house isn't big enough to accommodate them all." He raised his voice. "Mama? We're here!"

Vita hadn't been quite sure what she expected of Hap's mother. Somewhere in the back of her mind, an undiscovered memory came to her aid: the woman was a seventy-nine-year-old widow who had given birth to her first and only child at the age of thirty-six. After seeing the house, Vita anticipated a frail, regal, birdlike lady with Victorian lace up to her chin and an effusion of silver-white hair piled high on her head. The person who emerged from the kitchen, however, couldn't have been further from that image if she had deliberately aimed at its opposite. About five-four, with dazzling blue eyes and short hair in that platinum shade of blonde going to gray, she looked to be seventy-nine going on sixty. She wore faded blue jeans, a blue and purple striped rugby shirt, and Nike running shoes.

"Ah, Mama, there you are!" Hap went to her and kissed her on the cheek. "Sorry we're a bit late; the auction was a big one and went on longer than we thought."

"That's fine; I only got back from my tennis game an hour

261

ago." She gave Hap a poke in the ribs. "Hampton James Reardon, Junior, where are your manners?"

Hap grimaced. "Oh. Right." He pulled himself together and began a formal introduction. "Mother, I'd like you to meet Vita Kirk. Vita, my mother, Mrs.—"

"Oh, posh," she interrupted. "Stop this nonsense." She pushed him aside and hauled Vita into a hug worthy of a Kodiak bear. "I'm so glad to meet you, my dear." She released Vita and cast an acid look in Hap's direction. "*Finally*. I was beginning to suspect that Number One Son here had made you up entirely from his imagination."

"I'm happy to meet you, too, Mrs. Reardon—"

"None of that 'Mrs.' business, now," she interrupted with a wave of one hand. "I may be a certified antique, but I won't have my son's fiancée calling me 'Mrs.' as if I'm some prudish nineteenth-century dotter."

Vita's brain had flooded out on the word *fiancée*, and it took her a minute or two to pull in enough oxygen to get the engine running again.

"—Roe," Mrs. Reardon was saying when Vita's attention returned. "Please, call me Roe. All my friends do, and I want us to be friends. Good friends."

"Yes. Roe. Thank you." Vita's mind spun. It was one thing to like Hap, to be friends with him, even, perhaps, to have romantic feelings for him. But *marriage?* Could she possibly have agreed to marry him?

Hap's mother led them both back into the kitchen, all the while carrying on a spirited conversation with her son, but Vita couldn't hear a word of it. Somehow, in the midst of her mental fog, Vita helped Roe get dinner put on the table, going through the motions like a wooden wind-up doll. An animated discussion about antiques and the auction and Hap's plans for enlarging the shop swirled around her. Then they were sitting at the table—Hap at the head, his mother and Vita on either side. And Roe said, "Hap, would you like to say grace?"

Vita felt Hap's hand close around hers and saw Roe reach across the table to complete the circle. Vita started to bow her head, but with a sidelong glance she saw that Hap had his eyes open, his gaze drifting from the food on the table to his mother's face and then to hers. "God of the Universe," he prayed, "you give us many gifts. The bounty of the land for our nourishment, the warmth of family, the joys of work and play. Thank you for all these blessings, for laughter, and for love." He smiled in Vita's direction. "Especially for love. May we ever live with a grateful heart. Amen."

Vita felt something tear at the seams of her mind—not another small rip, but a violent pulling apart of the whole fabric of reality. The entire curtain rent in two, from top to bottom. The darkness lifted, and from the depths of her soul came a shuddering, like an inner earthquake with Vita at its epicenter. On the outside, nothing had changed, but within, she sensed herself standing in the presence of some glorious celestial occurrence.

She had heard this prayer before, not once, but many times. Jacob Stillwater's prayer. The prayer that Hap had offered before every meal they had shared together. Hap didn't remind Vita of Jacob because of similar physical characteristics. He reminded Vita of Jacob because of his *soul*.

Vita had once thought—a long time ago, it seemed—that if she could ever give her heart to any man again, it would be a man like Jacob Stillwater. Now that man sat next to her, holding her hand, and all the years of disillusionment and suspicion retreated into the background. It didn't matter anymore that Gordon Locke had betrayed her, or that Derrick Knight had betrayed both Rachel and Cathleen. The pain and distrust she had harbored for so many years seemed but a distant storm dissipating on the far horizon.

Vita could feel the old memories getting weaker, losing their hold on her. She could still envision herself as angry, bitter, and isolated, but that person didn't seem to have much to do with her anymore. She could recall being cynical and distrustful and having no patience whatsoever for anything that reeked of religion, but she could no longer quite remember why.

Her mind wrapped around the words of Hap's prayer: *Thank you for these blessings, for laughter, and for love. May we ever live with a grateful heart.*

And her own soul responded: *Amen.*

25

FAMILY LEGACY

Vita smiled across the table at Roe Reardon. Now that she was able to relax a little, and quit obsessing about her newly discovered status as a woman engaged to be married, she found that she really liked Roe. The woman was intelligent, incisive, sensitive, and down-to-earth—much like the son she had raised.

"So tell me, Vita," Roe said just as Vita had forked up a mouthful of the tenderest pot roast east of the Continental Divide, "what's your family like?"

Hap choked with laughter as Vita tried to swallow and answer at the same time. She elbowed him in the ribs to shut him up, took a sip of iced tea, and tried to compose herself.

"Well—" Vita hesitated for a moment, then said, "Both my parents are deceased. I have one sister, three years younger, who lives in Asheville with her husband. Her children, my niece and nephew, are twins. Mary Vita and Gordy. They're eleven."

"You must be very close if your sister named her daughter after you."

Given the events of the past few days, it wasn't an easy question. Which was true—the years of estrangement from Mary Kate, or the recent development of having a sister she could talk to, confide in? The earlier memories—the enmity, the resentment, the alienation—were still there, but they were rapidly fading into the background, like remnants of a disturbing dream from which she had finally awakened. The good relationship—the laughter, the love, the shared secrets—now seemed much more real. Vita heard Mary Kate's voice reverberate in her mind, calling her *Sis*, saying, *I love you.*

"We *are* close," she answered at last. "I'm very proud of Mary Kate. She's bright and beautiful and has raised two wonderful, loving children."

"Who, incidentally, adore their Aunt Vita," Hap said.

Vita grinned. "Mary Kate has just decided to go back to school, to get her master's in counseling."

Roe's blue eyes turned wistful. "I always wished for a sister," she mused. "Didn't want Hap to be an only child, either—it just turned out that way."

"Your mother wasn't able to have other children?" Vita blurted out before she realized how insensitive the question might seem. "Sorry, I didn't mean to—"

"It's all right." Roe waved a hand. "I never knew my mother or my father, so there aren't really any painful memories involved.

266

My aunt and uncle raised me, and since they were the only parents I ever knew, I always called them Mom and Dad. They wanted to have other children, but Mom had two miscarriages, and the doctors told her it would be safer for her not to try again."

"They've passed on, I gather?"

"Yes. But they lived to see me married, and to see their grandson. Dad died when Hap was a boy, but Mom lived to see him graduate from college. She lived with us the last few years of her life." Roe flashed a wry grin in Vita's direction. "But don't worry, dear—I won't expect you and Hap to take me in when I'm old and feeble."

"I can't ever imagine you as either old or feeble," Vita countered. "But as far as I'm concerned, there would be no question about your living with us if you ever needed to do so." Vita heard the promise come out of her mouth before she could stop it. She glanced at Hap, who was smiling and nodding. And she realized that the words were true. She sat there, unable to speak, amazed at what was happening to her. Where most people had what the psychologists called *boundaries,* Vita had always had *fortresses.* She had spent a lifetime keeping people not just at arm's length, but as far away as possible, outside the walls, beyond the barriers. And now not only had the gate to her walled garden been unlocked, but the walls themselves were coming down, stone by stone.

"Do you see your sister's family often?" Roe was asking when Vita tuned back in.

It took Vita a minute to realize that the topic of conversation had circled back to Mary Kate and the twins, and she stumbled for an answer. "Not nearly often enough," she answered truthfully. "But I expect that will change, now that—" She stopped suddenly, realizing that the logical conclusion to the sentence was a revelation about the transformations that were occurring in her own life. She would never be able to explain *that*. "Now that I'm almost finished with my new book," she ended lamely.

Roe brightened. "Yes, Hap tells me you're working on a guide to Alaska, and that you and a friend are going up there at the end of the summer."

I'm going to Alaska? When did that happen? Vita's mind lurched into overdrive, and then latched on to an indistinct memory . . . an envelope in her desk drawer, bearing the logo of Norwegian Cruise Lines. Reservations. A suite with a private balcony. In August. With Hattie. The trip had been booked for more than a year, ever since she had decided that Alaska would be her next project.

Fortunately, Hap saved her from looking like a total idiot. "Hattie Parker," he said. "She and Vita have been best friends since—since when, honey? Grade school? Hattie lives in Atlanta, and every year she and Vita take a trip together." He grinned. "I'd love to think I might be able to join in on one of these great adventures, but Vita and Hattie have been doing this forever, and although Vita has had the good grace not to say so, I'm sure they'd rather not have a poky old husband horning in on their fun."

"Very smart, my boy," Roe said archly. "Never come between

a woman and her best friend." She wagged a finger in his direction. "And I have one more piece of motherly advice for both of you. But first, let's move into the living room. Who wants coffee and pie?"

Vita said no to the coffee but accepted the pie, which turned out to be a heavenly concoction called French silk—a chocolate mousse made, of all things, with tofu. Roe wisely kept this tidbit of information from Vita until she had eaten every morsel and was eyeing the plate, wondering if licking off the remains would be impolite.

"Tofu?" Vita repeated.

Roe laughed. "Tofu. Amazing, isn't it? A low-calorie, low-fat dessert that tastes so good you'd think it must be sinful. Just goes to show that things aren't always what they seem." She collected the plates, refilled Hap's coffee cup, and returned from the kitchen with a small blue box in her hands.

"I have something for you," she said when she resumed her seat. "Something I've been saving for a long time." She handed the box to Vita and sat down.

Hap scooted closer to Vita and put his arm around her. "Mother," he said, "are you sure you want to do this?"

"You don't have to accept it if it doesn't suit you. I won't get my feelings hurt, I promise."

Vita turned to Hap, the box still closed in her hand. "You know what this is?"

He nodded. "Open it."

With trembling fingers Vita pried up the lid. There, on a

cushion of dark blue velvet, was the most beautiful ring she had ever seen. A wide, ornately-worked wedding band—clearly hand-made and one of a kind—with a diamond in the middle and two small rubies flanking the center stone. The diamond, perfectly cut and flawless, caught the lamplight and sent out multi-colored reflections around the room. She looked at Hap, and then at Roe.

"Hap's father had this ring made for me—it was my wedding band. I always hoped Hap would have a sister, and I could pass it on to her." She smiled, her eyes filling with tears. "Now I finally have a daughter to give it to."

"It's beautiful," Vita whispered. She looked into Roe's eyes. "Are you sure you want me to have it?"

"I'm sure. You don't have to use it as your wedding ring, of course—"

"No!" Vita interrupted. "I'd—I'd be honored." She turned toward Hap. "If it's all right with you, that is."

Hap grinned. "Absolutely."

Vita got to her feet and went to kneel beside Roe's chair. "Thank you. I don't think you can know how much this means. I feel—I don't know, as if I belong."

Roe gathered her into a hug and held her there. "You do belong, my dear," she whispered into Vita's ear. "To Hap, and to me. That's what family is all about."

After a minute or two Roe released her, and Vita went back to the sofa and sat down at Hap's side.

"Now," Roe said briskly. "I have something else to say. Are you listening?"

Vita dragged her eyes away from the diamond and ruby ring. "Yes ma'am."

"All right. I promise not to be an interfering mother-in-law, but there's one bit of unsolicited advice I feel I must pass on to the two of you. Marriage isn't a merging of two halves—it's the joining of two wholes. Ideally, marriage is a covenant between two people who draw out the best in each other, heart, mind, soul, and body. If you help each other become better, nobler, truer, more faithful individuals—in short, to develop into the kind of human beings God created you to be—you will have created something between you that is bigger than the sum of its two parts. But that kind of love is highly uncommon, and nurturing it is the work of a lifetime."

An alarm went off in the back of Vita's mind, a vibration, very faint. Where had she heard those words before?

"You're a wise woman, Mother," Hap said.

Roe shook her head. "I'd love to take credit for that, but it's your grandmother who was the wise one. She endured a lot of heartache in her life, and used it to build a faith as immovable as a mountain. If I manage to become half the woman she was before I die, I'll consider my life well spent."

"She must have been a remarkable person," Vita said. "I wish I could have met her."

Roe looked at her watch. "Good grief! It's nearly eleven

o'clock. I've kept you children far too long, rattling on with my old-lady blather."

"We probably do need to go," Hap conceded. "I need to get up early to unload the van and get the new stuff into my shop before nine."

Vita got to her feet. "Won't you let us help with the dishes before we go? I hate to leave you with all this cleaning up to do."

"Nonsense. I'm a little fussy about my kitchen, anyway. I'll have it done in a flash." She hugged Vita and gave her a kiss on the cheek. "Come see me often, dear," she said, "with or without Hap. You're welcome any time."

Vita returned the hug, strangely warmed by the woman's display of affection. "Thank you for the ring," she said. "And for—well, for everything."

Hap kissed his mother and herded Vita to the door.

Roe stood on the front porch, watching as they made their way to the van. Just before Vita climbed into the passenger's seat, she called out, "Vita! I forgot to ask you something."

Vita turned. "Yes?"

"Hap tells me you now have possession of the Enchanted Treasure Box."

"That's right." Vita wondered how Roe knew about the box. But of course Hap must have told her about it, or shown it to her in his shop before the day Vita found it.

"Good. It belongs with you. Take care of it—that box holds

great value and significance. Someday I'll tell you about it, so you can pass it on to that niece of yours when it's her turn." - - -

Her turn? Before Vita could respond, or voice the hundred questions that rose up in her mind, Roe waved and went back into the house. Vita climbed into her seat, Hap put the van in gear, and they drove away.

Vita awoke the next morning in a clouded half-light, with the sounds of thunder rumbling in the distance and rain pounding against the bedroom window. Roe Reardon's parting words swirled in her mind. *That box holds great value and significance. It belongs with you.* And, *I'll tell you about it someday.*

What could Roe possibly have to tell her about the Treasure Box that she didn't already know?

After a quick shower, she brewed a pot of coffee and went to her office, carrying a plate of toast in one hand and her coffee cup and the blue velvet ring box in the other. She clicked on the computer, and while it booted up turned her attention to the wedding band.

She withdrew the ring from the box and watched as light from the lamp caught the diamond like a prism. A beautiful stone, flawless to the eye, and clear as ice. But there was nothing cold about it; it held fire and brilliance at its core.

Fire and ice. Robert Frost had written a poem by that title—

a debate about whether the world would end in fire or ice. The poet had claimed, "From what I've tasted of desire, I hold with those who favor fire."

Vita considered the verse, intrigued by the personal implications she found in it. All her adult life, she had favored ice, keeping well back from the fire, not risking any chance of being burned again. And yet now that she had embraced the flame, she could barely recognize the ice maiden she had always been. Her years of self-imposed isolation seemed like a dream, a dim reflection of someone else's life, someone she couldn't imagine liking, much less being.

She ran her fingers over the gold and tested the heft of the wedding band in her palm. And suddenly Vita realized that the decision had been made, once and for all. There was no question of returning to the old way of life. Not one. Inasmuch as it lay within her power, she was never going back. Never.

Vita slipped the ring onto her left hand and found it smooth as satin, a perfect fit. She couldn't wear it, of course—she had to wait for the wedding. But there was no harm in trying it on.

She sat there for a full five minutes, turning her hand this way and that. If it hadn't been pouring buckets, she would have gone outside into the sun to catch the various plays of light across the diamond's face. Even on a rainy day, and in dim light, the wedding band was nothing short of magnificent.

But it could have been the prize from a Cracker Jack box, for all the difference it would have made to Vita. She had never felt so giddy, so much like a schoolgirl before, not even when she had *been* a schoolgirl. And now, as a mature woman of thirty-eight, she had to resist the urge to giggle, to write Hap's name on the front of her notebook, to dash out into the storm to carve their initials in the oak tree outside her window.

Idly she opened the middle left-hand drawer of the desk. There, atop a stack of pale blue legal pads, lay the thick white envelope from Norwegian Cruise Lines. She opened the envelope and scanned the contents: an itinerary, some brochures from various ports of call, and two tickets, one in her name and one in Hattie's. August 2–10.

In the drawer next to the envelope was a small appointment book with a tan leather cover. Vita flipped through the book and scanned its contents, feeling a bit like a detective investigating someone else's personal items. Yes. There it was. The first two weeks in August were blocked off for the trip; apparently she and Hattie intended to spend a few days in Seattle before and after the cruise.

She turned pages in the calendar. *August 20, Florist. August 23, Caterer. August 27, Fitting.* For her wedding dress? Vita's heart did a little skip. *September 3, Deadline for Alaska project. September 21, Rehearsal Dinner. September 22, 4:00 P.M., WEDDING.*

Wedding. Her wedding. She should be frightened, Vita knew. By all rights she ought to be scared out of her skull. But the closest she could find to fear was a small twinge of nervousness at the very back of her brain.

This was right. The right person. The right time. She would be ready on September 22.

Vita put the appointment book and cruise tickets back into the drawer and swiveled her chair around to face the computer. The booting-up process was done, and silver stars on a deep blue field winked at her from the screen, like an old friend welcoming her home.

Amazing, how much a simple computer program could change a life. Love, indeed, was the key that unlocked every portal. In learning to care about Sophie and Rachel and Cathleen and the others, Vita had opened her heart to a whole new reality. She was no longer afraid, no longer compelled to keep the walls fortified and the gates locked. She knew the risk of being wounded, but now it no longer seemed such a terrible threat. Broken hearts healed. People got over being hurt. They learned to trust, learned to love again.

She pushed the Enter key and waited, increasingly aware of a change in her attitude toward the Treasure Box program. Vita was interested in finding out what happened with Sophia Rose, of course—the same way she might be interested in a well-crafted novel or a particularly compelling movie. But the recent turn of events in her life seemed much more real now than anything that might take place on the screen.

The scene that came up on the monitor was, evidently, a party of some kind. Music playing. People laughing. Couples jitter-bugging on a dance floor while the strains of "Boogie Woogie

Bugle Boy" emanated from the speakers. Several of the men—people Vita didn't recognize—wore army uniforms.

The 1940s. World War II. More than twenty years had passed since the day of Rachel and Michael McCall's wedding, Vita's last glimpse into the Treasure Box program.

This was quite the celebration—V-E Day, perhaps? Everyone seemed happy and relaxed, but the location didn't look like a USO. More like a ballroom in a hotel, with chandeliers overhead and tables covered with white linen tablecloths.

A pinging noise, like a bell, got the crowd's attention, and the band faded into silence. Vita's view zoomed in on a long table on a dais at the front of the room, where a gentleman in formal morning attire was standing, tapping a spoon against the side of a crystal glass. He was middle-aged, with a slight paunch and a bit of a receding hairline, and on his left sat a lovely woman in a fawn-colored dress, her brunette hair done up in curls, with just a few streaks of silver at the temples.

Vita leaned close to the monitor and peered intently at the woman. Rachel Woodlea, maturing beautifully, a vision of elegance and charm. And the man standing beside her was Michael McCall.

"I'd like to propose a toast," he called out, "to a woman who has always kept my life—well, interesting—" A wave of laughter rippled through the room. "And to the man who has now bravely taken up the challenge of living with her." He raised his glass. "To the bride and groom!"

"To the bride and groom," the guests echoed.

"Son," he said, turning to the couple sitting to his right, "the woman you have married bears a special name: Sophia Rose. Sophia for wisdom, Rose for beauty. And she is both wise and beautiful."

Vita smiled. A wedding reception. Sophia Rose, all grown up, had just gotten married.

The guests applauded, and the groom gave his bride a kiss on the cheek. "My darlin' daughter has brought me great joy," Michael went on, "and taught me many important lessons. And so in the spirit of the moment, I'll pass a little bit of my own experience along to you. You may be a Commander, sir, but don't even try commanding this one. The fact is, you've chosen a lass who thinks for herself—"

"Ain't that the truth!" someone yelled from the back of the room.

The hall broke out in gales of laughter, and as the bride blushed furiously, Vita had the chance to study her features. She bore a remarkable resemblance to a young Cathleen, with golden blonde hair and startling blue eyes. But her expression held none of the perpetual sneer that had marred her mother's beauty early on. She exuded wit and intelligence, and Vita realized that the best of both Rachel and Cathleen had come together at last in the person of Sophia Rose.

The groom stood, handsome and debonair in Navy dress whites. He pounded his father-in-law on the back and raised a hand to quiet the crowd. "I already knew that, Michael, and it seems that everyone else did, too. But thank you anyway. Now, my mother-in-law, Rachel, tells me that true love is highly uncommon, and nurturing it is the work of a lifetime." He grinned in Rachel's direction. "And everyone knows that a wise man always heeds his mother-in-law's advice."

Another roar erupted from the crowd, and for a minute or two he couldn't go on. "And so I pledge myself," he continued when the noise subsided, "to my lovely bride. May we never stop growing, and may we help each other become all that God has created us to be."

The guests applauded heartily, but Vita barely heard the commotion. Nor did she take more than passing notice of the thunderstorm gaining momentum, pelting rain like gravel against the sunroom windows. Her mind was fixed on the words: *"My mother-in-law tells me that true love is highly uncommon, and nurturing it is the work of a lifetime."* Hap's mother had said the same thing, just last night. And what else? *"I'd love to take credit, but it's your grandmother who was the wise one."*

Vita jumped as a peal of thunder cracked nearby, and a bolt of lightning strobed through the dense, heavy air. On screen, the bride was standing, acknowledging her new husband's words, laying her hand on his arm. And then Vita saw the ring.

Sophia Rose was wearing a wide band, intricately worked, with three precious stones set in gold. A center diamond flanked by two small rubies.

279

The storm front rumbled nearer. A final toast. Applause. The band playing "Sentimental Journey."

Vita's breath caught in her throat. Real. It was all real.

Lightning rent the sky, and thunder followed in an ear-splitting crack. There was a blinding flash, and everything went dark.

26

AFTER THE BLACKOUT

Although the storm passed on through shortly after noon, the blackout lasted all day and into the night. Phone lines were down and streets were blocked with fallen limbs. No traffic was moving anywhere.

While she had the benefit of daylight, Vita tried to read, to do manual work on the Alaska project—anything to keep her from being bored out of her mind. She ate peanut butter and jelly sandwiches and made a point of opening the refrigerator only when absolutely necessary. Finally, around nine-thirty, Vita abandoned hope of finding anything to occupy her mind and went upstairs to her bedroom.

The rain had washed the air clean; a cool, fresh breeze blew in Vita's open window and stirred the flame of the single candle that burned on the bedside table. In the light from the flickering flame, she studied the diamond and ruby wedding band, then replaced it in its velvet case and stretched out across the bed.

Sleep eluded her, and she lay on the bed with her eyes wide open, thinking.

Roe Reardon was Sophia Rose Woodlea. The Treasure Box program was real.

And her memories—the new memories, the ones that included a sister and niece and nephew, a best friend, a fiancé—those were real, too. Vita could still recall the years without them, but that life now seemed like a bad dream, a nightmare of solitary confinement and isolation.

She flung a hand over her eyes. If she let herself analyze it, her mind got muddled and confused. But when she just accepted it, embraced the new life as the one she was meant to live, everything made perfect sense. Never mind that it was impossible. It felt . . . true.

Maybe that was the key. Perhaps the question she should be asking was not "What is real?" but "What is true?"

The Treasure Box was true. She had been lured in by the story. And once inside, the truths of the fiction became her truths, working their way outward into her life. Changing everything.

Perhaps that was exactly what faith was all about. Making the big leap into something that couldn't be quantified or proved by scientific formulas. And once the leap was made, once you were on the other side of the chasm, your perspectives shifted, and your point of view was altered. Once the miracle had happened, it worked backward as well as forward, transforming the past as surely as it changed the future.

Vita's world had certainly been transformed. Love had been the key that unlocked all her bolted steel portals. And now, as she looked back on the person she once had been, she could barely recognize herself.

Vita didn't know all the answers. If she were to be perfectly honest, she had to admit that she didn't even know all the questions. But that didn't matter. Some day, when she was ready to talk about her experiences, she might ask Roe to fill in the missing details about the Treasure Box. But for now, she simply needed to revel in the miracle, to hold it close like a secret gift from the One who loved her.

Somehow, miraculously, her life had changed. And she meant to keep it that way.

By the time the sun rose, Vita was in her office at the computer. A little after five, the power had been restored, and the dark silence of the early morning had been shattered by the humming of electricity through the wires and the jarring shock of lights coming on unexpectedly.

The first rays of dawn shot the big oak outside her window with a rose-hued light. Vita opened the window, took a deep breath of the cool, charged air, and leaned forward to watch. The sun came up behind the tree, suffusing its branches in pink and gold—a giant burning bush, with every green leaf ablaze. She held her breath, waiting like Moses to hear the voice from heaven, but no voice came. Just a whisper on the morning breeze, invisible footsteps across the wet grass, leaving a trail of diamonds in their wake.

The show didn't last long—nature's demonstrations of glory never did. You had to keep your eyes open and take in the details before they vanished.

Vita offered up a silent heartfelt *thank-you,* then turned back to the computer.

The boot-up was finished, and there on her screen was her desktop with its wallpaper of the Blue Ridge Mountains surrounded by program icons. No starry sky, no voice from the speakers.

She rebooted the computer. Still the same. Her Blue Ridge wallpaper, her word processing and research icons. But no Treasure Box program.

For a moment Vita felt abandoned, bereft. She hadn't the foggiest idea what to do next. For two weeks her work had been delayed and her life suspended because of the Treasure Box. How could it be gone, just like that?

"What am I thinking?" she muttered to herself. "If it won't come to me, I'll go to it. I have the Web address. I can get back to it whenever I want."

She clicked the Internet icon and waited while the computer logged on. She had e-mail—twenty-seven new messages, but only six of any importance. Impatiently she scanned the list:

one from HarrietP@CDC.org—that would be Hattie. One from HRPastimes—that would be Hap. One from MKate35—her sister. Two from her editor, one from her agent.

Vita closed the mail window. She'd come back to that later. Right now she was more intent on finding out the details of Sophia Rose's marriage to Hampton Reardon. She typed in the Web address—http://www.enchantedtreasurebox.com—and hit the Enter key. After a minute or two, a message box appeared:

 CAN'T FIND WEB SITE

- The site you requested is not available. It may have moved, or may no longer exist.

- If you typed a Web address, double-check for any misspellings, punctuation errors, or extra spaces.

- If you believe your address to be correct, try adding http://www at the beginning. If you still cannot connect, close all programs currently running, restart your computer, and try again.

Vita's eyes flitted back and forth from the message to the Web address she had typed into the box above the window. Her spelling was accurate. No punctuation errors or extra spaces. Everything was correct.

She shut down the computer, rebooted, and tried again. No

sign of the Treasure Box site anywhere. No links in a general search, no hits on "Treasure Box" or "Enchanted Box" or any other configuration of the name. No rotating icon. No starry sky. Nothing.

Vita sat back and let out a frustrated sigh. After three minutes of idleness, the screen saver kicked in, and she watched the swirling spiral move around the desktop, distorting the icons in a lethargic whirlpool. What had happened to the program? How could it have taken over her computer—and her life—for so long and then just disappeared? And why now?

Well, she thought, *sitting here glaring at the monitor isn't going to help me figure it out. I might as well answer my e-mail while I'm on-line.*

Vita opened her mailbox, deleted the junk without reading it, and went directly to the e-mails from her editor and agent. The first one from the editor was a download of the preliminary cover design for the Alaska project. The second informed her that, due to a change in the production schedule, her deadline had been extended by two months. That was good news. Her agent was just checking in.

She sent back a brief response to the business messages, then clicked on Hattie's name:

Hi, Vita—

Wanted to know if you're up for a visitor this weekend. I'm sick of Atlanta, and it's been too long since I've been to the mountains. I thought I'd take a weekend off. If you'll have me, I'll drive up Friday afternoon. We can rent movies and eat popcorn and stay up all night—just like the old days. Let me know.

Love,
Hattie

Mary Kate's was next:

Sis—great time talking with you the other day. Thanks again for keeping the kids. Gordon and I are going to counseling—that's a step in the right direction. And I've been accepted in the MSW program at UNCA. Can we celebrate? I'll take you out to dinner and we can resume our discussion about "many paths." How about this coming Monday?

The twins send their love and want to know when they can come back for another visit. I love you, too, by the way—

MK

Vita backtracked, sent a response to Hattie inviting her to come, and answered Mary Kate's message, telling her that Monday would be perfect. Then she opened the last one—Hap's e-mail—to find a single line:

I love you. That's all. Hap.

She let her eyes linger on the message, then put a finger to the screen to trace the words, *I love you.* The Treasure Box program might be gone, but something else—something far more important—had appeared in its place.

Vita would never have all her questions answered. But the big ones, the really important ones, about love and faith and God and family, had somehow resolved themselves in her mind. *I love you. That's all.*

She clicked on the "answer" button and typed in her response:

That's enough. More than enough—more than I ever hoped,

dreamed, or had the sense to pray for. More than I deserve.

But isn't that the definition of grace?

I love you, too.

Vita

Vita looked at her watch. It was nearly five, and she was supposed to meet Hap for dinner in an hour. All afternoon she had been at work in the garden—weeding, planting pansies, marking off a space next to the willow tree for a small pond and fountain. When she was finished, it would be beautiful—peaceful and serene, a paradise. Except for one thing.

The garden gate.

Carrying her toolbox in one hand, she went to the gate and

stood there looking at it for a minute. The padlock was gone, and the empty hasp hung like a broken finger from the frame. *No more locks, no fortress towers, no more protective shields,* Vita thought. *I've had enough of bolted doors.*

She fitted a screwdriver into the top hinge and smiled. Robert Frost had written about mending walls, repairing the breach, and here she was creating one. *"Before I built a wall,"* she quoted under her breath, *"I'd ask to know what I was walling in or walling out."*

All these years, Vita had never thought to ask what she was walling in or walling out. Now she knew. She had experienced firsthand the claustrophobia that came with too much safety.

The white picket gate, once removed, might make a nice backdrop in the corner of the garden to accent her irises. But no more walling in or walling out. She would put in an open arch in its place, perhaps. Or an overhead trellis. Some climbing plants—pink cottage roses or purple clematis. But no gate that could be latched.

The top hinge fell free, and the gate sagged at an angle against the ground. She had just removed the bottom hinge when the hairs on the back of her neck prickled, that sensation of being watched. Slowly she lifted her eyes and found herself staring into the gaze of a small dog. Sable and white, with keen, intelligent eyes and a beautiful face.

A Sheltie. Like the one in her dream.

"Hello, there," Vita said quietly, intent on not startling the animal.

The dog wagged its tail and regarded her curiously, its head cocked to one side. One of its ears flopped over, and the other stood straight at attention. Vita laid down her screwdriver and extended a hand in the dog's direction. It sniffed her palm, then gave a polite kiss to her fingertips.

"I see you two have met."

Vita looked up. Hap stood over her, clad in gray dress pants and a navy polo shirt.

"I had to go to Asheville to buy some antiques from some old friends of mine," he said. "They're moving to the Cayman Islands and can't take her with them." He stooped down to scratch the dog's ears. "How would you feel about an addition to our little family?"

Vita leaned back against the wall, and the Sheltie edged nearer, resting her head on Vita's knee. The dog's dark eyes held an expression of deep wisdom, and Vita could have sworn she was smiling.

Vita stood up and slapped the dirt off the knees of her jeans. "Does she have a name?"

Hap nodded. "Joy. Her name is Joy."

"Of course." Vita laughed. "What else would it be?"

Joy bounded ahead of them to explore her new home. Vita took Hap's hand, and together they followed her along the path, through the opening in the stone wall, into the garden. A garden with no gate. A garden which would never again lock a soul in or shut love out.

EPILOGUE

As the sun rose on a brilliant autumn morning, Vita sat in the garden swing, watching a breeze stir the tendrils of the willow tree. Last night's early frost had melted with the dawn, and a perfume of wet grass and mulching leaves wafted on the morning air. The oaks were beginning to turn bronze, and across the alley, in the neighbor's yard, the big sugar maple glowed red and yellow, as if each individual leaf had been painted in the night. In the distance, the undulating layers of the Blue Ridge Mountains rose up in mist, decked out in all the glorious shades of fall.

Upstairs, in the guest room, Hattie Parker still slept. Out in the yard, near the back wall, Joy was getting a drink from the fountain.

Vita gazed at the blue drift of sky over the mountaintops. She smiled as the dog returned to her, leaped into the swing, and settled her dripping chin across Vita's thigh.

Tomorrow was Vita's wedding day. Tonight everyone would gather for the rehearsal and dinner. Vita and Hap. Hap's mother, Roe. Mary Kate and Gordon and the twins. Hattie.

Vita's family.

Gratitude welled up in her soul and overflowed. The old man in Pastimes had been right. She held in her hands something more rare and valuable than she could possibly imagine. A miracle. A mystery. A wonder.

She stroked Joy's silky ears and pondered—had there ever been an old man? Vita seemed to think, now, that she had not bought the Treasure Box at all, but that Hap had given it to her that night up on the Blue Ridge Parkway. The night he asked her to marry him. A gift from him—and from his mother, and from his mother's aunt, all the way back to Sophie, who had sacrificed her life for the love of a friend.

Vita knew she'd never sort it all out, and at last she was content not to try. The Treasure Box program was gone—if it had ever existed at all. Everything had changed, and the person she had once accepted as herself now seemed a mere skeleton of who she was intended to be, a heap of bleached bones in an arid, barren place.

She didn't know how it had happened. Only that her ears had been opened and the mud washed from her eyes. For the first time in her life, she really saw, really heard.

Saw the pieces of the distant past, memories of anger and isolation and disconnection, dry bones scattered in the desert. Heard a voice out of the emptiness: "Daughter of earth, can these bones live?"

But no answer was required, because the miracle was already happening.

Like a reel of film run backward, she saw it all. Bones assembling. Ligament and flesh and skin attaching to a skeleton of memory, rising up whole and strong.

Yesterday, today, tomorrow. Past, present, and future. What might have been, or was, or is, or is to come. It was all a unity, all one, bound together by the Lover of Souls, the Creator who sees every possible then and now and hereafter.

Vita Kirk had walked through the labyrinth and come to its center. To a past with the gates removed and the walls broken down. To a present where pain and heartache had already given way to healing and hope. To a place where joy nipped at her heels and the silent, neglected baby had grown into a vital, living soul.

And over the hill, behind the bend, beyond the farthest place her eye could see? She did not know what waited there.

Only that the future—whatever it turned out to be—would be rooted in the rash, outrageous, unimaginable claims of love.

Also Available from Penelope Stokes

THE WISHING JAR

Abby Quinn McDougall is a Southern lady whose once picturesque small-town life seems to be shrinking. Abby wishes her life were simpler and her responsibilities fewer. Abby's daughter, Neal Grace, devastated by the loss of her father and the illness of her beloved grandmother, wishes for change. And Abby's mother Edith wishes only to be liberated from life itself. But wishes often backfire. As their wishes begin to come true, the Quinn women start to wonder: Could it be that their old life wasn't so bad after all? Is it possible that the answer to their deepest longings has been right in front of them, all along?

THE TREASURE BOX

Vita Kirk is a travel writer who has never left her hometown. In fact, she rarely leaves her house. Due to deep wounds and bitter losses, Vita has chosen isolation over vulnerability. But when she stumbles across an antique chest in a hole-in-the-wall boutique, she discovers a puzzling link to her past and her physical surroundings mysteriously begin to change. Inscribed in the treasure chest are the words, "Love is the key that unlocks every portal." The power of these words prove to unlock a part of Vita she thought had died years ago.

THE MEMORY BOOK

Phoebe Lange has it all – a Master's Degree, an adoring fiancé, and a future with unlimited possibilities – but something is missing. Orphaned at age five and raised by her grandmother, Phoebe longs for a past and a sense of connectedness, but it is not until she stumbles upon a scrapbook dating back to the 1920's that she discovers a terrible secret about her family's history which triggers an identity crisis. Phoebe becomes obsessed with a mysterious ancestor, whom she is convinced is the key to answering the questions that have plagued her. But the answers may not be what she has in mind.